I0760454

Praise for DDC Morgan…

"With each new book, the Calloway Series is developing into a tour de force of British noir – a must-read…"

"A terrific addition to the English Mean Streets school…"

"A brilliant piece of post-war noir…"

"A gem of a find and highly recommended."

"As I read, I had that feeling that I haven't had since I read chandler for the first time."

"I literally couldn't put this down and read the whole thing in under 24 hours."

"A fantastic read, stylishly written."

"Exciting, gripping and enjoyable - what more could you want!"

This edition first published 2023

ISBN: 978-1-914475-56-6

10 9 8 7 6 5 4 3 2 1

www.Fahrenheit-Press.com

F 4 E

Cover Design & Manuscript Typesetting by www.SkullStarStudio.com

Blood & Cinders

By

DDC Morgan

A Reg Calloway Mystery

Fahrenheit Press

Also available from Fahrenheit Press

- *Pills & Soap*
- *Rope & Canvas*

To my wife, without whose inspiration, wisdom and unfailing encouragement this novel would never have been written.

ONE

When Des Fenton hit the barrier at seventy miles an hour, his bike had bucked him, thrown him and snapped him like a twig. This wasn't meant to happen to Des. Dashing Des had the luck of the devil. He was Pattie Moxon's lucky star. In twenty years of speedway riding he'd never copped more than a few broken fingers. Des was good. Des was the Bullets' ace. Quick off the tape, king of the first bend. Nothing could touch him. Until tonight.

He had hit the barrier head-first, crumpling like a jack-in-the-box in reverse, before flopping face down onto the cinders. The stretcher bearers of the St John Ambulance knew it was a bad one. They sprinted across the centre green and over the track towards the prostrate rider, looking fearful. Pattie, the Bullets' boss, followed close behind. She too knew it was bad. She'd been in the business long enough. She threw her fur coat to the ground and knelt by Fenton's side as the St John's men examined him. One of them looked up at her and shook his head.

The heat had started well. Fenton was first off the tape, taking the lead on the first bend and holding it like it was his divine right. His teammate Ray Simpkins was a hair's breadth behind. He hugged the star's rear wheel like a hound at heel until their two wheels touched in the third lap. Fenton and his motorcycle spasmed as one, as if shocked by a high voltage current. Twenty thousand fans let out a collective gasp that bounced off the stadium walls. His wife let out a shriek that could be heard above the crowd. She scrambled out of the VIP box and ran towards the scene in quick faltering steps. She'd seen him come off before, but this wasn't the same. This one was bad. A speedway wife knows the difference.

Ken Kilminster knew the difference too, as he quickly ushered his photographer onto the track, hoping this might be the story that would make his career as a speedway correspondent. As the first flashbulb popped, it lit up Simpkins standing at the edge of the track watching, a cigarette dangling from his lower lip.

Simpkins had been twitchy that night. Uptight and tetchy. Something on his mind. Something that had been building for a while. Fenton clapped him on the back and wished him luck before the heat. Simpkins had blanked him. Now he stared blankly in the glare of the floodlights, as the ambulance crew eased Fenton's limp body onto the stretcher and covered his face with a blanket. He watched Pattie consoling Fenton's wife, who was gasping hysterically, her hand to her cheek and tears welling in her eyes. He saw Kilminster, notebook in hand, his pudgy fist squeezing a pencil stub as he captured the moment in shorthand. And he watched the stretcher bearers lift Fenton into the ambulance and slam the doors, leaving no doubt that this was Dashing Des's last race.

A hush descended on the stadium, the cheering and chanting of the crowd turned to ghoulish whispers as the ambulance drove slowly over the centre green towards the main gates. Simpkins flicked his cigarette butt towards it as it passed, spat the cinder dust from his mouth and walked back towards the dressing rooms. 'Not your night, was it Des?' he muttered under his breath.

TWO

Reg Calloway wished the morning over. He'd seen enough burials for one lifetime. He'd spent the past hour waiting for a break in the proceedings so he could smoke. When he lit a Navy Cut he realised he had company.

'Did you know Des well?'

'Only as a name over the tannoy.'

She leaned in to accept a light, letting the small veil of her mourning hat brush his cheek. He caught her scent but couldn't name it. It was a long time since he'd bought perfume for a woman.

'A great loss to the club,' she said.

'Not to mention to his wife. I hope he was insured.'

Dashing Des, star rider of Bermondsey Bullets, always drew a big crowd. Today was no exception. They had lined the streets from the stadium to the cemetery. Fifteen thousand had turned out to watch the funeral procession. Men, women, children. So many women, all made up and in their best coats. Dashing Des was the Bullets' ladies' man. Roguish good looks chiselled into a well-worn face. All flash suits and too much brilliantine. He'd walk onto the track before each fixture in top hat and tails, a red carnation in his lapel. He looked swell and had a swagger to match. The crowd would sing Putting on the Ritz as he plucked the button-hole from his lapel and threw it into the stands. The women would reach out to snatch it. They were all Des's girls.

'I value my riders, Mr Calloway. They're all insured. And the club will make a contribution to the widow.'

'Very generous, I'm sure. What is it they call speedway

promoters? Merchants of manslaughter?'

'They know the risks. And they live well. They enjoy the spoils.'

Calloway stole a glance at her. He put her past thirty and then some, like him, but she wore it well. Clothes from town, hair too he reckoned, and good shoes. Very good. Nothing you'd find on the local women. Shoes were always a tell. They set off her calves and ankles. She noticed him looking but didn't react. She was Patricia Moxon, speedway aristocracy. He was a glorified commissionaire.

He had walked in false solemnity ahead of the cortège. He didn't know Fenton in anything but name and he cared little for the Bullets. But as track security officer he was obliged to join in, taking his place alongside the promoter, the pit crews and the county commander of the St John's Ambulance. The procession reached the cemetery, the Bullets flanking the hearse in race jackets and leathers. They rode slowly, revving staccato to stay steady. Calloway counted six, three riders a side, plus Fenton in the hearse. One rider missing from the team of eight.

In the four months since taking the job, Calloway had grown to hate the stadium. It was a tinny colosseum for a shilling's worth of vicarious danger to punctuate a dreary existence. Fans came from the docks and the railways and the Peek Freans biscuit factory, scarves around their necks and rattles in hand, ready to sing oft-sung anthems to their adopted heroes. Their four-stroke gladiators. Their champions of the cinders. A pint or two in the Dun Cow before the races, then saveloy and pease pudding from George's Hole in the Wall on the way home. A ritual to blot out the grimness of life on the ration.

Calloway watched Fenton's widow as she dismounted the funeral car. Tight-jawed, more numb than sorrowful, her tailored black two-piece worn like armour to shield emotion. It was the onlookers who cried tears, perhaps for Des Fenton, more likely for loved ones lost to the war, to the Blitz or to the hardship of their tenement lives. Their collective grief on this crisp April Saturday had purpose. Have a good cry, love. Get it all out. Dashing Des's reckless demise was the spark to ignite a tankful of hurt.

As the final mourners passed through the cemetery gates, a woman stepped forward from the crowd and fell in line. About twenty, with a doll face and dyed-blonde hair, she wore a dark grey suit with a full skirt over rounded hips and a narrow-waist jacket. She wore it well but wore it local. This was New Look style through the shop windows of the Old Kent Road. Too full in the shoulders, padded in the bust, with clumsy stitching that lacked the finesse of its couture inspiration. The birdcage veil of her pillbox hat hid little of her common good looks. She gave the crowd something new to gawp at. She held her head proud, her small lips pursed with a hint of defiance.

The riders peeled off and parked their motorcycles in two neat lines flanking the cemetery road. They removed helmets and bowed heads. They snuck looks at the young woman and exchanged glances with their teammates. All except Simpkins. His head hung lower than the others, his eyes fixed on the damp bitumen of the road.

Calloway watched Patricia Moxon and the widow exchange the meaningless words the situation required. Hushed and insincere but better than morbid silence. Only then did Fenton's widow notice the young blonde who now stood at Calloway's side. The widow's eyes flashed through her veil. Her body squared up as dignity fought the urge to advance. Patricia Moxon gripped her arm, the meaning clear. Don't, love. Whoever she is. Calloway looked sideways at the young women. She stared purposefully into the middle distance with parade ground detachment. Oblivious, the undertakers' men beckoned the riders to the hearse to lift the coffin. It broke the line of hostility from the widow to the blonde. The county commander of the St John's Ambulance sighed, relieved that a scene had been avoided. Calloway caught his eye and raised a quizzical eyebrow. The commander shrugged. Pat Moxon saw the exchange. She flickered disapproval.

The proceedings were dismal, the eulogy long and inauthentic, the priest working to a script prepared from the customary fag-end biography of a man he knew little of. The widow wept a little but her composure held out. Calloway was grateful.

Between the eulogy and the lowering of the coffin, a grey mist drifted in from the river and under its shroud, the young woman had withdrawn unnoticed. Calloway looked for her among the headstones and the vulgar statues that mocked them, but she was gone.

'Who was the bottle blonde?' he asked when the formal proceedings were over.

Patricia Moxon shrugged, as if indifferent to his question. 'Perhaps she's the other woman.'

'So there is one?'

'They're speedway stars, Mr Calloway. Odds on there's another woman, on the side or just for the night.'

'Nice boys then.'

She considered this, drawing on a cigarette she held between well-manicured fingers and exhaling with deliberation.

'They enjoy taking risks. It goes with the job.'

Calloway glanced back up the cemetery road. The undertakers' men were rearranging the floral tributes and the grave diggers shovelled earth into the hole. He could see their breath as they panted from the exertion. Spring had yet to clock on for its shift. Moxon pulled the collar of her fur coat tight against the chill. A handsome woman, Calloway thought, and expensively dressed, but in a way that said she wasn't born to it. The lady Pat enjoyed new money. Beneath the couture there was a grafter.

The riders buckled helmets and mounted their bikes. Matchless, Triumph, the mighty Vincent, marques etched in gold and chrome polished mirror-bright. Their four-cylinder engines pounded brutally through the hush as the Bullets left the cemetery two abreast. Moxon and Calloway stood aside to let them pass.

A car was waiting outside the cemetery gates, its engine running. Moxon gestured to it. 'Where do you live? I'll drop you off.'

The invitation seemed premeditated. Calloway tried to duck it.

'No thank you, ma'am. I'd prefer to walk.'

She snorted. 'Don't be silly.'

She held the door for him. He accepted and eased his big frame into the back seat. It felt awkward going first. He was used to holding the door for ladies. She flicked a gloved hand, waving him to the far side of the seat before sliding in next to him. The driver asked for instructions. Calloway gave his address. He caught a look of disapproval on Moxon's face. She must have known his street. The driver nodded with a shortfall of enthusiasm. He was thin, shabby and smelled of coal tar soap. He gripped the wheel with nicotine-stained fingers, nails chewed short. His Burton's suit was ready for retirement. Calloway knew this type. A demobbed drifter down on his luck. Someone you wouldn't lend money to.

'Does he drive you everywhere?'

'Good lord, no,' she said, removing her beret and shaking her hair loose. 'The Bullets are good but they're not that good.'

'Why the chauffeur today?'

The title was generous.

'An excuse for a quick exit. I didn't want to hang around for the wake. I've seen them drink, and worse. Best I don't hang around. What the manager doesn't see, if you get my drift.'

The car swept past Saturday shoppers along New Cross Road, a bustling normality against the strange rubble landscape that was post-war London. The Kinema was showing Hollywood movies again, now the tax dispute with America was over. Now showing: The Sands of Iwo Jima. Coming soon: I was a Male War Bride. Still suffering the hangover of war yet revelling in the glory and the romance.

The car swung a sharp right at the Marquis of Granby. Pat Moxon leaned into Calloway on the turn. He felt her warmth through the flannel of his suit and caught her scent again - jasmine and roses.

'I need to talk to you, Mr Calloway. I suppose you'd call it a security matter.'

'Someone been skimming your turnstile take?'

'Something rather delicate, about the team. I'd appreciate your help.'

The driver caught a look at them through the rearview mirror, his interest piqued. Calloway returned the look. The driver read the signal and feigned disinterest.

'I work for the stadium, ma'am. This sounds like a club matter.'

She slipped off her shoes, then leaned forward in her seat to massage her feet. They were small and neat, her painted toes visible through the sheer silk of her stockings.

'I lease the stadium, Mr Calloway. I'd say you work for me.'

'Then I'd say you share me with the greyhounds on Saturdays.'

She laughed and sat back in the seat, toying with the expensive-looking pearls around her neck.

'Come to see me on Monday. We can't talk now in any case.'

The driver shuffled in his seat. Calloway tapped him on the shoulder.

'You can drop me here. I'll walk the rest.'

The car pulled up alongside the curb, just short of the turning into Calloway's street. Patricia Moxon looked out of the side window with seeming disinterest, as if noticing the place for the first time. Calloway sensed she knew the area well, but it would be unbecoming of speedway royalty to admit it. It was an unloved street, bombed into unintended blocks and connected by cleared sites, the rubble on some still to be removed. The exposed flanks of party walls lacking their neighbours bore a clumsy patchwork of paper and paint. Fireplaces floated in pairs at each floor level, like the plaintiff eyes of vagrants. It was a street of single rooms and lightless basements.

'Are you married, Mr Calloway?'

He climbed out of the car, placed his big hands on the dusty roof and leaned in to reply.

'Put it this way. If I broke my neck like one of your riders, there'd be no widow to mourn me. And no other woman.'

She smiled with what might have passed for warmth.

'You should do something about that.'

He turned away. 'Goodbye, ma'am.'

'Goodbye, Mr Calloway.'

Calloway glanced backwards as he walked towards the dilapidated street and caught the driver sneering.

THREE

They were filming at the track. A Pathé news crew had set up close to the inner boundary. With speedway stars back in the ascendant, there was appetite for newsreel in the cinemas. The crew was meant to interview Des Fenton. Pat Moxon had substituted Bert Webber, her number two rider since young Billy Riley started losing form at the start of last season. Webber didn't have Fenton's swagger, nor his rough diamond looks, but he was cocky and tenacious. The director had him making repeated broadsides, trailing dirt then stopping in front of the camera. The show-off in Webber was enjoying himself. The cameraman had to wipe the lens with each take and the producer tutted, picking cinder specks from the Harris tweed of his overcoat.

Webber removed his helmet for the interview and the director had him perch casually on the seat of his motorcycle while he answered questions. They rehearsed some lines beforehand with Pat providing the words for her rider. Webber removed a glove and scraped his hand across his head to sweep his hair back. He was no matinee idol. He was a snaggle-toothed grease monkey, wiry and bow-legged like a jockey, with the dull parchment skin of a chain smoker. But his hair was thick and lustrous and his eyes were steely and keen, his pupils darting shiftily like beetles on a hot plate.

'Oh yes, there's money in speedway racing and a good rider can make five thousand a year if he gets the breaks. It's a risky old game and you've got to have guts, but I wouldn't swap it for the world.'

He spoke the lines in a self-conscious monotone, oblivious to the rhythm of punctuation. Patricia Moxon coached him off-camera between the retakes. With each successive take he would fluff the lines, each time in a different place.

Reg Calloway leaned on a stand rail and watched the scene play out. A female member of the Pathé crew was adjusting Webber's scarf, untying the outlaw-style bandana favoured by the riders and knotting it into a rakish foulard. Webber wriggled like a child whose mother had spat on a hankie to wipe the smut off his face.

The frustration on the small rider's face grew with each successive retake. The producer feigned patience, but it was wearing thin.

'I'd be alright if it wasn't for that fucking camera putting me off me stroke.'

Moxon's voice echoed off the empty concrete stands. 'We'll have less of that language Bert Webber!'

Webber jumped, as if some all-seeing goddess of speedway had spoken.

'I've warned you before. None of your effing and blinding on my track. Otherwise you'll go straight back where I found you.'

Calloway crossed the stands towards her. 'So where did you find him?'

'The arse end of Rotherhithe, via The Hammers for a couple of seasons. They might tolerate his uncouth ways at West Ham but I'm not having it here.'

Webber gave it one last take before dismissing himself with a shrug and wheeling his machine towards the starting line.

'Still, he won the London Cup in forty-seven. Fearless little fella. An old-style leg trailer. It's a miracle he still has all his limbs.'

'Missing a finger, though.'

'You're observant. And two toes on his left foot. But that's small change for a rider like him.'

The film crew were setting up for cutaway shots at the side of the track. Webber was summoning two of the Bullets' crew, gesturing that he needed a push-off.

'They tell me Bob Danvers-Walker is going to narrate it,' said Moxon. 'I hope he does a better job than poor Bert. Do you follow the news, Mr Calloway?'

He nodded. 'On the radio and in the papers. I'm not one for the news theatres.'

'I don't blame you. Full of courting couples and queers. Still, good luck to them. It's not like there's many places they can do it.'

She was blunt, Calloway gave her that.

'You wanted to talk to me.'

She didn't respond. She was distracted. Two riders were ripping up the track with practice laps and Moxon was seeing something in their riding she disapproved of. He waited for her to answer. His impatience showed and she noticed.

'We've not spoken much have we, Mr Calloway?'

'Not much, ma'am, no. I look after the stadium. You look after the club. It suits me that way. I've not much time for the antics of these maniacs.'

She flicked her cigarette onto the stand and ground it into the concrete with her heeled shoes.

'You make me wonder why you're here at all.'

He had wondered the same thing himself in the few months since taking the job. But he knew the answer. Peacetime didn't suit him and opportunities to make a living were scarce. God knows the war hadn't been kind to him, but the past three years had been worse. He'd stuck with the army until forty-six. He had had no place else to go at the time. After the episode in Nuremberg, there had been no choice but to leave.

'I look after the pen, ma'am. Don't expect me to love the animals.'

She laughed.

'Some of them are beasts at that. But I like that in a man, Calloway. It suits me well. This game's about aggression as much as skill.'

'I think I've seen enough aggression, ma'am.'

She offered him a cigarette, which he accepted. She had a man's cigarette case embossed with the initials PRM and a matching lighter. They looked expensive but not ostentatious.

'You're right. I did want to talk to you.'

She turned to lean back on the railing. She closed her eyes and inclined her head to face the mid-morning sun, which had broken through the cloud. A wolf whistle cut through the noise from the track. Without opening her eyes, Pat said: 'Get back on that bike, O'Donnell. You've been slow off the tape for the last two fixtures. You of all people need the practice.'

The rider O'Donnell was stretched out on the upper tier of the stands in full leathers, taking the last drags of a cigarette held inwards between his oil-stained thumb and finger.

'But baby, the view from here is too damn good.'

'You'll get a view of the back of my hand in minute. Get your overpaid Yank arse down to that starting line or you'll be back in Pasadena before you can say Chattanooga Choo-choo.'

The rangy American put on a show of looking hurt, then lolled his way down each tier of the stands blowing kisses at his boss. She shot him a look, the kind a foreman gives when he's caught an apprentice smoking on his shift.

'They're still overpaid and over here then, ma'am.'

'And the other, I've no doubt, Mr Calloway.'

She watched O'Donnell as he straddled his bike like a western hero saddling up and shouted instructions for his push start to the track crew.

'I brought him over in forty-six. I needed some glamour in the team. His face has been advertising shaving soap since we won the league.'

'I've seen the posters. Do you take commission?'

'He gets to keep his fee. It pays for his lifestyle. He's got expensive tastes that one.'

She watched the American ride laps, pulling Looney Toons faces at the crew on the home straight.

'Outwardly they behave as if nothing's happened. But Des Fenton's death has rattled them.'

'Surely that's not surprising.'

'You'd think not, but this is a tough old life and not without its tragedies. Riders take the rough with the smooth. Deaths are few and far between, thank the Lord, but when they happen, well there's a sort of heroic acceptance of the inevitable.'

'But not this time?'

She shook her head. 'They're talking.'

'Saying what?'

She lit another cigarette and took a long and deliberate drag on the hot tar. 'They're poring over the details. The track conditions, the speed Des was coming out of the turn, why Ray Simpkins was on his tail the whole time.'

'It's the Bullets' first fatality. They're bound to be rattled. Anything show up on the club's investigation?'

'The track conditions were fine. We'd laid new cinder over the summer and the depth was tested at the start of the race. Deeper than the requisite six inches. The chief mechanic confirmed both bikes were in proper condition when they left the pits. Des Fenton was in good shape too. The trainer confirmed it. So was Simpkins.'

Moxon had installed a gym at the stadium and put the Bullets on a fitness regime. A former Charlton Athletic trainer put them through their paces twice a week and kept fitness records.

'Have your insurers investigated?'

'Yes, and the association. Neither found anything untoward.'

She turned and looked across to the track. The American rider was performing tricks for the cameras. She drew on the cigarette and exhaled hard.

'I've been around this business a long time, Mr Calloway. This is something different.'

'Different how?'

She paused for a moment, as if reluctant to continue. 'They're saying Des Fenton's death wasn't an accident.'

The statement hit him like a punch to the guts.

'Who's saying?'

She ignored the question. He pressed her. 'Who is saying this to you?'

'I can't tell you. I was told in confidence.'

'You were told that Ray Simpkins ran Fenton off the track deliberately? That's a serious allegation. It's a matter for the police.'

'I don't want the police involved. I want it not to be true.'

Calloway let this sink in. He changed tack. 'What's Ray Simpkins saying?'

'He's keeping his head down for the most part.'

'Was there something between Simpkins and Fenton? Bad blood?'

'Competition certainly, but that's not unusual. And they were different types. Fenton was gregarious. The life and the soul. Simpkins is quieter, a bit surly when he wants to be. The chippy type.'

'Did he resent Fenton's success?'

'Not so you'd notice. They were business-like around one another, but wouldn't call them pals.'

'Always like that?'

'They became distant over the last few fixtures, maybe since the end of last season.'

'You don't run a man off the track for being distant.'

'Maybe not, but I need to know more, Mr Calloway. If something's not right, I need it dealt with and dealt with quickly.'

She looked towards the track at the practicing riders. 'I can't have a jinx on the club, not this season. I've too much to lose. I need you to make some enquiries.'

'Why do you think they would talk to me?'

'You strike me as the persuasive sort. And I've asked around about you, what you did in the war. There's more to you than filling the fire buckets and locking the gates.'

She didn't know the half of it, he thought.

'I work for the stadium not the club. If there's anything in this, which I doubt, it's club business.'

It wasn't the answer she wanted.

'What do you earn, Calloway? Don't bother answering, I've read your personnel file. It takes you a month to earn what my riders can make in a night. If you help me, I'll pay you what I pay them, from now until the end of the season.'

Calloway snorted. 'Worth that much to you?'

'For the right result.'

'And what if I get the wrong result?'

‘Then we’ll need to fix that.’

He was inclined to leave it right there. But Patricia Moxon could be persuasive too. She was all persuasion from where he stood. She worked hard at it. From the fit of her dress to the height of her heels, her boldness of speech and her confident tone. Even the studied way she held a cigarette.

‘I’ll make some enquiries but I won’t take your money. I’m not one of your prize stallions and I won’t be bought.’

‘It’s good money, Calloway.’

‘I’ve no need for it.’

She raised an eyebrow. It was plucked to the width of a pencil point. ‘You could spend it on proper digs. I don’t see you as the “furnished room for single gentleman” type.’

‘It suits me fine.’

He stubbed his cigarette against the metal stand rail. O’Donnell clunked past them in lead-soled boots and sat on the stands a few yards away. He ran his fingers through the pile of helmet-sweaty hair on his big skull.

‘Give me a week,’ Calloway said. ‘If I don’t find anything, I suggest you draw a line under it. Tell your lads you’ve ordered a safety review. Any suggestions where I should start?’

Moxon looked over at the snaggle-toothed Webber, who chatted cheerily to the mechanics in the pits.

‘Start with Bert. He knows everyone’s business and he likes to talk. Whatever you find out, you tell me first. No one else.’

Calloway nodded an acknowledgement. She looked him up and down. Six foot and broad, with a firm jaw and all his own teeth. Dark hair shorn short, Brylcreemed close to his scalp in the no-nonsense fashion of an ex-NCO. Barrel-chested, with strong-looking hands balled into fists by his side. A powerful man, but in control, at least that’s how he appeared to her.

‘You know I’d never thought of you as a stallion, Reg.’

She took a long last draw on the lipstick-stained stub of her cigarette. Then she winked.

‘Well not until now anyway.’

The American laughed. Calloway wasn’t the laughing kind.

FOUR

Local women shouted at a thick-set man who stood at the front step of his narrow, smog-blackened house. He wore old suit trousers with braces over an unwashed vest, which showed off broad shoulders and taught, muscled arms. Thirty years old or so, his thinning black hair was combed flat across his scalp, with jagged, uncombed tufts sticking out where he had slept. He said nothing, staring back with mean detachment. Still in his hand was the wooden post which he'd used just a minute ago to strike a stray dog repeatedly on its head, as the stunned creature skulked motionless beneath the blows. The dog now crawled in deranged circles on half-crouched legs, blood dripping from its mouth onto the dusty stone paving.

Reg Calloway and Bert Webber had watched the scene play out from the table they were sharing in a cafe on the opposite side of the street. Neither seemed shocked, just distracted by the brutality of it. Webber broke the silence.

'That's Wally Whitby. I used to work with him down the rope factory. That was before the war.'

Even from across the street, Calloway recognised the look on Whitby's face, expressionless but with a certain kind of mania behind the eyes. He'd seen that look on men during the war.

'Whoever he is, he's a troubled soul.'

Webber took a slurp of tea and nodded. 'He was on the Burma railway. Never been the same since he come back from that POW camp. Fucking Japanese. I was in North Africa me'self. Them Italians weren't a bad lot. Half of 'em didn't want to be there. Same as us really.'

The two men ate fried food, smearing grease and egg yolks around thick plates. Webber spoke while he ate, saliva smacks punctuating his bad grammar, which he delivered cheerily.

'Was you overseas, Mr Calloway?'

Calloway nodded. 'Europe mostly. Normandy, the Ardennes, Germany.'

'What was you?'

'Army.'

'Same here. Service Corps. Driver. Not a bad mechanic too as it happens. You?'

'Airborne.'

Webber sat up, his eyes alight. 'Paratrooper?'

Calloway put his knife and fork together and lit a cigarette from the plain gunmetal case he had carried throughout the war.

'Gliders.'

Webber frowned. 'Blimey. Fucking death traps.'

Calloway flicked ash into a chipped metal Players ashtray, which stood in a moat of slopped tea on the pale blue Formica of the tabletop.

'Yep. I reckon they killed more of my lot than the enemy. What with that and the jeeps rolling over.'

Webber rolled his eyes and nodded. 'I don't know why they got rid of the Tillies. Granted they wasn't so good on rough ground, but on the roads those old utility cars handled like a proper motor.'

Webber slurped his tea and used the barbed end of a broken matchstick from the ashtray to pick tiny gobbets of bacon from the crevices between his crooked yellow teeth.

'Jeeps. They looked flash enough, but you couldn't trust 'em on the bends.' He sniggered. 'A bit like Six Gun O'Donnell.'

The waitress passed their table, half sashay, half slouch. Webber wolf whistled as she passed. The waitress turned and Bert leered. She stuck out a hip, crossed her arms and glared.

'That house coat's a bit on the snug side, Vera. Showing off your curves something lovely.'

She raised a thick eyebrow then threw a sodden grey cloth in the small man's direction.

'Who pulled your chain, Bert Webber?'

Webber caught the cloth like a fielder and let out a wheezy smoker's laugh.

'See you Sunday, Vera,' he shouted.

'Not if I see you first.'

She was about Webber's age, thirty-five but looking forty, with cheap lipstick on plump lips. A floral wrap-over housecoat restrained an ample bosom and clung to her hips. She had a menial seductiveness, the stuff of rushed encounters in back rooms. Groping and giggling with milk-stout breath. A thought forced its way into Calloway's head, base and filthy. He shook it off.

'One of your fancy women, Bert?'

'Leave it out. That's Vera, me sister-in-law. Coming to our place Sunday with her husband Stan for dinner.'

Dinner meaning lunch, Calloway noted. Just as tea meant supper. He'd used the same lexicon before the army and over time was re-educated into the ways of the mannered classes after his temporary commission. That and don't drink tea with your food. Webber looked his sister-in-law up and down as she walked back to the counter.

He leaned forward and whispered. 'Not that I wouldn't mind.'

Calloway had Webber down as the talker of the team, at least when he wasn't in front of a camera. There was no training on Tuesdays so Calloway had taken him for breakfast. The cafe was the rider's choice. It was dimly lit and a fog of cheap tobacco and smoking lard hung in the air. Webber was at home here, not like the places up West where his teammates would go to swank, as he put it. This place was favoured by drivers from the bus garage and posties from the sorting office. Painters and decorators, skilled men. The unskilled labourers had their own caffs, places the young Bert would go before the war when he worked at the factory. This was his concession to the rarefied life of a speedway rider with cash in his pocket. It was a very small concession. But Webber was content with this modest rung up the ladder, shunning the ostentation of his fellow track stars.

'Tell me about O'Donnell.'

'Typical Yank. A bragger. When he's not telling you why he's the club's best rider, which he ain't, he's telling you about getting his leg over. A different bird every Saturday. Acts like a movie star and they fall for it too.'

'Working his way through the fans?'

'Nah, his tastes are more upmarket. He goes dancing in town. Says he's good at that an' all.'

Calloway let him talk, mostly harmless anecdotes about his teammates. Calloway interjected with prompts until the conversation, virtually one-sided once the little man got into his stride, reached the death of Des Fenton.

'Des was a good rider and he knew that circuit better than any of us. He was with the Bullets in the thirties, before Pat took it over. He'd rode at Catford, under Eddie Dandridge, before the club moved to Bermondsey. He was the first one to really master the new track. The Dustbin Lid, they call it. Shortest track in the country. Tight as a gnat's arse, pardon my French. All bends and no straights. One big fuckin' broadside all the way round. The away clubs hate it. They're used to more straight riding in a lap. That's the Bullets' advantage. We know our own track and when we're away, well, it's a bleeding luxury. Room to breathe if you know what I mean.'

Webber lit a new cigarette from the burned down butt of the one that dangled from his dry lips. Calloway ordered two more teas.

'Shame Des Fenton didn't have more room the night he died. Did you see the accident?'

'Nah, just heard.'

'So what happened?'

The small rider stubbed the butt of his last cigarette onto the dirty breakfast plate in front of him.

'Des was bombing down the back straight. Simpkins was hanging onto his tail. Ray's front wheel touched Des's rear and sent him into a skid. Des couldn't pull out of it. He piled into the back of the Harringay rider, Alfie Biggs. Biggs hit the barrier but was okay. Fenton was thrown over his handlebars and landed smack on his head. Dead on the spot. Broken neck.'

The waitress, Vera, banged the teas down onto their table. Webber spooned in three sugars then slurped noisily. Pans crashed in the kitchen, followed by profanities. An old man with a veined and mottled face at the table opposite jumped. He peered with rheumy eyes over the counter into the kitchen. Amused by the sound of the ensuing argument, he grinned with too-white false teeth, a present from the National Health.

'There's a rumour Fenton's death wasn't an accident,' said Calloway.

Webber looked out of the cafe window as if distracted. The man who had beaten the dog had disappeared into his house leaving his neighbours on the pavement to gossip. There was tut-tutting and shaking of heads.

'I know. I've heard,' he said.

'Who from?'

He evaded the question. 'It's going around.'

Calloway pressed him. 'Around where? Around who?'

Webber didn't budge. 'Just around.'

Webber fidgeted and looked around the room. Calloway lowered his voice and leaned across the table. 'Any truth in it?'

Webber shrugged, showing discomfort at the question. 'I'm keeping out of it. It wasn't my race. I was in the pits with Hale, the chief mechanic. I'd come off me'self in the previous heat. Nothing serious, but me handlebars needed adjusting. I didn't see nothing of the accident. Just heard the commotion after Des came off.'

'Is Ray Simpkins a good rider?'

'Rocket Ray? Good as any. Was on good form start of last season. Got right sluggish halfway through and finished fourth on points overall. He's not rode so well this season either.'

'How was his riding in the heat?'

'The heat? Fenton copped it. He was showing a bit of muscle. Quick off the tape but not enough to get out front. It's been a while since he could beat Des to the first bend.'

'Was he being reckless?'

'Like I said, I was in the pits.'

Calloway changed tack. 'How did Simpkins get on with Fenton?'

'Alright I s'pose. Simpkins isn't exactly the friendly type. A bit on the chippy side you might call it.'

'That's what Pat Moxon said. Was he chippy with Fenton?'

'Fenton's flash ways got on his nerves. Nothing serious. I can only recall them ever having one barney.'

'What about?'

Webber thought for a moment. He rubbed the stump of his missing finger. 'You remember Joe Smoke? No, thinking about it, that was before your time.'

The small rider leaned back and rocked on the legs of his chair. 'There was this tramp. A proper smokey Joe, hence the name we give him. Blackened face and stank of wood smoke like he'd been burning a brazier on a bomb site. He had a big scar down one side of his face, all laced up. It looked like a fork of lightning. Army deserter, we reckoned. Anyway he used to kip under the west stand. He'd made himself a little camp out of old crates and blankets up one corner where it was dark. He'd come and go through a hole in the fence down by the railway line. We never knew he was there at first. He'd been there ages before the management realised. Then they turned a blind eye for a bit. He wasn't any bother and the last fella to do your job was a bit on the slack side. When he wasn't swinging the lead, he was half pissed. The manager, that is. Fell asleep at his desk one night with the safe open and Saturday night's takings there for anyone to help himself to. Prat. So one day this Joe Smoke came out of his hole and hung around the track when we was practicing. Des Fenton took the piss at first then he got talking to him.'

He was in his stride now. Calloway pushed him gently. 'Talking about what?'

'Dunno, but it happened on and off for a few weeks, Des and Joe Smoke having little chats. After a bit Ray Simpkins started to get the nark about it. Telling Des not to encourage him. Des carried on until this one time Simpkins has a right old go at the tramp. Telling him to fuck off and not to come back. Making a right fuss. Des Fenton wasn't having this and they started having a go at each other.'

'What happened then?'

'A bit of shovin'. Seemed to blow over. Joe Smoke never came back and Simpkins and Fenton kept out of each other's way. They've sort of stayed that way since. A bit distant. Whatever it was I suppose it's resolved itself now, with Des being gone.'

'Did this tramp every show up again?'

Webber shook his head. 'Nah. Not seen him since. They patched up the hole in the fence and took down his camp and burned it.'

'Where do you think he went, this Joe Smoke?'

'Probably on a bomb site somewhere. Or up the spike.'

Calloway looked quizzical. 'Spike?'

'Carrington House, the men's hostel.'

Webber grinned to himself then sang, husky and croaking.

'Dimly the lights of the city are gleaming,
Drear is the night and so cold.
Grimly the walls of the workhouse are frowning,
Frowning on mis'ry untold.'

He chuckled to himself. 'Thinking about it, Carrington House might be a bit upmarket for him.'

'And you've no idea what Fenton and the tramp used to talk about?'

'No, mate. You can't hear nothing on that track when there's bikes going round. He did show Des some pictures once though. Old Joe had these photographs in this grubby old album.'

'Speedway photographs?'

Webber shrugged.

'Did you ever see this album up close?'

The other man recoiled. 'You're joking. I wouldn't go near him. He stank of piss. I'm surprised Fenton had anything to do with him, what with all his flash ways.'

Calloway paid the bill and left half a crown tip on the table. Vera spied it from across the room.

'Thanks, lovely. You can come again.'

Calloway doubted he would. As the two men stood to leave, he said to Webber: 'Why didn't Billy Riley show up for Fenton's funeral?'

Webber rubbed at the stump of his missing finger. 'Said he was ill.'

'You think he was?'

'Dunno. It was odd that he didn't show up. Didn't show for training on Monday neither.'

They left the cafe and walked across the street, passing the house where the incident with the dog had occurred. There was a trail of dark red blood leading down a passageway to the side of the house. Somewhere the dog lay dying.

FIVE

Wednesday. The Bullets at home to Wembley. Twenty-five thousand pale white faces crammed into the stands. Flat caps and hair oil. Girls crushed against the barriers, arms hanging over the sides trailing black-and-red scarves. Gas rattles clapping out a machine-gun brat-a-tat. Young voices chanting in unison over the tinny crackle of the tannoy.

'One-two-three-four, who are we for? B-U-L-L-E-T-S, Bullets!'

Expectant faces hoping for the first glimpse of the riders. Banners and flags, the black flying bullet emblem of the home team waved euphorically, as if in some rally for a people's empire.

Calloway shouted orders to his staff. Boys had climbed the tannoy tower for a better view. They clung keenly to the scaffold, their chins resting on the cold metal. He sent men to bring them down. He didn't want a child breaking their neck on his watch.

The stand lights dimmed. A hush descended. A single spotlight beamed into the darkness, bathing the home riders in a sphere of white light. The crowd let out a roar. The tannoy blared Marching Along Together as the riders strode two abreast across the inner track and onto the manicured oval of grass within the circuit. They walked with the slow swagger of heroes, helmets slung by their sides swinging on the straps. Polished race leathers glistened, silk scarves shimmered.

Webber led the team, waving to the crowd. O'Donnell blew kisses to the girls, who shrieked a collective retort. The track crews took up their positions alongside the St John's

Ambulance, who stood like sentinels in black uniforms with blancoed cross straps at regular stations around the inner perimeter. Their furled blankets and stretchers lay in ordered rows ominously beside them.

The pit crews swarmed around the riders' machines, rear wheels spinning as they made their pre-race checks. They adjusted gear ratios to suit the track conditions. The riders entered the pits to the din of the engines, conferring with their crews in short shouted bursts. They fastened helmets, strapped on lead boots and slapped each other's backs for luck.

Marshals in white coats busied around the start line. Crew members in matching buff overalls and black berets paired up to give push starts. Engines fired up, filling the air with methanol. Castrol R, the smell of speedway. The first four riders nudged up to the tape. Chromium forks and silver spokes signalled like mirrors in the bright track light, which hung over them in a lattice of black wire. Webber and the South African rider, Jack Duiker, were first up for the Bullets, against the two Wembley Lions. Webber wore the blue race cap, Duiker the red. They edged their machines back and forth along the start line, digging into the dirt with their heels. The start marshal gave the signal and the tape snapped upwards. The four machines lunged forward in unison like a single mechanical being. Within three seconds they were leaning into the first bend, lead boots down and rear wheels showering cinders. Then three seconds of straight before screaming into the return bend.

Calloway looked on from the tower. His eyes tracked the black-and-red race jackets of Webber and the South African. Their opponents had the edge. As the four riders passed the final lap flag, the Bullets lagged by a motorcycle's length. The crowd screamed encouragement, desperation in their blood-lust roar. Webber responded, riding with pure aggression, throwing his bike into the final bend, his left leg trailing so that the toecap of his boot dug grooves in the dirt. It failed to count and as the chequered flag waved, Webber finished third to the two Lions ahead, with Duiker inches behind him. The cheering turned to a deflated groan as the riders left the track. Calloway saw Moxon in the pits, her body tense, her face contorted. Riders and crew kept clear. They knew this look.

The tower door opened and a uniformed commissionaire, breathless from running, called over to Calloway. 'There's trouble under the west stand, down by gate five. I think you need to come.'

They double timed along the underside of the tiered concrete, jostling fans. Calloway signalled to two of his boys to leave their gates and follow them.

'What's happening, Sid?'

The commissionaire, fifty, ruddy-faced and unfit from too much standing around, spoke between gasps.

'Cosh boys, sir. About ten of 'em. Started cutting up rough in the buffet. Some of the regulars turfed 'em out and now there's a standoff.'

A small crowd had formed a ring around the commotion. Calloway pushed his way through.

At one end a gang of youths jittered, their mouths tensed and eyes set firm on the group of burly older men that faced them. Some of the youths held weapons, a leather cosh, a bike chain, no knives Calloway noted, despite the stories he'd heard. They wore jackets cut long in the body in herringbones and flecks, some with velvet pocket flaps. High-waist trousers, narrow at the ankles with loud socks in plaid and spots. They dressed like cavalry officers, Calloway thought, only cheaper and nastier. Their matching hair was long and piled high on top. They were fifteen or sixteen years old at most. The men that had them cornered, dockers by the looks of them, were in their thirties and forties, just looking for an excuse to exert their rightful seniority over theses sneering pretenders. Calloway stepped between the two camps. The older men would be quicker to see reason. They would also be the most dangerous if things kicked off. He tackled them first.

'At ease, gentlemen. Don't let this spoil your night out,' he said, and then more quietly, 'Make some room and we'll have these little bastards out of here. You've done your bit, now go and enjoy yourselves.'

The older men exchanged looks, weighing up whether they should comply. One of them stepped forward to face Calloway.

'These little fuckers need a good talking to.'

The shortest of the mob, he was broad-shouldered and packed with muscle. His shirt was half unbuttoned beneath his jacket revealing an old swallow tattoo on his freckled chest. A seaman, or used to be, and a leader. The rest squared up behind him, acknowledging his superiority. Bold enough to pick a fight on two fronts, he was staring Calloway down, challenging him to his face.

'Language, gentlemen. Speedway's a family night. Now I need you to let me do my job.'

But there was pride at stake here and principle. The older men had confronted the younger to establish a natural order among the local males. Calloway's intervention was denying them justice. He signalled to the security staff to standby, which they did without enthusiasm. They didn't relish the thought of taking on both groups. Calloway spoke softly to the sailor.

'Look around you, pal. Girls, kids, their mums and dads. It's no place for a fight. Do the decent thing. Let us deal with this.'

The sailor looked to one side thinking and ran a big stub-fingered hand through his wiry blonde hair. He looked back at Calloway and nodded. Calloway turned to the youths.

'Now I can call the police or you can leave with my lads and save yourselves a lot of bother.'

'Who the fuck are you, cunt?'

He was the tallest of the group, standing with what passed for a chest all puffed out, his acned chin jutting forward. A bike chain swung by his side from his bony hand.'

Calloway leant forward and whispered in the cosh boy's jug ear.

'I'm the cunt that's going to stop these big lads here turning you and your mates into a pool of piss on the floor. If you leave now, standing tall, you'll save face. If you don't, the St John's Ambulance will be taking you out on a stretcher and all your mates will get to watch.'

The boy snapped 'Fuck off' and swung the chain at Calloway who sidestepped to avoid it. He kicked the boy's legs from under him so that he toppled back onto the concrete. The older men moved forward but their leader signalled to them to stay. Calloway bent down and hauled the boy off the deck by the lapels of his cheaply tailored coat and slapped him twice, good and hard across the face. The boy lay stunned, unhurt and unsure of his next move. Then he grinned, a forced grin for the benefit of his mates. He stared up at Calloway, cocky and defiant. Calloway should have left it there, but the switch had flicked. The switch that sent him back to the war, to the things he'd seen and the things he'd done. The stadium faded to the edge of his consciousness and his past closed around him. It was an angry past and the anger found a way out through his fists. The boy on the ground spasmed with the first blow. The second blow was harder and the face that recoiled from it had changed. It was not the boy's face. It was a face from the past, imprinted on Calloway's memory. A loathsome face. He raised his fist a third time. A hand on his shoulder snapped him back to reality.

'That's enough now, Mr Calloway. I think the boy's learned his lesson.'

It was Les Birkett, the most senior commissionaire and Calloway's effective number two on the security staff. An old and even-tempered veteran who commanded respect, not least from his boss. Calloway lowered his arm and rose to his feet, panting. He faced the boy's gang mates.

'Anyone else?'

His violence had them rattled. Some looked terrified. They shuffled and looked to their leader on the ground who offered no response, just rubbed his pockmarked chin and muttered profanities through split lips. The sailor spoke to the boys with a calmness he'd not shown up to now.

'Alright lads, we've had our fun. Now piss off before this big fella here calls the Old Bill and we all get a night in the cells.'

Birkett shouted to his lads to open up gate five and nodded towards the boys.

‘See these gentlemen the off the premises,’ he said. ‘They won’t be coming here again.’

Calloway took a slow walk under the stands. Ruddy-faced Sid caught him up and fell in beside him.

‘Nasty little Herberts,’ he wheezed. ‘If they were mine, they’d get a taste of the strap. If their fathers were here now I’d give ’em a piece of my mind an’ all.’

‘Too many boys without fathers these days. And mothers too busy holding house and home together to keep them on the rails. That’s the trouble with war, Sid. We’re too busy remembering the dead to see what it’s done to the living.’

‘The back of my hand, that’s what they’d get.’

And they’d probably return the favour, thought Calloway, looking for an excuse to be alone. He told Sid to check on the turnstiles and ducked under the tunnel that led to the circuit. The engine noise echoed off the bare concrete walls. He crossed to the outer track, leant on the wire mesh fence and pulled out his cigarette case. Four riders lined up at the tape. He recognised the lanky American O’Donnell from his height, even as he sat astride the skeletal bike. Calloway picked a discarded programme from the ground and opened it. The second Bullets rider was Chip Bellman according to the list of heats.

The tape shot up and Bellman took an early lead. The fans roared. Calloway turned to face them. It was a capacity crowd, crammed into the stands, pressed against the fences by the weight of the bodies behind them. Penned like livestock. To Calloway there was an obscenity about it. An unwelcome echo of his past. He turned again to face the track as Bellman came out of the bend showering cinder. Calloway spat the dust from his mouth. Bellman held his lead for another lap with the American close on his tail. The crowd sensed a much-needed win. They sang Oranges and Lemons, Clanger Bellman’s given anthem. Their hope was short lived. O’Donnell wobbled out of the final bend hitting Bellman’s rear wheel. It sent the machine sliding sideways across the path of the oncoming Wembley rider, throwing Bellman into a roll. He lay still where he fell until the second Wembley bike clipped him. He jolted as if given an electric shock. Two of the track crew leapt from their stations to remove the bike while the St John's Ambulance lifted the downed rider off the dirt and onto a stretcher.

Calloway had seen enough. Maniacs, the lot of them. He'd spend six years in Europe hoping to God that he and his colleagues would be spared death or wounding. This lot threw themselves in harm's way willingly for a few thousand a year. And their fans cheered them on as they went. He tossed the programme onto the ground and walked back through the tunnel towards his office. Giggling girls with plump faces and head scarves stuffed their mouths with hot dogs. Calloway caught the sickly whiff of fried onions. Two young boys in hand-me-down shorts and snake belts sang 'One-two-three-four, who are we for...' then screamed 'Bullets!' over the ear-splitting clack of the gas rattles in their grubby hands.

The altercation with the youths had rattled him. He regretted slapping the boy. As a gesture to appease the older men and a warning to the younger ones, it was effective enough in diffusing the situation. That was his job after all. But the violence came too easily to him, as it had in the past. He thought of the man he'd watched beating the dog. They weren't so different.

Bert Webber slouched in the doorway of the riders' dressing room, smoking and staring at nothing. Sweat trickled from his hairline making streaks in the smuts on his face. He had an expression like a slapped child. Calloway gave him a What's up? look.

'It's a fucking rout. The Lions have won every heat bar one.' He sucked hard on the fag. 'Clanger's bust up his wrist so he ain't gonna be fit to race for weeks. Pat's doing her nut.'

Calloway wished he hadn't asked. He shrugged and left him to it. Not his problem.

By eleven o'clock silence was descending on the emptying stadium. The main gates clanged in the distance as his lads shut up for the night. Calloway made his final rounds and tested each door. The surgery, the workshop, the supporters' club kiosk. As he approached the door of the riders' changing rooms, he heard rhythmic knocking and audible voices from within. Clasping the handle, he eased the door open.

'Christ, Calloway. You picked your moment.'

Jack Duiker was naked save for motorcycle boots and a red spotted neck scarf. Beneath him on the team's massage bench, a young woman half his age wearing his leather jacket and his goggles over her mussed-up hair. Her dress and shoes lay in a pile on the floor next to an empty gin bottle.

'If you'd like to finish what you're doing, Mr Duiker, I'd like a word,' Calloway said. 'And you,' he nodded to the young woman, 'what's your name, love?' 'Maureen,' she replied. 'Maureen Baxter.' 'You need to be out of here Maureen,' he said. He took a bunch of keys from his pocket and unlocked the door to an adjoining room. 'Get yourself dressed in there. It's not much but at least it's private.' She scooped the pile of clothing from the concrete floor and staggered into the adjoining room, closing the door behind her. Duiker slid off the bench. Calloway turned to face him. 'Not on my watch Duiker, you got that?' Duiker rolled his eyes and nodded. The bestial rapture on his face of moments before had turned to an irritable sulk. He pulled on suit trousers and a vest and leaned back against the lockers.

'So you wanted a word, Mr Calloway. You going to give me a lecture now?'

'Stow it, Duiker. I'm not in the mood. I want to talk about Des Fenton.'

'Ah, pretty Pattie's got you sniffing around hasn't she. You're the boss lady's little bloodhound. You want to know about Fenton? Okay, Calloway, I'll tell you about Dashing Des. He was no gentleman.'

'That's quite some condemnation coming from you.'

The rider pulled a pair of expensive-looking shoes from the locker behind him and dropped them carelessly onto the floor. He pushed a foot inside each one without bothering to bend down, treading the backs down as he did so.

'The fans might have adored him, but all they saw was his

public face. Wearing that fucking top hat. Beneath all that Dashing Des bullshit was a different guy altogether, I can tell you. He was a bloody bastard.'

'He seemed popular enough.'

'Popular? He was a speedway star. A real ace, I don't deny. The fans hung round him like flies on shit. That doesn't mean he was great bloke.'

Duiker tugged at the trodden-down shoe backs with his oil-stained fingers, swearing under his breath, then laced the shoes up. He spat on the palm of his hand and wiped smudges off the toe caps.

'So what kind of bloke was he?'

The South African swivelled to face him.

'He had to have something on you. Something that gave him the upper hand. If he found your weakness, he'd use it. He could be a right devious little shit. He was...' he groped for the word, '...manipulative.'

'Did he find your weakness?'

Duiker laughed. 'He thought he had.'

Calloway nodded in the direction of the door behind which the girl was dressing. 'Notching up autograph hunters?'

'I wouldn't be the first.'

Duiker pulled a pack of Navy Cut from his suit jacket, which hung on the peg behind him. He flicked a Zippo lighter and took a long drag.

'It wasn't that. It was something else. Something from the old days back in South Africa before the war.'

'Tell me.'

'It's no great secret. I did time. A couple of years inside. Stealing cars. I was just a kid and I've not stepped out of line since. Des Fenton found out. He'd taunt me with it, joking at first. Seeing how I'd react. Then he threatened to tell Pattie Moxon.'

'Or else what?'

'He didn't get the chance to tell me that. You see, Pat already knew. Nothing much gets past her. She couldn't care less, provided I kept my nose clean over here. All she cares about is whether riders win or lose. I'm a winner, Calloway. I'm one of her golden boys.'

'Not tonight you weren't.'

'We all have off nights.' He nodded towards the inner door. 'And hey, my night didn't turn out so bad.'

'I hope young Maureen feels the same way once she's sobered up. So why didn't Fenton push his luck?'

'Because I told him Pat knew about me and I also told him I'd tear him a new arsehole if I ever heard him mention it again. I had to give him a proper warning. He backed off. He was a coward. It wasn't Pat I was worried about anyway. It's that I was getting good press. A rider with good press gets good money. I couldn't afford for any old dirt on me spoiling that. You know what, Calloway? There's a cigarette card with my face on it. That buys you a lot in this game.'

'A cigarette card, eh? That's quite an accolade. You must be very proud.'

'Get out of it.' He snorted up a gobbet of phlegm and swallowed it. 'Do you buy this story that Fenton's death wasn't an accident?'

'Is that what people are saying?'

'The only person saying it is Pattie Moxon as far as I'm aware.'

The girl stepped back into the dressing room, fully dressed and her hair back into some semblance of style. She moved awkwardly towards the door, swaying a little on her heels and avoiding eye contact with the two men.

'Don't forget your autograph book,' Duiker said.

Calloway waited for the door to swing closed.

'So why is Pat Moxon suspicious?'

Duiker shrugged. 'Search me.'

'You've been with the team over two years. You must have some idea.'

Duiker stood up and stretched. Then he picked up the gin bottle and held it to the light, checking for any last drops. Disappointed, he tossed it onto the pile of soiled towels in the corner.

'Listen, do you know how easy it is to come off a bike in this game? How easy it is to hit another rider? We're doing seventy miles an hour around a dirt track the size of a cat's arsehole with one gear and no brakes. The only thing stopping us from sliding all the way from here to the shit house is our left fucking leg. Accidents happen, mate. Sometimes riders die. It's tragic, but it doesn't make it someone's fault.'

He flicked his cigarette onto the dressing room floor and stubbed it out with his shoe.

'Pat just can't accept she's lost her prize pony.'

SIX

Ray Simpkins slammed a beaten-up toolbox on the workbench. He pulled a spanner from the tray.

'I do my own maintenance. Always have,' he said, as if responding to an unspoken criticism.

It was the morning after the mid-week fixture. Calloway had waited until Simpkins was alone in the stadium workshop and shown up uninvited. He watched Simpkins working on the skeletal JAP motorcycle, which was raised up on a wooden lift table.

'Don't trust the mechanics?'

'My bike. My life. Simple as that.'

He was about five foot eight and slim built. His face was thin with mean features. A sharp nose, narrow eyes, narrow lips. He had red-brown hair, thinning at the sides, which he Brylcreemed back without a parting. There were navy tattoos on his forearms and the kind of scars that a man who falls off motorcycles for a living tends to collect.

'Des Fenton looked after his own bike too, didn't he?'

Simpkins held the butt of a roll-up cigarette between his thumb and forefinger and drew hard on the damp end with compressed lips.

'That was his living. At least before speedway. Had a workshop under the arches down Deptford. Stands to reason he'd do his own work.'

He gripped the roll-up in his teeth and worked on the bike's rear wheel.

'He'd have the mechanics running round after him though. He was good at ordering people about. Lording it over them.'

‘Ever lord it over you?’

Simpkins crouched behind the JAP, checking the wheel alignment by sight. ‘Not likely.’

‘Did the two of you get on?’

Simpkins shrugged. ‘We were teammates.’

‘That’s not the same thing.’

‘We were teammates, like I said. We didn’t have much in common. He was flash and liked to get around. I keep myself to myself.’

He leaned back against the bench, blinked hard and stretched his neck muscles. The sinews tautened through pale white skin. He looked as if he could use more sleep.

Calloway stood in the workshop doorway and watched the rider work. By now word had gone round that Calloway was conducting his own investigation, so he was direct with his questions.

‘What happened the night Fenton was killed?’

‘Why d’you wanna know?’

‘My stadium. My business.’

Simpkins sighed. His irritation showed. He turned towards Calloway and spat shreds of tobacco from the wet fag end onto the workshop floor. The workshop smelled of grease but it was tidy and well lit. Tools hung in orderly rows on pinboard along the far wall. Alfie Hale, the Bullets’ chief mechanic, was a stickler for order. A true engineer. This was Alfie’s place. With the shop to himself, Simpkins used it with an air of surly contempt. He tossed tools around noisily and dropped debris onto the floor. His locker door hung open. The bright pendant lighting illuminated a gallery of oil-smudged pinups. Simpkins liked a fuller figure. The adjacent locker had a broken lock, Calloway noted.

‘I told Pat, like I told the association and the insurance, I got too close to his tail. He went into a skid, hit the rider in front and came off. Accidents like that happen all the time. This time someone died. That’s all.’

Simpkins wiped his oily palms on a rag. He wore buff army overalls like the track crews, with the top half rolled down and tied at the waist, his torso covered by a vest. His chest was broad for a man his build and his arms were muscle-packed. He dropped the rag onto the bench.

'They say you hung on his tail the whole race.'

'What was I supposed to do, keep a polite distance? You don't know much about speedway, do you Mr Calloway?'

'It makes a lot of noise and sometimes people die. But maybe you could enlighten me on its finer points.'

Simpkins gripped a heavy-looking wrench and adjusted it. It gave him somewhere to look.

'When you're out there on the track, you don't think, not in the normal sense. You just go with it. We talk about tactics but really we just ride. When that tape goes up it's like throwing yourself off a cliff edge. Something inside you takes over. Sixty seconds later, the chequered flag goes up. Everyone cheers. It's instinct that keeps you going but by the time you've slowed up, it's just the blur of a memory.'

He turned to face Calloway, the heavy wrench hanging by his side, just like the chain in the hand of the cosh boy. He wore a similar expression too.

'You want to know why I clung onto his tail?' His tone smacked of provocation. 'I've got no fucking idea.'

'It must be difficult for you, knowing you killed a teammate.'

Calloway knew he was prodding at a raw nerve. He wanted a reaction.

'Difficult? How d'you think I felt riding alongside the hearse Saturday? Knowing his wife was in the car behind, looking at me.' He prodded his chest with an oil-stained finger. 'Me, Calloway. The rider that put her husband in the ground. How's that supposed to feel?'

'How well do you know Fenton's wife? Close were you?'

'What's that supposed to mean? I hardly knew her at all. He'd bring her to the club's annual dinner, that sort of thing. She never had much time for me and the feeling was mutual, seeing as you ask. I was too common for her, with her pearls and her semi-detached.'

'Probably makes it easier for you.'

'I might be common but I'm not callous.'

That's not how he looked to Calloway. The tensed lips, the narrowed eyes, the inability to look you in the eye unless it was to confront you. A hint of sneering resentment was constant in his manner.

'Did you see much of Fenton outside the track?'

Simpkins tossed the wrench back on the workbench. 'No more than the other lads. The usual drink in the members bar if we'd had a good night. I'm not one for socialising.'

'What are you one for?'

'I mind my own business.' He looked Calloway in the eye. It could have been a warning. Calloway ignored it.

'You and Fenton ever argue?'

'No. Why should we?'

'This is a tough old game, so I've heard. There's bound to be fallings out.'

'Well there wasn't between me and him. What are you getting at?'

'I have to write a report.'

'Why would me and Fenton arguing be in your report?'

'You said you didn't argue.'

'And we didn't.'

Calloway changed tack. 'What did you do before speedway?'

Simpkins seemed relieved by the diversion. 'Merchant navy, since I was fourteen. Started off shipping coal from Wandsworth to South Shields for the gas company. Then war broke out and one of my mates signed on for the convoys. I decided to go with him.'

He drew up phlegm and spat on the workshop floor. 'Worst decision of my life, looking back on it.'

'How come?'

Simpkins relaxed a little. He dropped the hard man act, but he didn't lose the surliness. That was ingrained.

'I was on a five-thousand tonner running between Liverpool and New York.'

He glanced over at the plus-size pinup on his locker door with a predatory sneer.

'I met a lot of American girls. Those Yank bints know how to put out, if you know what I mean. Then the Admiralty put the kibosh on that. Sent us to the Arctic, making runs to Murmansk. We had a pretty clear run for the first few crossings. Then the Kriegsmarine deployed more U-boats and started hunting in packs. We'd try evading them, zig-zagging you know, but we couldn't avoid them in the end. We were hit about fifty miles off the Norwegian coast. The starboard engine had started playing up so we'd stopped to fix it. We lost our escort because the fucking navy said they couldn't spare a corvette. Had to protect the convoy, they said. So we were on our own just floating there, like a turd in a toilet bowl. It wasn't long before a wolfpack found us. Put two bloody great holes in our hull. Once we started taking on water, that was it. It was all over so quick. No time to launch the lifeboats. Half a dozen of us made it clear on a Carley float.'

'How long were you adrift?'

'About three days. We were picked up by a German cruiser.'

'You were lucky then.'

'Was I? I spent the next four years in a prisoner of war camp.'

'Unlike the rest of your crew.'

Simpkins thought about this. He forced a smile like a sulking child who's been made to thank the host at a birthday party.

'Yeah. We were treated alright as it happens. But there's only so much football and cards you can play before you go stir crazy. It did my nut in.'

He started tinkering with the bike again.

'And after the war?'

'Drifted for a bit. Didn't want to see another ship, not from the inside anyway. Got work up the Surrey Docks.'

'How did you get into speedway?'

'I started coming here to watch, when the stadium opened up again after the war. I got talking to some lads in the pits and one thing led to another. They were short of younger riders at the start. There was no speedway after 1939 so the club was a bit on the old side. Bellman was nearly fifty even then. Pat gave me a tryout. I'd done a bit of riding during the war so I knew my way around a bike. I must have impressed her.'

'Is there much motorcycling in the merchant navy?'

Simpkins shot Calloway a look. The hard man act was back. 'I bought myself a bike in Liverpool, to use when I was on leave. Have you got enough for your report now?'

Calloway planted himself on a stool and lit up. 'Almost. What do you know about the dosser that used to sleep under the stands? The one they called Joe Smoke.'

Simpkins thought too long about the question. He shuffled where he stood and busied himself with tools without using them. When he replied, he sounded like one of the Three Stooges playing the innocent.

'Yeah, I remember him. That's was a few months back. The last bloke who did your job slung him out.'

'Did you ever speak to him?'

He shook his head with too much emphasis. 'Why would I?'

'Fenton used to talk to him. What was that about?'

Simpkins scoffed. 'Fenton would talk to anyone if he thought there was some reflected glory in it. What's this got to do with the accident?'

'I'm reviewing security. We can't have unauthorised personnel hanging around the stadium.'

''Spose not. And while we're at it, I can't have you hanging round here. I've got work to do if you don't mind, Mr Calloway.'

Simpkins slammed tools around to make his point. Calloway backed off. He'd heard enough to know he wasn't getting straight answers. He returned to his office. Wally Gurney, one of the pit crew, was there waiting. There was a toolbox on Calloway's desk, like the one Simpkins had been lugging around but in better condition.

'What's this, Wally?'

'Des Fenton's tools. I dunno what to do with 'em. Not sure his wife will want 'em. Mr Hale said to bring 'em to you.'

'Where did Des keep these?'

'In his locker in the workshop. Only the door was bust and I was worried, well you know, light fingers.'

'Do you have many light-fingered folk round here?'

Gurney looked sheepish. 'One or two. They don't mean nothing by it. Just use what's there sometimes.'

'It's the same with scotch in the members bar.'

Gurney grinned through crooked yellow teeth embedded in his dull parchment face.

'When did you notice the locker door was bust?'

'This morning when I got in. I've been lugging this toolbox round with me since.'

'Who was around?'

'Just me and Rocket Ray. He always works on his bike Thursdays.'

'Was Ray there when you arrived?'

'Yeah.' Gurney hesitated. 'I reckon he was first in. Listen, I'm not saying anything. Just thought you better have Des's tools for safekeeping.'

Calloway had been in London long enough to know the code. Grassing was worse than thieving. Gurney's hesitation said as much.

'Good man, Wally. This stays between us.'

Gurney shuffled off, visibly relieved to be leaving the security boss's office.

Calloway sat behind the big metal desk and opened the toolbox. He removed the tools one by one and laid them on the desktop. It was a standard mechanic's toolkit. Good-quality tools by the looks of them but well used. He also removed several receipts and laid these flat on the table. He ran his hand over the bases of the expanding tool trays and pulled out stray nuts and bolts until only the butterfly nuts in each corner of the toolbox floor remained. There were three receipts. One for inner tubes, one for gaskets and one for two bottles of chemicals, acetic acid and ammonium thiosulphate. He put the first two receipts back in the box along with the tools and slipped the third into his jacket pocket.

There were files on his desk too that morning. Manila folders containing the Bullets' points tables for last two years plus the current season to date. He had requested them from Patricia Moxon and she must have sent a lad up to his office to drop them off. He lit a cigarette and turned the pages one by one.

In forty-seven the Bullets finished fifth out of seven in Division One. Last year they were National League champions. This was the title Moxon was so keen to defend. Calloway read down the club results for each fixture. The Bullets started last season with outstanding results, a run of unbroken wins and stellar points averages for the top riders. Things had wobbled badly during July and August but they had clawed back some of their form by the Autumn, in spite of noticeably poor performances by Simpkins and Riley. Bert Webber and Des Fenton had led an assault on Belle Vue in the last two fixtures of the season and clinched the trophy. There were photos of the team celebrating their victory, in dusty leathers with white teeth grinning through cinder-blackened faces. Fenton beamed, Webber sniggered, Billy Riley smiled like a self-conscious boy in his school photo. Ray Simpkins forced an uncomfortable smirk.

This season told a different story. The club hadn't won a single fixture. True there had been some strong individual rides, with Bert Webber a clear contender for the season's star man, but Moxon was right. What victories they enjoyed as individuals belied the team's performance.

Calloway took a wooden ruler from his desk drawer and read across the individual scores. He compared each rider's results with those of their team members. He looked especially at the performance of riders paired with each other in each heat. He pulled out the small black police notebook he carried in the inside pocket of his suit jacket and made notes. Names and numbers. He slipped the notebook back into his jacket alongside the receipt he'd taken from Fenton's toolkit.

There was a pattern in the numbers that needed an explanation.

SEVEN

Calloway slept in on Saturday. At least he tried to. Sleep didn't come easily to him and the sounds of the house starting its day were especially intrusive this morning. He lay in bed gazing at the ceiling of his single basement room, imagining the domestic chaos in the flat above, where the young war widow Mrs Cobb was failing to keep breakfast on the table. Children's feet thumped on bare boards as the widow's two young boys fled from the scolding their mother struggled to make heard. A minute before, there had been the sound of breaking crockery, a reflex smack, leading to tears then rebellion. Calloway wished the noise would stop. At the same time the pang of regret for the family life he'd been denied pained him.

The Cobb family chaos clashed with the comforting sounds of morning. Milk bottles jangled on the stone steps above the door to his basement. Women in the street exchanged cheery good mornings and reported on their plans for the day. Bicycle bells rang as boys left home for their half-day Saturday shifts. But echoes of his past did their best to drown out the pleasing normality of the present and on mornings like these he relied on a routine of distractions. He abandoned his lie-in and took a gramophone record from the collection he kept on a makeshift shelf on the chimney breast. The plain card record sleeve felt soft with damp. There was only one dry wall in the room and that was reserved for a curtained off wardrobe and rail on which he hung his clothes. An old army habit. Dry clothes trumped everything, in this case even a prized collection of heavy shellac discs.

A gentle Mahler symphony rose from the inadequate speaker

of the portable HMV radiogram he had guarded zealously in the final weeks of war. He lit the single gas ring to boil water for coffee and tied the cord tightly on his old wool dressing gown before venturing into the light of morning to retrieve the newspaper carelessly dropped into the basement well outside his door. He was glad to have his own entrance. It spared him too many encounters with the neighbours in his building. The overwrought Mrs Cobb and her fatherless children, the painted Miss Logan whose past career in the theatre was as dubious as her frequent gentleman callers, and the O'Sheas, who Calloway knew only through the obscenities they exchanged during booming, unrestrained arguments that were the talk of his street.

The music soothed him as he took in the news from the paper. The signing of the Treaty of London had formalised the Council of Europe, which was to sit in Strasbourg. Winston Churchill claimed it as a victory in his campaign for European integration. Calloway had seen firsthand the consequences of a divided Europe and wished this new council every success. He trusted Mr Churchill's judgement, but as a nation we weren't taking any chances. A separate item confirmed peacetime conscription would be introduced under the National Service Act, with the first lads getting their call-up papers in two years' time. Pattie Moxon better make the most of her novices before they swap their leathers for battledress, Calloway thought. What with that and the signing of the North Atlantic Treaty the previous month, it felt to Calloway like we were back on a war footing. Victory in Europe seemed more like a temporary ceasefire while the powers that be swapped a couple of the sides around.

He filled a basin with warm water from the kettle and strip-washed over the stone sink. He shaved in the small mirror which hung on a nail over the sink, focusing on the task in hand and avoiding his own eye, as was his habit. Then he dressed in one of the clean shirts Mrs Cobb had brought down the previous afternoon. She topped up her meagre widow's pension by taking in laundry, a menial service but more savoury

Calloway suspected than one Miss Logan provided to callers.

After breakfasting late on boiled eggs, he left the house. Bert Webber, who in the past few days had become a benign source of information on the Bullets' movements, had told him Billy Riley habitually took a pint with his sister in the snug of the Four Bells at opening time on a Saturday. Calloway wanted a chance encounter. Riley's failure to show as an outrider at Fenton's funeral a week ago needed an explanation. So too did the numbers in the Bullets' points tables.

Calloway ordered a pint of Courage and settled himself in the public bar with a view of the snug. He was the sole customer save for three Caribbeans in bus company uniform who sat in silence at a table in the corner. The barman, Wilf, with whom Calloway was on nodding terms from his occasional post-work drink, gazed at the three men, transfixed. 'What d'you reckon then?' he said.

'About what?'

Wilf, a diminutive elf of a man with a jutting chin and oversized ears, nodded to the three men in the corner.

'The darkies. They've started coming here from the bus garage. Been working the night busses. I wasn't sure whether to serve 'em at first, but they don't cause no trouble. What d'you reckon?'

Calloway had read about the Jamaicans and the Trinidadians who had arrived at Tilbury the previous year on the Windrush. Like Wilf the barman, these were the first he'd seen in the neighbourhood.

'I reckon you've got three new customers, Wilf. And someone to drive your busses.'

The pub started to fill up, as workers clocked off from their half-day shifts. They trailed the smell of sweat and industry as they trooped to the bar shouting orders to Wilf and the barmaid, Dinah, a robust and red-faced woman with arms like a docker. The customers eyed the three Caribbeans with suspicion as they entered. Some muttered quiet words, but were soon distracted by their first pint of the weekend.

Calloway ordered a second pint and nodded along with

Wilf's narrow world views with a grudging interest. It passed the time, but wasn't the type of company he'd choose. Mind you, he was no longer sure what type of company he would have preferred. His life after the army had become increasingly solitary as the years progressed.

The chat in the pub turned to Millwall and became more heated as drinks were downed. True to Bert Webber's word, Calloway saw Billy Riley slip through the far door and into the snug, accompanied by a pale but pretty girl. Riley bought a pint for himself and a milk stout for his sister and the pair settled themselves at a table. They conversed in an unhurried, almost bored way, but they looked content. They were comfortable in each other's presence and looked pleased to be away from the throng that had filled the public bar. Calloway let them enjoy their drink for now. He would wait for Riley to order a second round before approaching him.

As he waited, the far door opened and a well-dressed woman walked into the crowded bar. Heads turned, cutting animated conversations short. Calloway recognised her from the funeral. Des Fenton's widow. Her outward suburban respectability drew looks from the regular clientele, whose common masculinity made the well-dressed woman more out of place than the three black bus drivers who drank quietly in the corner. Ignoring the looks, and a few coarse mutterings, the widow slipped into the snug. From his vantage point at the bar, Calloway watched her approach Riley, who excused himself to his sister and followed the widow back into the public bar. She looked agitated, verging on combative. As they spoke, Riley appeared uncomfortable. He responded calmly but tensions were clearly rising. Calloway wished he could hear their words, but the hubbub in the bar made that impossible. The widow pointed a finger threateningly at the boy rider, who responded plaintively. The drinkers nearest the pair watched the escalating argument. Riley turned to leave but the widow grabbed him by the arm and pulled him back. She mouthed at him in anger and he responded in kind before wrenching himself from her grasp and heading for the snug, slamming the door behind him.

Fenton's widow stood for a moment, weighing up whether to follow him. Instead she pushed her way through the cluster of onlookers and left.

Calloway slid his big frame off the bar stool and nudged his way through the crowded room to where the scene had taken place.

'What was all that about?' he asked a two of the drinkers who'd been closest to the scene.

'Search me, chief, but the lady wasn't happy,' said one. The other chipped in, 'Said he owed her money.'

His mate snickered.

'I'd give her money.'

'Save yourself the trouble, Spike. Her sort don't put out. Too busy polishing their silverware.'

The man called Spike winked. 'I'd give her something to polish.'

Calloway left them to their ribaldry. He'd spent his army career keeping out of conversations like that. It had earned him the nickname Reverend for a while, until the stripes on his arm earned him more respect, to his face at least.

He crossed the public bar into the snug.

'Hallo Billy. It thought I saw you come in.'

Riley was surprised by the sudden appearance of the security boss.

'Didn't know you drank in here, Mr Calloway.'

'You know how it is, Billy. I found myself at a loose end.'

He was a good-looking man of twenty or twenty-one Calloway estimated, with dark, well-cut hair swept back from his face. His hairline formed a sharp V on his forehead pointing downwards to two dark, deep-set eyes. With a slender nose and strong, chiselled jawline, his classic good looks were a stark contrast to the back-street rakishness of the better-looking Bullets.

Riley was courteous. 'This is my sister Doreen, Mr Calloway.'

The young women smiled awkwardly. 'I only come here on Saturdays,' she offered, as if making the point that she didn't frequent pubs habitually.

'Nice quiet spot in here. Away from the rabble.'

'It's the only time I get to see Billy these days. The rest of the time its speedway, speedway, speedway.'

'Not easy having a star in the family, eh Billy? I expect you get stopped all the time. Even in here.'

Riley smiled politely but looked uncomfortable. Calloway couldn't tell whether his sister knew about the altercation with Fenton's widow. Doreen answered for him.

'I can't say I'm not proud, Mr Calloway. But I'd be lying if I said I wasn't scared for him when he's out there on the track.

'Dangerous business.'

Doreen sipped her stout. Its head was as pale as her freckled face. 'Seeing that poor Mrs Fenton just now. How she must be feeling.'

Riley looked at Calloway like he owed him an explanation. 'Des's wife popped in here, as it happens.'

Calloway played dumb. 'Joined you for a drink?'

'No, just wanted to say thank you. I sent flowers.'

It hadn't looked like gratitude to Calloway.

'Billy couldn't make it to the funeral. He wasn't well.'

Riley shrugged in acknowledgement. There was an awkward silence. Calloway broke it. He had noticed Doreen had laid a coloured team scarf on top of her coat, which was folded on the seat beside her. But it wasn't the familiar red and black of the Bermondsey club.

'Not a Bullets fan then?' he said pointing at the scarf.

'That's the Rattlesnakes. Billy is a club patron. We're going along to support them later, aren't we Bill?'

Riley explained and Calloway feigned interest.

'You should come along,' said Doreen. 'They're away to Peckham Stars at East Surrey Grove. It's just up the road. Starts at two thirty but they're always late.'

Riley cut in, too quickly Calloway thought. 'I'm sure Mr Calloway has better things to do Doreen.'

Calloway made a play of thinking about the offer for a moment. He clapped Riley on the back. 'Like I said, I'm at a loose end today. I think I might just come along.'

Doreen seemed pleased. Her brother managed a courteous smile, which looked like it hurt.

East Surrey Grove was a street in name only. The Blitz had replaced its familiar built forms with a boulevard of rubble and dust. Calloway found it by following the elated screams of a thousand children huddling five deep around an oval of track, marked by a border of single bricks laid end to end. The stadium was no more than a picket fence and a hundred yards of bunting, with a blackboard and chalk to keep score. This was cycle speedway, a bomb-site sport improvised in the rubble. Riders lined up at a makeshift start line of knicker elastic stretched between white painted posts. They wore skid lids and race jackets like their motorised counterparts, with white socks turned over the tops of long boots. They shielded their faces from the dust with bandanas worn bandit style over their nose and mouth. Their bikes were stripped bare, with long cow-horn handlebars and no brakes.

Billy Riley was at the start line. Young fans pushed and shoved to get a closer look. Pure joy beamed from their undernourished faces. They chanted 'Riley, Riley, he's our man, if he can't beat them no one can.' Riley signed autographs and ruffled hair. With his lightweight American clothes and tortoise shell sunglasses, he was a bomb-site idol. He made his way down the line of riders from both teams, slapping backs and mouthing words of encouragement. Riley's sister watched him from the sidelines, with the same look of pride she'd shown in the Four Bells. Next to her a small boy with knotted hair stood on a broken chair to chalk Peckham Stars and Rotherhithe Rattlesnakes on the blackboard in his best block capitals. He left blanks for the scores. The boy jumped down and handed Riley the flag. As guest of honour he would start the first race. The riders lunged forward at the drop of the flag. They pedalled hard and took the corners with abandon, their worn down boots churning up dust. They were older than the fans, lanky teens, lean as whippets. Supporters cheered them as they passed with the shrill voices of children. Their excitement lit up the drab colosseum of street backs and half-demolished homes.

Doreen spotted Calloway across the track and waved. She tugged her brother's sleeve and gestured towards the big man who stood incongruously amid a sea of short trousers, scuffed knees and hand-knitted jerseys. Riley didn't seem to share his sister's enthusiasm at Calloway's arrival.

The heats continued in quick succession. Small boys and girls mobbed the winners each time they passed the homemade checkered flag. Riley walked around the poorly roped off perimeter of the track and shook hands with the handful of adults present. They seemed to know him. Calloway took this as his cue. He crossed the track between heats.

'Quite a show you put on here, Billy.'

Riley hid behind his courteousness. 'I can't claim the credit but I support where I can. It's good to see these kids enjoying themselves. Even if it's in the middle of all this mess.' He gestured to the barely discernible remains of the street, with its jagged half walls and overrunning buddleia. 'Mind you,' he chuckled, 'they probably did half this damage themselves. What the Germans didn't destroy, this lot would have taken care of after. Smashing up abandoned homes was the local sport, before the skid kids started up. That's why I encourage 'em. These kids need something.'

He pointed to one of the riders.

'See the tall kiddy with the Rattlesnakes bib? His house took a direct hit with his mum and sister still in it. Six weeks later his old man went down on a tanker crossing the Atlantic. He lives four to a room in a Corporation flat with his auntie now. She doesn't want him, poor sod. But he's wanted here you see. These kids love him. Listen to 'em cheer.'

It was true. They cheered like war had just ended. They lined the tacky little circuit five deep to get a better view of the lanky teen riders. They chanted like Bullets fans chanted, minus self-consciousness. Pure joy mixed with bomb-site mischief. The young ones screamed like pint-sized banshees. The older ones snuck behind the rubble to smoke cadged cigarettes. Urchins' paradise.

Riley watched keenly, doing his best to ignore Calloway. He

hoped he would leave. Calloway spoke above the din.

'Why did Irene Fenton come looking for you in the Four Bells, Billy?'

'I told you at the pub. To thank me for the flowers I sent.'

'Long way to go for that, don't you think?'

'Said she was passing.'

'She didn't look grateful from where I was sitting.'

The realisation Calloway had watched the scene spread over Riley's face. The look didn't suit him. Calloway pressed the point. 'In fact she looked quite upset with you, Billy. Everything alright between you two?'

'She was upset, sure. Still grieving I s'pose.'

'Perhaps she was upset you didn't show at her husband's funeral.'

'I was ill.'

'I thought you might have toughed it out, Fenton being a teammate. Were you and him close?'

'We got on.'

'Not good mates though?'

'Not particularly.'

'Des Fenton didn't seem to have many mates, from what I've heard. Why do you think that was?'

'He was popular enough.'

'With the fans, sure. Not too many pals among the Bullets though.'

'S'pose not.'

'I've yet to hear good word about him, in fact. I hear he liked to have the upper hand. Did he have the upper hand over you, Billy?'

Riley flushed red. Anger tugged at his good looks for a few seconds before he composed himself. 'He was a cocky sod. Yeah, he liked to have the upper hand. I s'pose that's what stardom does to some people. It never bothered me.'

The boy with the knotted hair rubbed the scores out with the sleeve of his jumper and chalked up new ones. Riley's sister whispered in his ear. He repeated the process this time with the scores added correctly.

'You a gambling man, Billy?'

Riley screwed up his face. 'What's that got to do with anything?'

'Ever had a wager with Fenton?'

'Why would I do that?'

'Friendly rivalry. A bit of fun.'

'Not me.'

'Ever borrow money off him?'

The anger flashed again and this time it won. Riley snapped. 'I don't need to borrow from anyone. I do alright.'

Calloway gave no ground. 'It's just that I heard you owed his missus.'

'You heard wrong. What's with all the questions? This isn't about track security.'

'I have to make a report.'

'Yeah, well, you're barking up the wrong tree. There was nothing between me and Des Fenton and nothing between me and his missus.'

'Whose tree should I bark up, Billy? You see there are rumours.'

Riley nodded. 'I've heard. I dunno what's got into Pat. An accident's an accident. But she ain't letting go. It's not like her.'

'What is like her?'

'Hard as nails that one. Whenever one of us gets bust up she's all "there, there, now get over it and get back on that track". This time she's scared of her own shadow.'

'She's lost her star rider. She's bound to be out of sorts.'

'Star rider?' He sniffed. 'Star turn, more like. He was flash off the track. Nothing special on it.'

Calloway had found a raw nerve. He prodded it. 'He saw you off more than once. You've not been able to touch him since the middle of last season.'

Calloway had studied the results from Moxon's file. This was one of the stories the numbers told.

'Just tactics, that's all.'

'Oh come on, Billy. You were Pattie's rising star this time last year. You mean to say your loss of form is tactical. Get away.

You're as hungry for glory as the best of 'em. You just can't cut it anymore.'

Riley turned on him. 'Oh, so you're suddenly an expert.'

'I can read the scores.'

'Yeah? Well read 'em to someone who gives a damn. What d'you come here for anyway? You're not interested in all this.'

'Your sister invited me, remember.'

'Too polite for her own good.'

'She's a nice girl. And you're a good man, Billy, I can tell. But you're not being straight with me.'

'Aren't I?' Riley looked him in the eye. His defences were up. 'Well that's too bad.'

A cheer went up from the dirt track. The tiny Rattlesnakes fans huddled around their star rider as he raised a cheap and tarnished trophy above his head. He was tall and confident, a diamond in the rough. This could have been Riley a few years back, Calloway thought. But unlike Riley, this kiddy had nothing holding him back.

EIGHT

Saturday. Greyhound night. Calloway watched the track-side bookmakers setting up. The main gates were not yet open and the stadium was quiet, save for the shouts of staff and the barking of excitable dogs.

The bookies set up easels for their chalkboards, hung their cash bags and fastened their decorative nameplates on top. One of them fumbled and dropped a butterfly nut, which bounced along the concrete landing at Calloway's feet. He bent to pick it up, turned it over in his fingers and flicked it into the air, catching it in his palm like a tossed coin. He handed it to the bookie who nodded his thanks.

'Thanks, chief. Tricky little buggers.'

Butterfly nuts weren't permanent fixings, it occurred to Calloway. So why were there four of them fastening the base of Des Fenton's toolbox?

He walked to his office, locked the door behind him and lifted the toolbox from the floor beside the filing cabinet and onto the desk. He pulled out the tools in handfuls and dumped them on the desktop. Then he twisted off the butterfly nuts one by one. He took one of Fenton's screwdrivers and used it to lever up the metal panel from the base. Between the panel and the floor of the box was a void an inch deep. It concealed a small marbled notebook and a brown envelope, unsealed and bound by an elastic band. He snapped off the band and removed the contents of the envelope. There were bank notes to the value of four hundred fifty pounds. He placed these on the desk. He then opened the notebook. There were handwritten notes on the first few pages, with three names at the top: Ron Sampson, Jack Ladbroke, Frank Belper. Calloway didn't recognise the names. They weren't Bullets men. The name Ron Sampson was underlined. Beneath the names was a list:

1943

Marlag Westertimke/Amerhsam
Genshagen, Berlin
Totenkopf/Belper

1944

Hildesheim
Dresden/Division Nordland
Lodz
Chelmno

1945

Lubeck

On the two pages that followed there was a ledger of dates and payments, starting in July 1948. The last entry was four days before Fenton's accident. Calloway looked down the column and made a rough calculation. The numbers added up to the four hundred fifty pounds in the envelope.

He put the cash back into the envelope, fastened it with the elastic band, and locked it in his safe. He took the notebook and dropped it into his desk drawer, then refastened the false panel to the base of the toolbox, replaced the tools and slid the box into the footwell of the desk where it was concealed from view.

They were testing the tannoy when he returned to the track. The sound of the announcer bounced off the concrete of the empty stands. The bookies nodded as he passed.

'All good, Mr Calloway?' shouted one.

'All good,' he replied, joining in the weekly ritual, which endorsed the track-side bookmakers' legitimacy.

The Saturday night crowd was gathering at the turnstiles. A tall and severe-looking commissionaire watched them from the top of the steps, which led up to the circuit.

'They're an excitable lot tonight, Mr Calloway. Millwall won at home. We can expect high spirits.'

'The high-spirited ones will still be in the Royal Archer, Les. This lot are the early birds. The Dandelion & Burdock brigade.'

Les Birkett acknowledged with a nod but failed to crack a smile. Good humour wasn't his strong point, but his dourness carried an authority which suited his role. At six foot one with a heavy build, the big ex-infantryman's presence was enough to dissuade the most high-spirited punters from any roughhousing. And the North African and Italian campaign ribbons sewn to his uniform testified to the hard-earned toughness of the former regimental sergeant-major.

Small talk wasn't Birkett's strong point either, so Calloway asked him a question outright.

'How well did you know Des Fenton, Les?'

He answered obliquely. 'Fenton? Bad business that accident.'

Birkett surveyed the line of punters at the turnstiles, his head swivelling on his sinuous neck like a gun turret seeking a target. He prided himself on his ability to spot trouble.

'Know him? Nope. No more than the rest of 'em.'

'Did he serve in the last shout?'

Calloway knew from past conversations that the one thing Les Birkett could be relied upon to know about a man was his war record.

'Gunner. Royal Artillery.'

'Overseas?'

'Manned an ack-ack battery at Dover. Cushy billet. Probably went home for his tea.'

'Dover, eh? Long way from Berlin.'

The old Regimental Sergeant Major looked quizzical. 'Sir?'

'Don't worry, Les. Thinking aloud.'

Calloway left Birkett to surveil the crowd, adding a brisk, 'As you were, sar'nt-major' as he left. This got him a smile.

They were training novices at the track the following Monday. Calloway watched from the stands as a pro rider demonstrated cornering, hitting full speed on the straight and letting momentum carry the bike into the bends. The novices paid close attention to the moves as the rider glided over the cinder with the aplomb of a veteran. Even with his scant interest in speedway, Calloway was impressed. He couldn't tell which Ranger this was. Their face was masked by a white silk scarf leaving only a slit between scarf and helmet. After two more laps the pro jerked the bike into an abrupt skid, stopping inches short of the novices.

The rider was Pat Moxon. She removed her helmet, tugged down the white scarf and raked her fingers across her tied-back hair. She leaned on the handlebars to address the would-be Bullets.

'You've got to get out of those corners fast, which means backing off the throttle to control wheel spin. If you hit that dirt with too much gas your bike will take off. Wait until you feel the grip of the track, then you give it a handful. Got it?'

The novices nodded like dutiful children.

'Right.' Moxon pointed to the slack jawed lad at the front. 'You. Show me what you've learned.'

She dismounted the bike and handed it to him. 'I've warmed the seat for you.'

The novices sniggered. The boy flushed red.

'Four laps then pass the bike to the next lad. Off you go.'

Moxon crossed the track to where Calloway stood leaning on the stand rails. She swaggered, swinging the helmet by its strap and tugging down the zip of the heavy black Lewis Leathers jacket.

'I know what you're thinking.'

'Go on.'

'It's no job for a lady.'

'It's no job for anyone with an ounce of sense.'

She leaned on the rail next to him, watching the young riders practice. 'I decided I'd better start training them myself. With Des gone, Clanger Bellman out of action and Billy Riley riding like a wet weekend, I've got to breed some new talent.'

'How long have you been riding?'

'That's like asking a lady her age. Let's just say long enough.'

'Why don't you race?'

She laughed. The laugh said he was being naive. 'Women

don't race, not anymore. They banned us in 1930. Speedway's a man's game, Mr Calloway, like everything else in this life. Unless it involves screaming kids or dirty dishes.'

She smiled at him, as if forgiving him his naivety, and offered him a cigarette from her monogrammed case. He accepted.

'Why did they ban women?'

'Modesty, Mr Calloway. A female rider took a fall at Wembley and broke her collar bone. The St John's Ambulance had to cut some of her clothes away by the track to treat her. The crowd got an eyeful. This was deemed most improper by the men that controlled the sport. That's all it took for them to ban us all.'

She hollered instructions across the track to one of the novice riders. She shook her head, unimpressed by his performance.

'What did you do then?' asked Calloway.

'After the ban, I took to demonstration riding. Showing off between races. A novelty act, or as good as. Pretty Pattie Moxon, Queen of the Dirt Track.'

'I bet there's a cigarette card with your face on it.'

She dropped the smile. 'Oh, there's more than that, believe me.'

She drew hard on the cigarette and exhaled slowly. 'So Calloway, you've had your week. What have you found out for me?'

'Nothing to suggest Fenton's accident was anything other than that.'

Moxon looked displeased with the answer. She fingered the string of pearls she wore under the leathers.

'So nothing up with the team?'

'Oh there's something up with the team. Plenty, I would say. But nobody's killed anyone yet. Not deliberately.'

The novice was demonstrating the wrong way to corner. His machine bucked beneath him, throwing him into a heap on the cinders. Moxon shouted words of encouragement, then turned to Calloway.

'So tell me.'

'They're a cagey lot for the most part. And you're right, something's got them spooked, some of them at least. Fenton wasn't well liked and there's no love lost between him and his teammates.'

'Why?'

'He was flash, manipulative, liked to have the upper hand. Qualities not conducive to camaraderie in my experience.'

He sensed this struck a chord but she was trying hard not to show it. 'That could apply to anyone in this business. Anything specific?'

'Two things. Fenton and Simpkins fell out over a tramp that used to doss down under the stands. I don't know why but Simpkins is denying it. And I saw Billy Riley in an argument with Fenton's widow, over money apparently, although he won't admit it. Any of this make any sense to you?'

Moxon shook her head.

'There's one more thing. Fenton had built a false bottom into the toolbox he kept in the workshop. He'd hidden four hundred fifty pounds cash and a notebook showing payments adding up to the same amount. The last entry was just before his accident.'

'Was he running a book?'

'Unlikely. The payments were for regular amounts. And there was a list of dates and place names which I can't figure out. Dates during the war, towns in Germany and Poland, and German military units by the looks of them.'

Calloway knew this for sure. As a member of an airborne field security section during the war, he had a good working knowledge of enemy formations. The Totenkopf Division was notorious. He had no recollection of a Division Nordland.

'Did Fenton spend any time in Germany after the war?'

Moxon considered this. 'Speedway started up in Germany quite soon after the war. Mainly forces clubs setting up impromptu dirt tracks. Then the locals joined in. It's big over there now. I know Fenton's racing career pretty well. He never raced in Germany. He was with the Bullets all through the thirties, then did his best not to get called up.'

'He was a gunner according to Les Birkett, but didn't make it past Dover. Had a good war by all accounts.'

'Sounds like Des. Probably bribed someone to keep it that way. He was always a bit on the wide side. He got back into racing pretty soon after speedway started up again. He's been with the Bullets since. Never ridden in Germany. Nor Poland for that matter. They only started speedway again last year. What do you make of it, this notebook and the money?'

'Not a lot right now. But I know someone who might make sense of the dates and names on that list. I can give them a call.'

'Do that,' she said, then added, 'I know you said you'd work for gratis for a week. I need to start paying you now.'

'I won't take your money.'

She looked him up and down. 'It won't make you any less the man, Reg. Or do you have trouble with lady bosses?'

'Can't say I've had one. I'll treat this as a stadium matter. My wages will cover the time.'

'Suit yourself. But allow me one thing?'

'Like what?'

Moxon glanced back to the track. Another novice had the bike this time and was showing promise. She seemed to approve.

'I have a party invitation this evening, in the West End. I'm short of a date. You seem like you could do with a night out. Care to join me?'

His instinct was to pass. But for the first time in a long while he ignored it. She was right. He'd spent too many nights with his records, polishing his shoes and listening to groans of Miss Logan and her gentleman callers. And he hated to admit that Patricia Moxon had started to appeal to a side of him that he'd buried away since the war.

'I'd hate to think of you at a party on your own. Not that I imagine you would be for very long.'

'A compliment? So there is a gentleman under there. I knew that parade ground manner was just an act.'

'Don't be so sure.'

She gave him an address in Mayfair. There was definitely

money in speedway.

'Call for me at eight. And leave that demob suit at home.'

'I think there's still a blazer in the back of my wardrobe.'

Probably damp, it occurred to him.

'Fine. Now run along and polish your buttons. And make that phone call. Whatever's going on, I want it cleared up.'

He clicked his heels. 'Yes, ma'am.'

Calloway strode back to his office with a lightness in his step. Part of him felt buoyed by her invitation. Another part of him already regretted accepting it.

It took Calloway an hour of calls to various government departments before he tracked down Sammy Mackay. They had stayed in touch for a while after Calloway left the army, but not to the extent that he had a current address or phone number. He had outsmarted a succession of officious telephonists with half-truths and a confident tone, until he was put through to an extension within one of Whitehall's less-public departments.

'Reggie? Good God man, how did you find me here?'

Calloway recognised the familiar tone of the gentrified Scot. 'Peasant cunning, Sammy.'

'Oh yes. It makes up for lack of breeding.'

'That and grammar schools.'

Mackay scoffed. 'Not so sure about that. What are you up to?'

'Stadium security officer.'

Through the earpiece Calloway heard the sound of a match striking, followed by the smack of lips sucking on a pipe, drawing in air.

'You work at a dog track?'

'Dogs and motorbikes.'

'Oh dear me.'

'Didn't have much choice, Sammy.'

The line crackled as Mackay paused.

'I suppose not. That Nuremberg business was a damn shame. You only did what any of us would have done.'

'Yes, but without the benefit of breeding.'

‘I suppose class does have its advantages. Christ, I sound like a Bolshevik.’

Calloway heard breathy chuckling. Mackay was the jovial type, on the surface at least. Beneath the joviality was a ruthless operator.

‘No one’s going to mistake you for a red, Sammy.’

‘That’s a comfort, especially in this place, although I suspect I wouldn’t be alone.’

‘Careful, Sammy, they might be listening.’

‘Very possibly,’ he whispered, then chuckled some more. ‘To what do I owe the honour?’

‘I’m after a favour.’

‘That’s not like you. You were always the stoic, self-reliant type. Well, fire away.’

‘I need you to make sense of something for me. Something up your street. Relating to the last shout. Got a pencil?’

‘The departmental budget can just about stretch to one. I use it to clean out my pipe.’

Calloway read out the dates, place names and the two German divisions from the marbled notebook. He heard the tapping of a pipe on teeth through the earpiece.

‘Not meaning much to me so far, old man.’

‘How about Ron Sampson, Jack Ladbroke and Frank Belper? They may relate to someone named Amersham.’

Mackay was silent for a moment. His tone had changed. The joviality was gone. ‘Still not ringing any bells, I’m afraid. Do you know their units or ranks?’ He paused for a second. ‘Or where they might be now?’

‘No, but I’m guessing you have access to the registry. Dig around for me, will you.’

‘I remember when I used to give a you the orders. Should I ask what this is about?’

‘Probably nothing. Call it a character reference.’

‘For a greyhound?’

‘Got it in one, Sammy.’

Calloway gave Mackay his contact details and hung up.

NINE

Patricia Moxon's mansion block was the kind people with interesting lives lived in. Double-fronted modernism, with curved bays, metal windows and travertine steps up to a grand entrance flanked by miniature conifers. The street number was carved large into stone relief in Broadway lettering. It said movie-star chic a little too loudly. Calloway imagined her neighbours were single folk of private means who dined out, threw parties and crashed borrowed sports cars. It wasn't the kind of place for a coal miner's son with a soon-forgotten battlefield commission and a blazer from Alkit. But the blazer, crisp white shirt and Tootal cravat earned him a respectful welcome from the building's doorman, who addressed him as sir and directed him to Moxon's apartment via the small cage lift.

She answered the door with a cocktail cigarette in one hand and a crystal tumbler of what looked like gin in the other.

'Reggie. Just the man I need.'

She turned her back to him. Her cocktail dress was unfastened, revealing a band of soft white flesh pushed upwards over a tightly cinched bra strap.

'Zip me up, will you love. My nails are still drying.'

He leant into her, eased up the zip and fastened the clasp, the backs of his fingers glancing over the smooth nape of her neck. He smelled the same fragrance she wore at Fenton's funeral.

'Fix yourself a drink. It's gin or gin.'

She drew on the gold filter of her cigarette waved it towards a bar in the corner of the room.

'Gin is fine,' he said.

'Ice in the bucket. The big pineapple. Tacky, I know. A gift from GI friend who was posted to Hawaii.'

She disappeared into what he assumed was the bedroom.

The pineapple was alone in its tackiness. The rest of the flat was decorated in an understated style. Clean, modern, quite masculine, he thought. Like a Hollywood director's office, at least the way they're depicted in films, but with overstuffed bookshelves. He looked over the book spines. Modern editions of American novelists, Steinbeck, Faulkner, some Chandler. Virginia Woolf, Hardy, the Brontës. Some art books.

The gramophone told a different story. Caribbean rhythms and sexual double-entendres. Calloway had never heard this music.

He shouted towards the open bedroom door. 'What the hell are you listening to?'

'Do you like it? It's Lord Kitchener.'

She sounded distracted. He imagined her in front of the dressing table mirror applying lipstick.

'The field marshal?'

'The calypsonian.'

'It's obscene.'

'All in the mind, darling. He's a wonderful man. I was introduced to him in a club in Soho. Straight off the boat. A friend and I spent a fascinating weekend in Notting Hill tracking down his records. I learned to smoke reefers. Isn't he wonderful?'

'I prefer your books.'

'Help yourself. But don't expect to spend the night in reading.'

She appeared at the door. 'Well, will I do?'

She wore an expensive-looking black cocktail dress, with a plunging neckline and tightly cinched waist. The dress clung in a way that held his attention too long. She noticed him stare but stood in the doorway regardless, hands on her hips, fingers with newly painted nails smoothing over wrinkles in the shiny fabric.

'You look very nice,' was all he could manage.

She shot him an exaggerated scowl. 'Damned by faint praise. For that you can fix me another drink.'

He poured two gins and failing to find a mixer, dropped ice into the straight liquor.

'There's a bottle of angostura behind the bar. Splash in a couple of drops for me, will you?'

'Did you learn that in the navy?'

'What, pink gin? No, but I've drunk with a few sailors in my time.'

She joined him on the angular, chromium-framed sofa, and slid across the polished leather to within a foot of him. The sofa was a triumph of style over comfort. She turned to him and chinked glasses.

'We're officially off duty. You can stop calling me ma'am now.'

'Are you Pat or Patricia?'

'Oh strictly Pat. Pattie sounds patronising and Patricia sounds like my mother. I'm calling you Reggie by the way.'

'As you wish.'

She swivelled sideways, crossed one leg over the other and swung her foot in time with the music. Calloway was about to make conversation when the doorbell rang. Pat didn't seem surprised. She patted him on the knee.

'I'll only be a moment.'

She crossed the room and walked down the apartment's generous hallway to open the door. The caller was a middle-aged man with watery blue eyes and a drinker's nose. A whisky man. He wore a tweed suit with brown suede brogues. The suit had been expensive and was now well-worn in. His tie may have been regimental. Calloway couldn't tell from where he sat. His greying hair was inches too long, swept back over his ears and tickling his shirt collar. He held a small package in his puffy hand.

Moxon took the package without looking. She took something from a handbag on the hall stand and passed it to the caller in return. She exchanged a few words, which he acknowledged with a knowing nod, before closing the door.

She called back to Calloway.

'Amuse yourself for a moment, will you.'

Then she disappeared into a room off the hallway, which he judged from its chequered tiling was a bathroom. She emerged a few minutes later straightening her skirt. She strode down the hallway and rejoined him.

'Now, about this do,' she said, draping an arm over the back of the sofa and leaning into him. Her foot tapped to the calypso rhythm, double time.

'We're going to Dennis Robinson's place in Belgravia. An old friend. He's a talent scout for Centurion Pictures. Recruits girls for their charm school. He swans around like a minor aristocrat but don't be fooled. His father was a bus driver from Maidstone. Still can't hold a knife and fork properly. He always throws a party for his latest cohort of starlets. A sort of passing out parade when they've stopped dropping their aitches and mastered the rudiments of RP.'

'Sounds like a cattle market.'

'Don't knock it, Calloway. Plenty of single young ladies with all the attributes.'

She sounded excitable. She prodded his bicep through the sleeve of his blazer. 'We might even find you a girl.'

'I thought I was your date. Or have I been demoted to chaperone already?'

'We're both free spirits, Reggie. Let's see what the night brings.'

She crossed room to the gramophone swaying a little in time to the rhythm.

'I'll change this for something that won't offend your puritanical streak. What do you fancy?'

'I like the German romantic composers.'

She screwed up her face like she'd smelled a bad smell.

'Dreary. We'll have jazz. Anyone who doesn't like Duke Ellington isn't allowed in here. It's the door policy.'

'Do you get many through the door here?'

She shot him a hurt look, then winked. 'That's my business. Let's talk about you.'

She spoke quickly and was now far more animated than when he'd first arrived. 'You like the German romantic composers and you're interested in books. You're not married when you really should be by now and you walk around like smiling is on the ration and you've run out of coupons. You don't have any friends that I'm aware of and you don't like letting people inside that hard shell sewn into the lining of the demob suit you're still wearing. So I'm guessing you're suffering either a bad war or a broken heart.'

'Try both and you might just be getting somewhere.'

She knew how to read a man. He changed the subject. 'You've an impressive library.'

She seemed pleased he had noticed. 'Thanks. I'd never read a book in my life until I was thirty.'

'What happened then?'

'The war came and I joined the ATS.'

'You got an army education?'

He had the Army Education Service to thank for filling the gaps in his own half-baked schooling.

She tutted. 'You think I had time for that? I was a dispatch rider. Working all hours. They billeted me with a pale young thing who had dropped out of Cambridge to fight the fascists. I'd be so full of adrenaline after riding all day I used to read her cast-off novels to get to sleep. I got a taste for it and haven't stopped since.'

'Does she still lend you her books?'

He doubted it, if the affluence her flat reflected was anything to go by.

She shook her head and took a sip of the pink gin.

'One night during the blackout she swerved to avoid a policeman on a bicycle. Wrapped her bike around a lamppost and died on the spot. It sounds silly when you tell it like that.'

'There's nothing silly about war. Just blood, death and bad dreams.'

She stubbed out the lipstick-stained filter of the cocktail cigarette in a large metal ashtray and with her other hand waved the tumbler in circular motions.

'Fix us both one for the road. We'll see if we can't get through to the real Reggie Calloway before the evening's out. Have you eaten?'

He shook his head as he mixed the drinks.

'Good. We'll meet Dennis at a Greek restaurant in Dean Street. His crowd always goes there before a party. I prefer Italian food but there's not been much of that around since the riots drove the Eyeties out. Italy's loss has been the Cypriots' gain.'

She talked as though he'd never eaten out in his life. He suppressed rising irritation.

'Will any of the Bullets be there tonight?'

'Only the house-trained ones, which narrows it down a bit. O'Donnell's bound to be there. Try keeping that one away. Brains in his trousers, or pants as he'd call them. Maybe Billy Riley. He scrubs up well and likes a night up West, although he's been a bit of a stop-at-home of late.'

'Something not right with that one.'

She nodded agreement.

'He does have a haunted look these days. But let's not talk shop. This is your night out.'

He passed her the drink and their fingers touched for second.

'Reckon I can allow myself just the one.'

He flagged them a cab to Soho, which wove its way through Kodachrome streets. London was alight again, now the ban on electric signs had been lifted. The city shone its colours into the night with pent-up defiance. He paid the cab fare and held the door for Pat as they entered the restaurant. The noise inside could compete with the stadium on speedway night. Excitable diners showing off and waiters playing up their foreign accents at full volume. Pat spotted Dennis Robinson and his crowd. They sat at the biggest table in the place, with a loud red gingham tablecloth and candles stuck into wine bottles.

'Pattie darling! Queen of the cinders! Come sit next to me.'

Robinson shouted across the room, shoving a male guest over and pulling up another chair in between them. He was late thirties and tanned, with hair cut en-brosse. He wore a broad-shouldered dog tooth sports jacket, the long collar of his primrose yellow shirt splayed California style revealing a hairless chest.

'And who's this big brute?' He looked Calloway up and down. 'Sit yourself over there fella, next to the delightful creature that's doing her best not to fall out of that rather common dress.'

A cutesy-faced girl with scarlet lips and dyed-blond hair that was lacquered brittle screwed up her face and threw a breadstick at Robinson. He caught it like an arrow through the heart and mugged death throes.

They ordered and ate. The food was good. Calloway joined in the chat. The girl next to him was a charm school graduate with leading lady ambitions. If her acting was as fake as her conversation, she wasn't going far. Pat kept catching his eye from across the table. He couldn't tell if she felt sorry for him or was worried he'd show her up in front of her cheap show business friends. Either way, her concern irritated him.

By eleven they'd left. Pat had picked up the bill he noticed and Robinson seemed happy to let her. She'd refused Calloway's own offer to contribute for both of them. The group divided up and took cabs to Belgravia. Robinson had the first two floors of a Nash-style townhouse. It was grandiose, scuffed and sparsely furnished. The flat was already full and the music cranked high. Calloway got the impression this was a place where bright things came and went. Pat had been right about the Centurion girls. Fresh from the charm school mint, all hips and bust, they talked self-consciously with professional smiles to men of varying ages. Some of the girls danced with eager young men, heavily Brylcreemed in sports jackets and twills. The girls danced like they were auditioning.

Pat took his arm and paraded him around the room making introductions. She called the people friends although he doubted they were. A shrill wolf whistle cut through the noise. O'Donnell gave Moxon and Calloway a film star's wave. He was leaning in a window alcove, his arm locked around the waist of one of Centurion Pictures' hopefuls. Of all the girls in the room, she looked like the one most likely. She had Betty Grable's legs, Jayne Mansfield's curves and Jean Harlow's hair, which tumbled down in platinum waves from her hairline to her cleavage. Her full lips looked pumped to bursting, like the rest of her. The nostrils of her turned-up nose flared slightly into an almost predatory sneer.

'O'Donnell's a fast worker.'

Moxon looked in the direction of the rider and the starlet. 'And an ambitious one too. That bombshell is Robinson's squeeze. They have quite an open relationship by all accounts, so old Six Gun might get lucky. But she usually aims higher when she plays away. Not sure my boy's speedway-star credentials will cut it.'

Other men in the room looked on enviously as O'Donnell tightened his grip on the bombshell's waist. A sharp suited and skinny young man with jet black hair and eyebrows that gave him a look of permanent mischief crossed over to them, trying his best to cut in. Calloway couldn't hear his patter but it looked slick and well-practiced. It made the bombshell laugh. She pinched his cheek. The skinny young man swooned. O'Donnell looked irritated and steered the girl towards the adjoining room. The young man made a quick about turn, swiped a wine bottle from the window sill and glided over to a lone brunette who was flicking disinterestedly through the host's record collection. He started up his patter again.

An hour passed. Calloway made small talk with a bunch of people he'd be in no hurry to meet again. Pat excused herself and Calloway poured himself another drink. A strong arm slapped him on the back.

'How's that investigation of yours, Calloway?'

It was O'Donnell. He had lost the blonde and sounded drunk.

'Detected any foul play?' He slurred the last two words in a bad English accent.

'I'm off duty,' said Calloway.

He waved the bottle at the big American. 'Can you fit any

more in there?'

O'Donnell thrust his empty glass forward. 'Fire away.'

Calloway poured neat scotch. O'Donnell belched and raised his glass.

'Salute.' He necked the scotch in one. 'Spider tells me you were airborne.'

'Spider?'

'Webber. All you Limeys have nicknames, right? What's yours?'

'Cab.'

O'Donnell whooped. 'As in Calloway? Yeah!'

The drunken American started to sing:

'The jim, jam, jump on the jumpin' jive,

'Makes you like your eggs on the Jersey side,

'Hep hep!

'You like your eggs on the Jersey side Calloway?'

'If I knew what it meant. I was intelligence, attached to the 6th Airborne Division.'

'Intelligence, that figures. I was with the 82nd. All the way from Normandy to the Rhine.'

'I'm surprised we didn't run into one another.'

'It was a big war.'

O'Donnell swayed but not in time to the music. He clapped a hand on Calloway's shoulder and pointed across the room with the other.

'Mr intelligence guy, you should talk to that one over there. She could tell you a few things about the late James Fenton.'

It was the young woman who had appeared at the funeral. She was dancing with a round and ruddy-faced man in his fifties. He was dancing as close as his gut would allow. Beads of sweat popped on his forehead as he pawed at her with pudgy fingers. In the absence of moonlight and romance, she managed a polite grimace.

'Who is she?'

O'Donnell shrugged.

'I dunno, but I've seen her around with Fenton in places where his wife was strangely absent. Places like nightclubs.

They seemed to get along.'

O'Donnell spied a face in the crowd, a female face. He knocked back the scotch and slurred, 'So long Cab' in Calloway's direction. He left humming the Jumpin' Jive.

Calloway crossed the room towards the dancing couple.

He tapped the fat man on the shoulder. 'Mind if I cut in?'

The fat man looked put out. 'Actually I do, squire. Push off, will you.'

Calloway gripped the man's fleshy arm. He squeezed so it hurt. 'But it's the gentleman's excuse me.'

He used a tone that ruled out any argument. The fat man complied, mouthing to himself as he retreated rubbing his arm. Calloway took the woman's hand and led her. He danced well, with a lightness of step which belied his big frame. The woman looked relieved to be shot of the fat man, but uncertain what to make of Calloway's intrusion.

'Forgive me, but you looked like you needed a change of partner.'

'Did I? And how would you know that?'

'He didn't seem like your type.'

'Really? So what is my type?'

'Oh I don't know, someone a bit more flash. A racing driver perhaps.'

He spun her under his arm and she responded, a half beat behind the rhythm. She was dancing under the influence.

'Or a speedway rider.'

She pulled back from him but he was too strong. He spun her again and felt her stiffen.

Her eyes narrowed and her lips tensed. 'Who the hell are you?'

'I should have introduced myself. My name's Calloway. I work at Bermondsey stadium. I saw you at Des Fenton's funeral.'

'Yes, I was there,' she said, as if responding to an accusation. Then she composed herself, as much as the drink would allow. She was remembering her charm school training. 'I'm Liz. Liz Francis.'

'Did you know Fenton well, Liz?'

'Des and I were friends.'

'Good friends?'

She started laughing. She was drunk and past caring.

'If you mean lovers, then yes. Oh don't look so shocked. We were going to get married.'

'I'm not shocked, but Mrs Fenton might have been.'

She let out a bored-sounding hiss. 'I couldn't care less.'

'Did Des care?'

'He was going to leave her. He promised me he would. He kept putting it off but he promised he would tell her that night. The night of the accident.' She laughed again. It was a dark laugh. 'So that was us finished.'

Calloway watched her retreat into the thoughts in her head. She was full of anger, grief and cheap wine. It wasn't a good look on a would-be starlet.

'How long had you and Fenton been going together?'

'It would have been two years next month. He was putting money aside for a flat. For the two of us. We were going to live up West.'

'Putting money aside? Fenton earned more in a month than most of us earn in a year. He could have paid for a flat without putting anything aside.'

'He wanted to keep the money separate from her. She had her claws into everything he earned. For her pearls and her nice house in the suburbs. He said he had a sideline that she didn't know about.'

Calloway thought of the cash in Fenton's toolbox.

'What kind of sideline?'

'He wouldn't tell me. Told me not to worry about it. Just said he had it all arranged.'

The tempo of the music had slowed. They danced closer and she leaned into him, rolling carelessly to the rhythm. He could feel fatigue and resignation in her limp body.

'How did you and Fenton meet?'

She looked up at him as if awoken from sleep. 'Through Dennis Robinson. I was at the Centurion charm school. Dennis invited me to a party here. Pat Moxon brought Des and some of the Bullets along. I didn't know he was married at first. Then I saw a photo of him and Irene in Speedway Gazette. Silly I know but I'd started buying the speedway press to read about Des. I must sound like a schoolgirl.'

'You're not much older.'

Her face hardened. 'I'm old enough.'

'So you're an actress?'

She shook her head and looked disdainfully around the room at the charm school hopefuls. 'I dropped out of the Centurion school. Convinced myself I was going to be the wife of a speedway star. Des saw I was alright, financially. And I've done some modelling.'

Calloway could imagine and he didn't imagine couture. 'Did Des get you into that?'

She shook her head, as if the suggestion was improper. 'Dennis fixed me up. Some glamour work.'

'Very tasteful I'm sure. So what now?' He nodded towards the other partygoers. 'Are you looking for the next Des Fenton?'

He felt her body tense as they danced. 'You're quite insensitive, did you know that?'

'It has been said.'

The needle zipped across the record that was playing and the music stopped abruptly. Robinson appeared and shoved his face between Calloway and Liz as they danced.

'Showtime, lovelies. Follow me if you would.'

He still looked immaculate but up close he smelled of neat liquor and too much cologne.

Calloway looked at Liz and shrugged. She seemed to know the form and led him into the hallway towards the stairs. Other revellers were heading in the same direction. They looked furtive. Robinson whispered in new ears along the way and the group grew, Pied-Piper style, to a dozen or so. At the piper's behest, they crammed into a darkened bedroom. It was void of furniture, save for some tea chests of what Calloway assumed were the occupant's still unpacked belongings. With a flourish of showmanship, Robinson drew back a dusty Persian rug. Beneath it, a hole of around three inches in diameter had been bored in the heavy floorboards. The people lined up and took turns in crouching down and peering into the room below. One of them was Billy Riley. They stifled giggles and exchanged salacious looks, except for Riley who looked awkward. It was Calloway and the girl's turn. She passed, rolling her eyes as though she'd seen this show before. Calloway peered into the circle of light. The skinny young man with the mischievous eyebrows was crouched on a bare mattress in the room below. This time he was naked save for his socks. Beneath him, the brunette he'd been making a play for earlier was doing a poor impression of rapture. Someone in the audience kicked a tea chest. There was shushing and laughing out loud. The skinny man looked up, in the direction of the noise. He spotted the spy hole and shook his fist at the ceiling.

'Robinson, you utter bastard!' he cried, as the brunette scrabbled on the floor for her clothes.

There was more laughing. It was the greatest show on earth, judging by the look on Robinson's satisfied face. Calloway pushed his way out of the room. Riley was ahead of him. Liz Francis had disappeared.

Calloway followed Riley as he made his way downstairs and into the dimly lit hallway. Riley stopped to talk to a young man about his age. He was a similar height and build, but better bred from the look of him. He had the sandy hair and healthy complexion of privilege. They knew each other but not well, Calloway sensed from the exchange. Calloway couldn't hear them over the sound of the gramophone, which had started up again, but their conversation had the air of conspiracy. The pair made to leave a moment later. Calloway found his trench coat in the pile that had formed beneath the bulging mass of garments on the hall stand and followed them, but at a distance.

TEN

It had rained and the streets gleamed mirror-black under the streetlights. Riley and the sandy-haired man flagged a lone taxi as it passed. Calloway hung back in a doorway and strained to hear their destination. They were too far away to be audible above the tick-tick of the taxi's diesel engine. Calloway watched as the twin red dots of the cab's tail-lights faded to a faint glow in the distance. Then a second taxi approached. Calloway stepped into its path and flagged it with a raised hand as the tail-lights of Riley's cab turned into a side street. He barked instruction to the driver to catch it up and follow.

The streets were empty. It was past two am. It made the tail easier. The cars passed through Victoria, around the back of the palace and along Piccadilly. They circled the statue of Eros and headed down Shaftesbury Avenue until the cab in front cut left into Wardour Street. It snaked its way through a tangle of Soho side streets before pulling up next to a darkened passageway. Calloway let his taxi continue for thirty yards before stopping. He paid the driver who took his cash with a knowing look. This was Soho after hours. Men didn't come here at this time of night for the Greek food.

Calloway double timed back to the passageway. En route he was propositioned from a darkened doorway by a woman in a fur that was as tired looking as her painted face. She smelled of Ma Griffe. He waved her off. Her scent followed him to the corner of the passageway.

The passage was poorly lit and empty, but there was music coming from a doorway set back a little with a spy hole. There was a small printed card pinned to the doorframe. It promised "all night gaiety in London's bohemian rendezvous". Beside it was a bell push. Calloway pressed it. He heard scratching at the spy hole then a bolt slid back. The door opened slowly, casting a swathe of red hued light onto the wet paving. A large man appeared in silhouette, his features emerging as Calloway's eyes adjusted to the light. He was big and foreign, Maltese most likely, who looked like his sole job at the establishment was to keep people like Calloway out.

'Are you a member?' the big doorman asked, with a heavy accent. More a warning than a question. Calloway mugged embarrassment. It bought him time to peer into the club over the shoulders of the goon. Through the reddened glow he could see a small and busy room, cheaply decorated like a Bedouin tent, with oriental throws over old sofas, low tables and lamps with red shades. The clientele were mostly men, draped over the sofas or leaning against the room's roughly painted wooden pillars, talking enthusiastically. There were a handful of women too but, Calloway noticed, they had size-nine feet and Adam's apples. Billy Riley and his friend were ordering drinks at a makeshift bar. Riley looked more relaxed than he had at Robinson's party. The other young man seemed to know everyone.

'I think I've made a mistake,' said Calloway, playing up the embarrassment.

The doorman gave a grudging nod and closed the door. Calloway heard the bolt slide back.

A voice from behind him gave him a start. He caught the smell of Ma Griffe again.

'Not your cup of tea then luvvie?'

Calloway shook his head.

'Are you sure you don't want some company? It's a filthy night.'

He did want company, but not this kind. The company he craved could never be. It left an empty place in his heart, which grew colder as the years wore on. Nothing the whore could offer could fill the gap, no matter how extensive her repertoire. He declined her invitation and started to walk. He'd reached the Embankment before it occurred to him to hail a taxi. It was the time of night for refusing fares south of the river but Calloway wasn't having it. He made this known when he barked his address, like an NCO to an errant private. The cabbie took the hint. It earned him a decent tip when they pulled up in Calloway's street a half hour later.

The basement room was as dismal as he'd left it. Perhaps he needed oriental throws and some red lamps. He should ask Miss Logan for advice. He laughed to himself as he sat on the narrow, creaking cot and pulled off his brogues. He was too alert for sleep. He poured himself a slug of London gin from the bottle he kept behind a curtain on a shelf under his old stone sink. The burn of the gin on his throat was comforting. He switched on the portable gramophone and chose a record while its valves warmed up. The heated valves smelled like burning dust. It brought back memories. Two peopled intertwined in the sanctuary of a requisitioned villa in Germany, soothed by gentle music away from the carnage of war. He poured a second shot of gin, necked it in one go and drifted off, fully clothed. The violin concerto soothed him even now, but the soothing was bittersweet.

He woke around eight. He'd slept poorly. It was cold in the basement and his damp clothes clung to him. He lit the old oil heater. It emitted a thick chemical smell, but it took the chill off the cold spring morning. He made tea and drank it black and sweet. Then he changed into fresh clothes, hanging the old set on the rail behind the wardrobe curtain. He heard the telephone in the main hallway above ring and Mrs Cobb's footsteps cross her ground floor room and enter the hallway. Small feet followed her excited by the sound of the shrill telephone bell. He heard her shout 'hush' to her boys before answering. Then the front door opened and feet padded down the stone steps outside and into the basement well. Calloway opened the door, anticipating the knock.

'It's the stadium, Mr Calloway. They say they need to speak to you urgently.'

The two boys clung to her legs and peered nosily into Calloway's room. He thanked her and followed the three of them back up the steps and into the hall. One of the boys stuck out his tongue. The other scowled.

'Calloway, it's Pat.'

She sounded tense. 'Morning, ma'am.'

'You can cut that out. Look, you need get yourself down here. There's been a break in.'

'Where?'

'The workshop lockers, my office, your office.'

'What's been taken?'

'I can't tell. The safes look to be untouched. But they've gone through the filing cabinets and desk drawers.'

'Have you called the police?'

'They're on their way. You need to be here when they arrive.'

'I'll be there in fifteen minutes.'

'Good.' She hesitated a moment. 'Calloway, I'd be grateful if you didn't mention the matter you and I have been looking into.'

'They could be connected.'

'They could equally be nothing of the sort. I don't want to set hares running. It's not good for the club.'

He thought about telling her where to go. He was head of security, not some cloak-and-dagger stooge.

'Understood, ma'am.'

He drove to the stadium and parked in Canal Road. A police Wolseley was already parked in front of the main gate. Les Birkett was there too. He looked uncomfortable on seeing Calloway arrive.

'They're waiting in your office sir.'

'Give me the gen on the break in first, Les.'

Birkett cleared his throat. 'Well, they must have come in overnight sir, They cut the fence.'

'Who was on nights?'

'Archie Hook sir. He...'

The old soldier hesitated.

'Spit it out, Les. I don't have time for tall tales.'

'I found him asleep, sir. Under the stands. Had an empty bottle of single malt in his hand.'

'Single malt? We must be paying him too much.'

'I've read the riot act to him sir.'

Calloway's anger rose. He let it show. 'You'll do more than that, Birkett. Get rid of him.'

'Sir?'

'A night watchman needs to watch. At night. He drank himself unconscious and slept. Get rid of him.'

Birkett frowned, his camaraderie fighting with his sense of duty.

'As you wish, sir.'

Birkett turned on his heels. Calloway called him back. 'Archie was with you in Italy wasn't he?'

'Anzio, sir. A right old mess that was. Ted machine guns had us pinned down on the beach.'

'Ted?'

'The Tedeschi, sir. It's what the Eyeties called the Jerries. We sort of picked it up along the way. Archie was caught in a shell hole with three pals. The other three copped it. Those MG42s took their heads clean off their shoulders. Archie's not been right since. He takes a drink to calm his nerves, sir.'

Calloway sighed and let the anger subside. He was too soft by half.

'Let him down gently, Les. I'll find him four weeks' pay and put in a good word for him for his next job. But I want him out, alright?'

'Yes, sir. There's one other thing sir.'

'What?'

'It wasn't Archie's bottle, sir. He said he found it in his hut, next to the kettle and the tea. I think someone knew he liked a drink and left it for him.'

'To knock him out deliberately?'

'It seemed to have had the desired effect.'

'Let's keep that to ourselves for now. Go and check the bar, the workshops and Miss Moxon's office. See if anything's been taken.'

Birkett turned on his heels and left, swinging his arms in parade ground time.

There were two uniformed officers in Calloway's office. One looked like he ate the other one's dinner habitually. The big one had sergeant's stripes. The skinny one looked straight out of Hendon. His uniform fitted him like a hand-me-down. Calloway took stock. The place had been turned over. The door lock had been jemmied and the doorframe was splintered. Drawers hung open. Files lay splayed on the lino. The safe was closed and looked untouched. He introduced himself as security officer.

'Security officer, eh?' the sergeant chuckled. 'Not your day then is it, sir?'

Calloway bristled. 'When I want a laughing policeman I'll go to the end of the pier.'

This drew a smirk from the boy copper. The cheer drained from his sergeant's face. 'Alright sir, alright. Now perhaps you can tell me what's been taken.'

Calloway pulled out his handkerchief and used it to open the safe. He felt stupid doing it, like something Basil Rathbone would do in one of those preposterous films. The weekend's turnstile and bar takings had been banked the day before and the petty cash was still there. So was the cash from Fenton's toolbox. He checked the filing cabinet. The marbled notebook was gone. It was the only thing missing. He turned to the police.

'Nothing missing as far as I can see. They probably heard the night watchman coming and scarpered. Kids, most likely. We get a few in here from time to time looking for things to nick.'

'Nothing gone form the safe?'

Calloway shook his head. Les Birkett appeared at the door. He gave a respectful nod on seeing the uniforms, before giving the laughing policeman and his malnourished apprentice the once over. The look on Birkett's face said they didn't pass muster.

'The bar's still locked, sir. The workshop's been broken into but Hale says nothing's been taken. Just one of the lockers prised open, but that was empty he says.'

Calloway rolled his eyes so the policeman could see him. 'This isn't a professional job, sergeant. More like vandalism. I think we can stand you boys down. I certainly don't think we should waste CID's time on a bit of high jinks like this. The stadium can deal with it.'

Birkett looked unsure. The sergeant looked relieved. He had one less thing to do. Calloway waited until the police had left before quizzing Birkett on the details.

'Which locker was broken into?'

'Des Fenton's. Nothing taken though. There was nothing to take. Mr Hale had already had it cleared.'

'I know. That's Fenton's toolbox there,' said Calloway nodding to the upturned box on the floor. 'How about Pat's office?'

'The door's been jemmied and it looks like Juno Beach on D plus one, but she says everything's still there.'

'A couple of chancers most likely. Ghoulish souvenir hunters looking for a piece of Fenton memorabilia. We'll get the doors and the fence patched up.'

'What about the whisky bottle sir?'

'I reckon Archie has a secret admirer. I'm not convinced it's connected to the break in.'

Birkett didn't buy this but Calloway was security officer. He was happy to let the buck stop with him.

'Right you are, sir,' he said, then hesitated. 'Do you still want me to give Archie his cards?'

Calloway sat on the edge of his desk and pulled out his cigarette case. He lit one and drew on it hard. 'Give him a final warning. But no second chances, Les.'

Birkett smiled, relieved.

'Thank you, sir.' He turned to leave. 'Oh, Miss Moxon has asked to see you in her office.'

Moxon's office was in the same state as Calloway's. She sat behind her desk, which was strewn with papers from rifled files. The lino told a similar story. Framed photos of Bullets' line-ups through the years had been pulled from the walls, their glass lying in splinters on the floor.

'Some date you proved to be.' She blew cigarette smoke his way. 'Last time I looked you were all over that little blonde piece.'

'I thought we were free spirits.'

'It certainly seems that way,' she snorted, righting an upturned ashtray and stubbing her cigarette out hard.

'She was Fenton's mistress,' said Calloway.

She raised her eyebrows. 'Available then.'

He shrugged this off. 'Fenton was planning to leave his wife. He was putting money aside for a flat. He had a sideline apparently. Something he kept from Irene. I don't know what.'

'That might explain the cash you found.'

He nodded.

'And the notebook that went missing in last night's break in. Seems like this was the only thing that did.'

She looked concerned. 'Did you share that with the police?'

'You told me not to. I sent them away. Blamed it on vandals.'

She leaned back in the chair. She looked tired. 'So I can rely on you for something at least. So what next?'

'I'm going to follow up the Joe Smoke angle. That connects Fenton and Simpkins somehow.'

For now he was keeping Billy Riley and the all-night gaiety at London's bohemian rendezvous out of the picture.

'Do that. Take off for a day. But hurry it up will you. You've had your week and we're none the wiser.'

He clicked his heels. 'Understood, ma'am.'

'Stop it. Call when you've got something to tell me.'

He acknowledged her with a half-hearted salute.

'Oh and Reg.' Her tone had softened.

'Ma'am?'

She held his eye for a few seconds too long. 'Thank you. I do appreciate your help you know.'

He turned to leave. 'Keep working on that Pat. You might just end up sounding sincere.'

ELEVEN

Carrington House was a sanctuary for single men who were down on their luck. A big brick fortress with a hundred tiny windows, it reminded Calloway of a military prison. He caught the smell of cabbage and carbolic as an earnest-looking man in his forties greeted him with a tolerant smile, introducing himself as the manager of the hostel. He had the demeanour of a disgraced clergyman. Calloway explained that he was trying to trace a rough sleeper. He described Joe Smoke and his scar. The manager's nostrils flared like he smelled something worse than cabbage.

'A vagrant? I'm not sure why you've come here.'

'I thought this was a spike.'

The manager recoiled. 'It certainly is not. This is a gentlemen's hostel. We provide clean and decent lodgings for working men. Quite respectable and not all of them labourers.' He puffed out his pigeon chest with an awkward pride. 'Some of our residents are from the clerkly classes.'

Calloway had already taken a dislike to him.

'That's not what they say round here.'

'People can be very judgemental,' he said, meaning people like Calloway. 'What's your interest in this gentleman?'

'We believe he may be an army deserter.'

'Are you with the army?'

'Field security.'

The best lies were the half lies based on a version of the truth.

'I see.' He seemed satisfied with the answer, to Calloway's relief.

'It's possible this man came to you looking for accommodation last summer.'

The manger considered this with the air of a man who really had better things to do. 'It's true that vagrants do come here looking for a bed or a hot meal. We can accommodate some. It all depends on...' he grappled for words becoming of the manager of respectable lodgings '...their state of mind. We have to think of the welfare of our residents.'

'So if they look mad or dangerous you turn them away?'

'A rather indelicate way of putting it, but yes.'

'And when they're turned away, where do they end up?'

'Bomb sites and abandoned buildings most likely. That's the harsh reality. And London has plenty of both these days.' He hesitated for a moment and thought some more. 'Actually I do remember the man you describe. That scar is hard to forget. He was very confused. He didn't make a lot of sense and his behaviour was unsettling. We couldn't help him here. We're not that sort of establishment.'

'Unsettling how?'

'He was rambling and incoherent. Fragments of memories mostly. Some moments of lucidity.'

'Did he say anything lucid when you turned him away?'

The manager took umbrage. 'Look, we're not equipped to deal with men in his condition. It's tragic I appreciate. Men like him need help and it's just not there for them a lot of the time. But we can't help everyone. Carrington House isn't a place for men like him. Our guests are hard-working, capable men in need of a helping hand. Your vagrant was way beyond our capabilities.'

'I appreciate that, but any thoughts you may have would be of tremendous help.'

'He was a deserter you say? Well that would make sense. I remember he talked about the marshes. There is a place, you see. I know it only by reputation.'

He described it and gave Calloway directions. It was an hour's drive at least. Calloway took Pat Moxon at her word and set aside the rest of the afternoon. He drove south east along the A2. London gave way to cheap suburbia before hitting Kent, not the Garden of England part. This Kent was a mess of gravel pits and quarries and scrubby fields with scrubbier livestock. The place was held together with rusting barbed wire and corrugated iron, with uninviting roadhouses for light relief. Following the hostel manager's directions, he turned north before Dartford and headed for the river. From there he navigated by instinct. If there had ever been signposts here then they had not been replaced after their removal during the war, under a plan to fox the enemy based on the assumption the German army couldn't read a map.

Short haul trucks spilling aggregates terrorised the narrowing roads. The surrounding terrain was barren and soggy, the air smelled of dust and chemicals. A cold spring sun was going down behind him. It lit up a string of abandoned coastal defences, which peeked from the overgrown marshland. Thank God we'd never had to rely on them, Calloway thought. He'd seen the Atlantic Wall the Germans had built in France. The Germans had built well. They had slave workers to do it. We had built pillboxes with all the defensive capabilities of a public convenience.

The road petered out, ending at a rotting five-bar gate, which gave way to a raised track through the open marsh. He cut the engine, took the torch from the glove compartment and left the car. He walked along the track towards the river, grey and cold in the distance. There was a brittle silence, broken only by the swish of the breeze through the reeds and the steam whistles of cargo vessels navigating the estuary. As the sun sunk lower in the sky behind him, the way ahead was turning to grey.

He had walked a quarter mile before he saw the first camp, an elaborate bivouac which had expanded over time, made of heavy canvass, crates and salvaged iron sheeting. Its owner peered through the half light at him over the smoke of a small camp fire. He wore a filthy greatcoat over layers of clothing. His face was hard and weather worn.

Suspicion flickered in his eyes before the opportunism

kicked in. 'Got an oily?'

A roll-up already hung from his cracked lips. Calloway pulled three cigarettes from his case. The man held his hand out as if this was payment due to him and slipped them into the greatcoat pocket.

'What do you want?' he wheezed.

'What makes you think I want anything?'

'You're not here for the view. You police?'

'Not police. I'm looking for a friend.'

'No friends here.'

He drew up a gobbet of phlegm and spat into the embers.

'I'm looking for an old army pal. He dropped out of sight. I want to see him again.'

The man looked wary. 'So you say.'

'My friend has a scar on his face, a big scar, shaped like a fork of lightning. He was sleeping rough in London then came out here seven or eight months ago.'

He cocked an eye, sensing another opportunity. 'An army pal, eh? Got any more of those smokes?'

Calloway handed out another three cigarettes from his case. The man in the greatcoat pocketed them with the others.

'Mad Carew,' he said.

'What's that mean?'

'We call him Mad Carew. After the rhyme.'

He stared out over the estuary and began to recite, like a drunken music hall act with an audience of one.

'There's a one-eyed yellow idol
'To the north of Kathmandu;
'There's a little marble cross below the town;
'And a broken-hearted woman
'Tends the grave of "Mad" Carew,
'While the yellow god for ever gazes down.'

He gave a small bow from where he squatted and said, 'You won't get much sense out of him. Speaks in tongues half the time.'

'So he camps out here?'

'Camps? He's a gentlemen of property.'

He pointed with a blackened finger towards a squat concrete cube just visible through the reeds.

'You see that pillbox? That's Mad Carew's castle.'

He laughed to himself until the laughter turned to coughing. The embers hissed with another gobbet of phlegm. Calloway continued down the sodden path. His shoes were soaked by now and the turn-ups of his suit trousers felt wet against his ankles. Eyes followed him as he walked, all with the same look of suspicion. Some had shelters like the one he'd just seen, others just simple bivouacs. The hostel manager had described it as a colony. Deserters had hidden out in the remote marshland during the war. Some had stayed, making homes among the abandoned defences. He'd counted half a dozen colonists before reaching the pillbox.

Up close he could see it was brick built with a concrete slab roof a foot thick. There were rifle loops on all sides and an aperture for a door on the landward wall. Discarded tins, bottles and the detritus of a sorry existence littered the doorway. Flies buzzed around him as he approached. Then he caught the stench. Something he'd not smelled since the war, when he'd smelled it far too often.

By now the light was all but gone. He lit the torch and took cautious steps through the doorway on crouched legs. Joe Smoke had been dead at least a week. Calloway had seen enough corpses to know. Flies darted in and out of his mouth, which hung open as though singing his own eulogy. His eyes stared at the underside of the concrete from his scarred and soot-blackened face, which was stiff from advanced rigor mortis. The concrete roof was heaven's foot-thick defence against an unwanted spirit. Joe's soul was consigned to an eternity in the North Kent marshes, hanging like fog over the stinking estuary mud. His dead hand clutched a half-drunk bottle of meths as if in celebration of the fact.

The stench was overpowering. Calloway choked back the urge to wretch. With his torch in one hand he rifled through the vagrant's few possessions. A tobacco tin, an empty and rusting paraffin lamp, soiled blankets and some dog-eared pornography. He opened up the dead man's greatcoat. The stench of the bloated corpse grew more intense. He shone the beam of the torch along the body. There was a deep poacher's pocket sewn to the inside of the rough wool fabric of the coat. He slid in his free hand and withdrew a book. It was the photo album Webber had described.

Calloway backed away from the corpse, ducked through the doorway and gasped down the damp mashland air. Setting the album on the remains of a brick outer wall, he shone the torch on it and turned the pages. A dozen pages in he found perhaps twenty small three-by-five prints. They were the kind of photos army buddies took, but it wasn't the army he'd expected.

TWELVE

It was past nine when he returned to his basement room. He poured a slug of gin and settled himself at the undersized drop-leaf table, which served as his desk and dining table. He set the photograph album on the table. The green sugar paper leaves were damp from successive winters spent in makeshift shelters. The pages tore as Calloway turned them.

The photos showed the same two men. The first few pages were cheery shots of comrades in arms, in bars, with girls, or sightseeing in unfamiliar towns. The backdrops were European, Central or Eastern. Images of military mobilisation followed, the two comrades posing on the tailgates of trucks or from the windows of railway carriages. The final two pages showed scenes only possible once war has desensitised its participants. Trophy shots, posing with their human prey like big game hunters. Rifles on hips, boots on the bodies of their kill, smiling for the camera. Civilians hanging from trees, nooses cinched beneath contorted gargoyle faces, with the two pals pointing, grinning or mocking the still-warm dead. And in every photo the they wore the same uniforms, which Calloway knew well. They were Waffen SS.

The photographs were water stained an indistinct, but some were clear enough for him to make out the insignia worn by the two men. The SS runes on their collar patches and death's head cap badges were clear enough. The cuff titles were typical of Waffen SS units although their script was illegible in the photos. It was the right-hand collar tab that Calloway couldn't make out. Three heraldic lions stacked vertically against a black background. Unit recognition had been part of his job as a sergeant in the Intelligence Corps and he could spot most units from the manuals he had committed to memory. But he'd never seen the three lions insignia before.

He turned the pages again from the beginning and this time read each of the handwritten captions. Though the ink had smudged, he recognised place names and dates from the notebook he'd found in Fenton's toolbox. Three photos were missing from the final page of the album, with only the small black photo corners and captions remaining.

Calloway tried to connect the photographs with the two riders, but neither Fenton's nor Simpkins's war records tallied with the locations, most of which were further east than the western Allies had advanced by 1945. They would have been under the control of the Red Army. There were other explanations of course. The album might have been seized from a POW who had been withdrawn from the eastern front to repel the Allies' westward advance. But the connection would need to be deeper if it was to link Fenton, Simpkins and the tramp in a way that was worth the two of them falling out.

He removed each photo from the album and stacked them in a deck. He took an envelope from the drawer and stuffed the photos inside. Then he licked the flap of the envelope to seal it, taking a swig of the gin to wash away the taste of the glue. Fumbling in a draw he picked out two drawing pins and used these to pin the envelope to the wooden underside of the portable radiogram cabinet. He stood back and looked at the gramophone from across the small basement room. Even with the cabinet opened to play records, the envelope was not visible.

The next morning he called Sammy Mackay from his office. Mackay answered in a musical brogue.

'Sammy, it's Cab.'

'I was about to call, but you've saved His Majesty's Government the tuppence.'

'The stadium coffers will cover it.'

'Yes, I'm sure there's money in dog racing. Now about your names and places. I've done some digging and frankly old man, it's something you might want to leave be.'

'Why?'

'You always were so wonderfully blunt. I can't go into detail but ties in with a bit of departmental business, if you get my drift. Pretty low-grade stuff but not worth meddling in. It could all get horribly complicated.'

Calloway ignored this. 'What can you tell me about a Waffen SS unit with three lions on its collar tabs?'

He heard irritation in Mackay's voice. 'Last time I had anything to do with the Waffen SS I was interrogating one of their Obersturmfuhrers from the Das Reich division. You stood behind him like a terrier that had cornered a fox. I had to stand you down as I recall. I always thought you enjoyed your job a little too much.'

Calloway let the comment go. 'So what can you tell me? Three lion insignia and a shield on the forearm.'

'What's on the shield?'

He could tell Mackay knew the answer already but was probing to see how much Calloway knew. Calloway had failed to make the emblem out. The watermarking and foxing on the photo was too bad.

'You tell me.'

There was silence on the end of the line for a moment, then a deep sigh. 'Cab, where have you seen all this?'

'Photographs.'

Another silence followed by a muffled humming. Mackay was smothering the receiver with his hand while he spoke to someone else. He came back on the line. 'Look, take my word for it, this is something that really shouldn't be your concern. You were in the game. You know how this works. Let it go, old man.'

Calloway didn't let it go. 'If it affects the security of my stadium and those that use it, then it's very much my concern. Goodbye, Sammy.'

He ended the call, left the office and walked down to the track. A couple of the Bullets were doing laps. Simpkins hung over the guard rail watching. He saw Calloway cross the centre green. As he approached, Simpkins flicked his cigarette onto the concrete and turned to walk away. Calloway stopped him.

'We need another talk.'

'I've said all I need to.'

'I'll decide that.'

The rider shrugged. His insubordination was well practiced.

'So talk,' he said.

Both men ducked to avoid the spray of cinders as the two practicing riders passed.

'I need you to be straight with me,' Calloway said. 'I know there was bad blood between you and Des Fenton. You fell out over the tramp that slept under the stands, the one they called Joe Smoke. I'm guessing you knew him. I'm also guessing Fenton knew that you knew him and this bothers you. Fenton wasn't well liked but you seemed to have more reason to dislike him than most. I don't know why yet. You need to tell me.'

Simpkins shouted above the clatter of the motorcycle engines. One of the riders had pulled up. A mechanic was making adjustments to his machine as the rider revved the engine.

'I don't need to tell you anything.'

Calloway stood to his full height. He was a head taller than the Simpkins. 'Oh, I think you do, Raymond. Because right now people are saying you ran Des Fenton off the track deliberately. Personally I don't believe it. But there are rumours and they're getting louder. Soon they will be so loud that the police will get to hear them and then, whether those rumours are true or not, you son will be in a lot of bother.'

Simpkins smirked. He stretched his neck and shoved his chin forward. 'So maybe I didn't like Fenton. He was a flash bastard, if you want my opinion. I remember the tramp, sure. Doesn't mean I know him. Is that all you've got? Not much of an investigation, is it?'

Calloway could see through the bravado. He played his hand.

'The tramp had a photo album. I've seen it.'

Simpkins switched off the surliness. He looked worried for a moment. Calloway noticed and pressed the advantage.

'Those photos don't make happy viewing, Ray. A couple of kamerads from the Waffen SS slaughtering their way across Europe. They were good at that. I met a few myself, although the boys in these photos were from a unit I don't recognise. Three lions on their collar patches. Strange that some tramp who hung around here had an album like that. Mean anything to you, does it?'

Simpkins lit a cigarette and tried to look disinterested. Calloway recognised the discomfiture beneath the sham.

'So what am I German now? This is bollocks and you know it.'

'What I know is that there were place names and dates under those photos. I found the same places and dates in a notebook hidden in Fenton's toolbox. The notebook was stolen from my office.'

The rider drew on the cigarette with tensed lips. Calloway sensed he was getting somewhere. Then a thought seemed to flicker behind Simpkins's eyes. 'Why don't you ask Joe Smoke about it?' he asked.

He sneered as if he'd scored a point with the question.

Calloway answered deadpan, 'Joe Smoke is dead.'

The rider smiled. He stood back from the stand rail and turned to face Calloway square on. 'Then I'd say you've hit a dead end. Best to forget about it I reckon.'

'Perhaps I should.' Calloway clapped a hand on the small rider's back and leaned in towards him. He spoke quietly into his ear. 'The problem is, Raymond, you're not the first person to tell me that today. And that just spurs me on.'

THIRTEEN

The away team rider slid a dozen yards along the rough cinder track before hitting the perimeter fence feet first. Sparks flew as his lead-soled boots scraped the metal posts. The crowd oooh'd and aaah'd. This was injury as entertainment. The ambulance crew scrambled across the track with a stretcher, as the remaining three riders scudded down the back straight at full throttle. The pit crews lifted the buckled bike out of the race's path. The three riders passed within feet of the stretcher party before it reached the centre ground and laid the injured man down. Calloway watched from the tower. The whole operation had taken less than twenty seconds. A lap later the checkered flag flew. Billy Riley took first place, O'Donnell second. Riley removed his helmet and waved to the crowd. They chanted 'Billy, Billy, he's our man', waving their scarves and cranking their gas rattles, which clacked like an ack-ack battery in an air raid. Riley played to the crowd. He made a victory lap, head held high, waving regally as he passed. O'Donnell followed, a respectful bike's length behind his winning teammate. He made the six-gun sign with his thumb and forefinger, firing off imaginary rounds into the night sky above.

The Bullets had ridden well. They had clinched a victory over the visitors by a narrow points margin and the crowd responded in full voice. The spectre of Des Fenton's death seemed to have departed, for the last few heats at least. Pat Moxon seemed pleased with her boys. She strutted around the pit in her fur coat like a lioness in her den. Riley was the man of the moment. There was much back slapping and ruffling of hair from his teammates. Later a horde of autograph hunters gathered outside the riders' changing room. Mostly girls. Calloway's men struggled to hold them back, such was the frenzy.

'I swear some of 'em pissed 'emselves,' said Sid Tanner, the ruddy-faced commissionaire, once the autograph hunters had dispersed. He was a man of few words and most of them indelicate.

Riley, to his credit, signed every book. He valued his supporters and treated them with respect. Duiker should take note, Calloway thought.

A good night for the Bullets meant a late night in the members bar. The lights still shone brightly through the long picture window above the west stand, which gave the more discerning punters a panoramic view of the track. Calloway would leave them to their celebrations for another half hour before closing the bar. He made his rounds. As he passed the members changing rooms, he saw Billy Riley coming towards him. He had bailed from the celebrations early.

'Hallo, Billy. You've had a good night.'

Riley didn't look pleased to see him. Since their talk at the cycle speedway, he had been avoiding the security boss.

'Not bad, I s'pose.'

'Not bad? A return to form I would say.'

'We all have our good nights.'

'Yes, but this is the first good night you've had since the middle of last season. What's changed Billy?'

Riley shrugged. 'I guess my luck just turned.'

Riley made to leave but Calloway blocked him.

'I don't believe in luck Billy. I prefer numbers. I've been studying the Bullets' form. Your results make interesting reading.'

'I didn't think you were a speedway fan, Mr Calloway.'

'I'm a recent convert. I've been following a couple of riders in particular and one of them is you. Your results puzzle me. You were flying high at the start of last season, none of the riders could touch you, home or away. Then something happened.'

Riley made a play of looking nonplussed. Calloway continued.

'Your form tailed off, Billy. But not across the board.'

'What do you mean?' Riley's voice wavered.

'You started losing to one rider in particular.'

Sweat beads popped beneath Riley's hairline. 'I had a run of bad luck, that's all. Every rider does.'

'Maybe. But you were only unlucky when you were paired with Des Fenton. The trouble is I don't believe in luck. I think you were pulling races, Billy. I'd like to know why.'

Riley flushed, half anger, half disbelief. 'That's rubbish. Sure, I had a bad season. I didn't just lose to Fenton.'

'True, up to a point. But when you were paired with another Ranger, your luck held up pretty well.'

Calloway looked to the side and ran his big hand through his hair. 'Ah, but there I go again talking about luck when I said I don't believe in it. Your numbers show above average form in all your races except for those when Fenton rode with you. You lost every one of those races. That's not bad luck. The pattern is too obvious. I think you were pulling races and Fenton was behind it. I think his widow was in on it too. She wasn't in the Four Bells to thank you for the flowers last week, Billy. I watched the altercation between you. I'll wager you weren't ill for her husband's funeral either. You were keeping out of her way.'

Riley rolled his eyes. 'What are you on about? Pulling races! This isn't boxing, Calloway. Riders don't take a fall in the third round, like they do in the films. You're seeing things that aren't there.'

'Perhaps. I'm sorry to have brought this up when you should be celebrating. I meant to talk to you at Dennis Robinson's party, but as I recall, you left early.'

The colour drained from Riley's face. He swallowed hard. 'I wasn't enjoying the party. I don't like Robinson, as it happens, or his friends. They're a bunch of fakes. Me and a mate went looking for a late-night drinking club.' He pulled a cigarette from the pocket of his blouson jacket and lit it. Calloway noticed his hands were trembling. 'Is that allowed, Mr Calloway?'

'It's allowed.'

'Look can't you just drop this Fenton business. Whatever Pat's got you chasing, it's got nothing to do with me.'

'I'd like to drop it. Genuinely I would. But when there's something not right on that track, or in this stadium, well that becomes my business. Things need explaining.'

Riley pushed past Calloway. 'Just blow, will you.'

The security boss called after him. 'Des Fenton and Ray Simpkins fell out over some photographs. Do you know anything about that?'

Riley stopped dead. Cautiously he turned to face Calloway. 'Photographs?'

The rider's mouth was dry and his voice rasped.

'From the war. German soldiers.'

Riley's face relaxed. 'Before my time, Mr Calloway. I spent my war in the shelters. I was even too young for the Home Guard.'

Two autograph hunters came bowling along the underside of the stands. They had spotted Riley and were offering up their autograph books to the one-time star rider. They were pursued by Sid Tanner. He was a furlong behind and wheezing. Riley made the most of the diversion. He played the star and signed the books. Calloway dismissed Tanner with a wave of his hand and told the fans their time was up. They skipped away, grinning. Calloway leaned in towards Riley and whispered, 'You need to trust me Billy, for your own good.'

FOURTEEN

The Fentons lived the mock Tudor dream. Their suburban house was a contrived apology for the humble roots they had earned enough to disown. Every house in the street told the same story. This was Merrie England with an Alvis in the drive. Calloway knew these avenues, although not in this town. He had visited his better-off school friends in similar surroundings back home, the perks of a grammar school education, sometimes finding yourself a guest in a home where your tea was called dinner and the lav was indoors. His own father called it bourgeoise. The foreign words he used were Marxist. At the time Calloway didn't care. These houses were warmer, the mothers more fragrant and the food more plentiful. He'd learned a new etiquette from his encounters with the middle classes. His father called it 'putting on airs'. He was a coal miner, a socialist and a staunch union man. About this time Calloway resolved never to follow his father down the pits. The army had been his escape.

Irene Fenton greeted him with an unfelt smile. Courtesy came with the house but it was as fake as the half-timbered facade. Calloway returned it in kind. She invited him into the front room. The chintz was fighting a style war with the American dream. The three-piece suite and curtains were a riot of pastel flora. The bar was Broadway in miniature. Chromium-framed photos of speeding bikes and scenes from the stadium lined the walls, an odd substitution for the customary Haywain and hunting prints. The Fentons' wedding photo stood on the bar, next to the soda siphon. Fenton wore battledress with Royal Engineers' insignia. He was one stripe up. Irene had done her best with dreary utility fabric. The picture gave no hint of celebration. This was a cheap wartime marriage. The trappings of motor sport stardom were a few years off.

They drank tea from china cups. Irene made small talk with the tight vowels of a telephonist. She held the cup with her pinkie extended. Her lips left a perfect pink bow on the rim. Calloway turned on the bedside manner. It was the best the jaded ex-sergeant could muster.

'I know this is a difficult time for you, Mrs Fenton. I will keep this short. There are some questions I need to ask as part of my investigation into your husband's accident.'

She gave him a condescending smile. 'It's no trouble, Mr Calloway. The Bullets was Des's life. He would want me to help you.'

There was no fragility in her voice, nor any hint of stoicism. She was hard, plain and simple.

'How did your late husband get on with his teammates?'

'What, my Des? He was the life and soul. Everyone loved Des.'

There was a hint of bitterness. It made him think of Liz Francis.

'Were there tensions with any teammates? Grudges or differences?'

She placed the cup and saucer down on the table between them and took a cigarette from the dark wood cigarette box beside it. Calloway offered her a light and she accepted.

'He got on with most of them. There were a few who resented his success.'

'Was Ray Simpkins one of them?'

She drew on the cigarette and spoke as she exhaled. 'You don't believe the rubbish about the accident do you?'

'What rubbish is that?'

'That it wasn't an accident.'

'I don't believe anything yet.'

'That's Pat Moxon, that is. Spreading rumours. She thinks

the intrigue will be good for business. You know why people flock to the speedway, Mr Calloway?' She toyed distractedly with the cup on its saucer. 'For the accidents. The smash-ups. The broken limbs.'

She glanced at the speedway photos on the walls as if she suddenly resented them being there. 'And the prospect of a death on the track. I've been a speedway wife long enough to know.' She corrected herself. 'A speedway widow now.'

She rose from the armchair and walked over to the window, pulling aside the net curtain and gazing into the street. It looked like bad amateur dramatics, a scene Noel Coward might have written while drunk. Calloway didn't doubt her grief. He just wasn't convinced by the play acting. He knew the real Irene Fentons of this world. They greeted death with savage emotion. They wailed and sobbed and cried, 'Why my Des? Why do the good die young?' Then they spoiled for fights. The claws came out and the accusations flew. Calloway sensed this grief was deeply suppressed in the widow Fenton. She had left that past behind, locked it inside her electroplated suburban shell and buried the key under the rose bushes in her garden.

'He was my Dashing Des, Mr Calloway. And now he's gone. I don't care what others thought of him.'

'What did Billy Riley think of him?'

She stiffened at the name, only slightly, but enough for Calloway to detect. He had learned to read the small signs during interrogations.

'I'm not sure Des had much to do with Billy. They weren't close.'

'Is that why Riley failed to show up for your husband's funeral?'

She leaned forward and stubbed her cigarette into the ashtray. The veins on the back of her hand protruded as she ground the stub into the heavy glass.

'You'll have to ask him.'

She pursed her lips revealing the lines of a lifelong smoker beneath her makeup and powder.

'I've not seen him since before Des's accident, and then only in passing. As I said, we didn't mix with people like him.'

'People like him?'

She skirted the question. 'I have no interest in Billy Riley's business and I'm sure he had no interest in ours. Like I said, I've not seen him.'

Calloway looked down, cradling his hands in his lap. 'That's odd, Mrs Fenton. You see I like a drink of a lunchtime, usually in the Four Bells on New Cross Road, and I'd swear I saw you speaking to Riley there last Saturday. In fact the two of you seemed to be arguing over something. What might that have been?'

She stood and straightened the skirt of her two-piece. It was a signal. 'I don't go to pubs, Mr Calloway. Especially not in New Cross. If you don't mind I'm really not feeling too well. My Des's not been in the ground ten days and now all these questions, well it's all a little too soon.'

She gestured to the door and he rose to leave. He'd heard enough. As he crossed the room he picked up the wedding photograph.

'Royal Artillery. Did your husband serve overseas? Germany, for instance?'

She shook her head. 'Des was stationed in Kent. Anti-aircraft duties.'

She took the photograph from his hands and replaced it on the bar. 'He would come back home whenever he could. We met at the New Cross Empire one Saturday night. He asked me to dance. He was a good-looking boy. I knew him from speedway. He rode before the war you see. He wasn't as big a name then of course.'

'Did Pat Moxon manage him in those days?'

Femton's widow scoffed. Her accent slipped. 'Her? She was just a just a show rider. Tarting herself around the circuit doing tricks.'

'Of course. That was when Mr Dandridge was promoter.'

Irene Fenton put on a playground voice: 'Pretty Pattie Moxon, Queen of the dirt track. Believe me, that one's no better than she should be.'

Calloway let this ride. He glanced around the walls. 'These are very good photos, Mrs Fenton. Someone has a real eye for a picture.'

'Des took them. Photography was hobby with him. When he had the time of course.'

'He takes a good photograph.'

'Took a good photograph,' she corrected.

Calloway thanked the widow for her time. They exchanged polite goodbyes. As he drove away he thought of Billy Riley and the exchange with Irene Fenton in the pub, the exchange she had just denied. He thought of Riley at the Soho club and the photos on Fenton's wall that the deceased rider had taken himself with an obvious talent for capturing the moment. And he remembered Duiker's claim that Fenton always liked to have something on you. On the Riley-Fenton front at least, things were starting to fall into place.

It was almost midnight. The pubs had long since called time and locked up. In the moonless night the streetlamps struggled against the blackness. A train whistle blew in the distance. The last train home. Otherwise the street was quiet.

Calloway had been waiting in a doorway, which gave him a view down the cobbled path beside the railway viaduct. Satisfied now that the street was deserted, he walked slowly towards the path, keeping a hand his raincoat pocket to ensure the tools inside did not clink against one another. In his other hand he held an old No. 4 battery lamp not yet lit.

The cobbled path was uneven and smelled of motor oil. The railway arches were infilled with corrugated iron, within each a peeling wooden door wide enough to take a car. Some had enamelled signs nailed to them for Castrol oil and Champion spark plugs. The fourth arch along had a painted sign above the door with white lettering that was just visible through the darkness: J Fenton, Motor Mechanic, with the phone number TID 0621. Checking behind him to see that he'd not been followed by a drunk looking for somewhere to piss, he twisted the selector switch on the side of the lamp and turned it on. It cast a red glow through its coloured filter, enough for him to examine the padlock which fastened the doors. He withdrew a small jemmy from his coat pocket and slid it between the wood of the door and the padlock bracket. He worked slowly and gently, easing the bar a fraction of an inch at a time to avoid the noise of scraping metal in the darkness. Then from behind he heard voices. He stopped work, extinguished the light and flattened himself against the doors as best he could.

'You're having a fucking laugh aren't you?'

It was a woman's voice, coarse and husky from too many cigarettes. She sounded drunk.

'You don't think I'm going down there with you. It stinks of petrol and Christ knows what.'

Calloway made out two figures at the end of the path, silhouetted against the glow of the streetlamps. The second figure was male and swaying, steadying himself against the woman as the pair stumbled towards the first of the railway arches. The man-made plaintiff grunts, barely able to form the words through his inebriation. He sounded pathetic and the woman cackled in derision.

'Come on then. If this is what you want.'

The silhouetted woman leaned with her back to the doors, hitched up her skirt and hooked one leg around the man. He had by now unbuttoned himself and was pushing his groin towards her in faltering jerks.

'What do you need, a map or something? Give it here.'

She grabbed between his legs and guided him into her. The doors banged against the frame as the pair bucked, bestial in their drunkenness. The woman mocked him with insincere encouragement as he went at her, frustrated with his own ineptitude. Before long he let out a yelp, high pitched and feeble. She patted his back as he slumped against her, like a disinterested mother consoling a sobbing child, before pushing him away and straightening her clothes. They stumbled off.

Calloway stayed flattened against the doors until the pair had disappeared from view.

He resumed his work on the lock. He put his full weight

behind the jemmy. The bracket snapped off easily, its screws wrenched quietly from the damp wood. Calloway slid the jemmy back into his coat and eased his way through the crack in the door, pulling it closed behind him. He turned the selector switch of the lamp to its normal position and shone a beam of white light through the darkness.

The workshop was tidy, the workbenches clear and tools hung in neat rows from pinboard. The trolley jack on the shop floor was squared away under the bench and all the drawers of the metal tool cabinets were closed, with small patches of rust bubbling up through their drab paintwork. The cans on the shelves were arranged neatly and the tyres on the racks above his head were lined up in order of size. The whole place was preserved in aspic, presumably as a fall back in the event Des Fenton's speedway career took a turn for the worse and he needed to go back to his old job.

In the centre of the floor were five loosely laid, oil-blackened planks covering a small inspection pit, just large enough for a man to crouch in. Calloway eased up one of the planks and shone his torch into the void. It was empty. He rifled through the draws and shelves and found nothing you wouldn't expect of a well-equipped mechanic.

At the back of the railway arch was a wooden screen with glazed wood panels. It was a typical workshop office, for paperwork and the telephone, but its windows were blacked out with paint on the inside of every pane. Calloway's heart rate increased. He had expected to see such a place and the discovery felt good. He tried the door, which was locked. A simple domestic lock. The key was most likely on a hook somewhere but he couldn't waste time looking for it. If the cobbled path outside was a favourite place for locals to fuck in the dark, there was a chance another two would come along before the night was out. Maybe even the same woman. He took the jemmy and levered it into the crack between the wooden door and its frame. He gave it a shove. The wood splintered with a crack, much louder than he expected. He stopped and listened. From the path outside he heard the rattling of doors. He judged the sound to be coming from the workshop in first arch, nearest the street corner. Above the rattling he heard a tentative whistling, a popular tune he recognised but couldn't name. He stepped quietly towards the doors, avoiding the lose planks over the inspection pit, and peered through the chink between the door and the frame. Against the glow of the distant streetlight he saw the outline of a police helmet. A copper making his rounds, checking doors. He whistled as he worked his way along the path, trying each door in sequence. He was too close for Calloway to slip away unseen. He looked back into the workshop for a hiding place. He eased up the first plank of the inspection pit, then heard a voice from the end of the path. He froze, gripping the heavy raised plank in his hand.

'Is that you 453?'

A young and surprised-sounding voice replied. 'Yes, Sergeant. Just checking locks on the workshops. They're buggers round here for swiping tools.'

The sergeant cleared his throat in disapproval. 'Language unbecoming, 453. Language unbecoming.'

'Sorry, Sergeant.'

'So lad, anything to report?'

'No, Sergeant. All correct.'

'Then get yourself down to Comet Street. Our old friend Ida is making a right old commotion. One of her clients is too drunk to find his wallet.'

'On my way, Sergeant.'

Calloway heard heavy footsteps disappear into the distance. He replaced the plank over the inspection pit and moved to the office door. He entered in darkness, closed the door behind him and felt along the doorframe for a light switch. With the blacked-out window-panes and door closed, it would be safe to turn on the light. He felt the cold brass switch cover under his palm and flicked the switch. The room lit up blood red. A darkroom safelight shone from a pendant in the ceiling. There was a bench along the far wall with three shallow rectangular trays in a row. An old photographic enlarger stood beside them.

On a shelf behind were bottled chemicals. He peered at the labels, already knowing what they read. Acetic acid and ammonium thiosulphate, the same as on the receipt he'd found in Fenton's toolbox.

Photographic prints hung from a cord above the bench. Speedway shots. Riders captured mid-race. Team shots and crowd scenes, like the ones in Fenton's living room. There was a metal filing cabinet on the adjacent wall. He tried the drawers, which were unlocked. There were files inside. Receipts, bills, accounts and catalogues for motors spares. The darkroom doubled as a working office. As he crouched to close the bottom drawer, he saw a tool cabinet like the one in the main workshop tucked beneath the bench. It was far enough back not to be visible when standing. He pulled it into the centre of the room and tried the drawers. They were locked. He took a screwdriver from his pocket and used it as a lever. The metal rim of the cabinet bent easily, enough for him to remove the draws without unlocking them. There were photographic prints inside, in a batch bound with elastic. He slid off the band and rifled through each print in turn.

He recognised Liz Francis, even without her clothes. The first few shots were cheesecake pinups, risqué but nothing that would frighten the censor. The rest were pornography. Francis acting out Fenton's private fantasies. Performing acts he doubted wife Irene would to be cajoled into. The second draw had several bundles of prints, each with a set of negatives labelled with names, locations and dates. The names belonged to men. The dates were within the last three years. Each set of prints told a similar story. Men meeting in public places, talking, laughing, but furtively, then touching and kissing. Some went further. The shots were taken from a distance, blurred through magnification but with the parties still recognisable. One of them was Billy Riley.

Calloway gathered up the prints and negatives and stuffed them into his coat pocket. There was a third draw, jammed shut. He pulled out the jemmy and used brute force on it. Inside was an envelope, old and dog-eared, some initials and the date September 1934 scrawled across it in pencil. Calloway pulled the set of prints and the strip of negatives from inside. The images showed the same eye for depravity Fenton has used for his private shots of Liz Francis. But the model was someone else entirely.

FIFTEEN

It was two am. The curtains on his basement window were drawn shut. They had been open when he left. From behind them he saw the glow of a torch moving around his room. He descended the basement steps, treading lightly. The door was open an inch. There were wood splinters sticking out from the frame. He drew the jemmy from his pocket, a lightweight crowbar a foot long, heavy enough to break a man's nose or put a dent in his skull. He let his eyes adjust to the darkness in the basement well before easing open the door an inch at a time. He placed his steps close to the skirting to avoid the loose boards creaking. In the near darkness of his single room he made out a figure, male, five foot ten perhaps, rifling through drawers. There was ten feet between the two of them. Calloway would need to be fast if he was to land the first blow. He raised the crowbar and sprang forward. The floorboards creaked, the intruder turned and dropped the torch, raising his arm to parry the blow. He swivelled his body, grabbed Calloway's forearm and braced it for an elbow break. Calloway stamped down hard on the man's shin, failing to snap the bone but causing enough pain for the intruder to loosen his grip. Calloway broke free. He grabbed the man's head with both hands and raised his knee. There was a sharp crunch as the knee slammed into his jaw. The man buckled. As he slumped to the ground, he reached inside his jacket and pulled out a Webley service revolver. Calloway flung himself at the intruder. It was harder to shoot a man at close quarters. He made a half turn and crashed his forearm down on the other man's gun hand. The revolver fell to the floor, illuminated by the beam of the torch. Calloway snatched it up. The intruder made for the door and Calloway followed.

Outside a car was waiting, engine running but headlights doused. The intruder shouted to the driver and fell into the passenger seat clutching his injured arm. The driver revved hard, slipped the car into gear and pumped the accelerator. Calloway gripped the butt of the heavy Webley in both hands, raised it to his eye line and aimed for the car's tyres. He fired off three rounds which echoed through the silence like iron doors slamming. The first two missed. The third burst a rear tyre as the car was making its sharp turn into the adjacent street. The driver lost control and the car piled headlong into a shop window, showering glass. Calloway strode towards it, the Webley still raised and the passenger door in his line of sight. Through the rear windscreen he saw the outline of the driver slumped over the wheel. There was movement in the passenger seat. The passenger leapt out, like a paratrooper on a green light. Calloway fired another round, which went wide. His target ran with adrenaline-charged energy towards the creek. Calloway pocketed the Webley and followed. He had twisted his ankle in the scuffle. A searing muscle pain shot through his calf. He pressed on at a fast hobble, favouring his good leg and trailing the bad.

Calloway was breathing hard, swallowing down the damp creekside air in big gulps. The other man was finding it hard to run, hampered by injuries from the fight or the car crash. They ducked through the courtyards of municipal flats, clawing through washing lines and crashing into bins, before emerging onto the Lower Road. Out of nowhere Calloway heard the screech of brakes. A lone car hit the man he pursued before skidding to a halt. The man rolled off the bonnet like a barrel off a dray. He landed feet first and the momentum carried him forward. He recovered by reflex and continued to run. The car driver leaped from his vehicle and into Calloway's path. He started to shout in angry panic. Calloway barged past him and ran towards the escaping man, gritting his teeth against the pain of the twisted ankle. They cut through a passageway between the backs of the old sailors cottages. The hard cobblestones jarred his injured leg. The intruder had slowed his pace. His injuries were taking their toll too. By the time they reached the river, Calloway had gained ground. There was twenty feet between them. As they rounded the corner of the dock wall, the silhouetted bulk of Paynes Wharf loomed into view. Beside it a dark alley, at its end only the Thames. There was no exit save for a leap into the stinking river. Calloway knew this. The intruder clearly didn't. He stopped dead and for a second and contemplated a leap into the high tide. This was Calloway's chance. He gripped the Webley barrel first and clubbed the other man across the side of the head with the butt. The pistol's lanyard ring gouged a deep wound across his scalp, but the blow failed to floor him. He struck Calloway's windpipe hard with the side of his flattened hand. The big man choked. From the corner of his eye Calloway saw his attacker reach down and draw a stiletto from an ankle sheath. It was a Fairbairn-Sykes knife and it had only one purpose, killing a man quickly and efficiently. He lunged towards Calloway in a move well practiced from the manual. Calloway took a reflex step to the side, stumbling against the wharf steps. The attacker lunged again. Calloway was trapped between the high wharfside and the steps. He still held the Webley and in a single move swivelled it on his palm, found the trigger and squeezed. The blast echoed between the high dock walls. His assailant slumped. The knife dropped from his hand, the black metal hitting the cobblestones with a dull clatter. The man grasped the wound in his gut with both hands and let out a wounded animal squeal. Calloway raised the pistol with a straightened arm and put the remaining bullet through his skull.

Calloway made a circuit of the neighbourhood to approach his street from the south. He clung to buildings, hiding in their shadows. Every hundred yards he stopped in a doorway or passage to surveil the route ahead. He couldn't risk an encounter with 453 or his sergeant. Not at three am with a blood-spattered trench coat furled under his arm.

He dumped the dead man's body into the river. There had

been no way of weighting it down. He just had to hope it would drift with the tide and not end up back in the same place, though this was entirely possible. Throughout history Deptford was a place bodies washed up. The currents brought them home. It was the resting place of the drowned. The Webley had sunk like a rock. He had wiped off his fingerprints then grasping the angular barrel in a handkerchief had hurled it as far as his muscles, weakened from the fight and the inevitable come-down from adrenalin, would allow. He did the same with the knife. He took comfort knowing these at least wouldn't be found. The river would ingest them, deep within its mud-lined gut.

His street was empty as he approached it. At the far end he could see a huddle of figures around the spot where the car had crashed. The car was gone, leaving a gaping whole in the shopfront, as if the window, with its glass-shard teeth, had swallowed it whole. Some of the figures were in uniform. Police, possibly young 453 and colleagues. Some looked half dressed, no doubt the shop owners. It was too soon for the vehicle to have been towed. The driver must have recovered and fled the scene in the crumpled car. This was not good. It meant a living witness, however culpable in the break in. As Calloway approached his house, the front door opened. Miss Logan bade a practiced farewell to a caller. He wore the cheap suit of a commercial traveller. He looked flushed and embarrassed. Miss Logan was wearing a dressing gown. It was silk and frayed at the neck and cuffs, its colours faded in the chink of light from the hallway. Beneath the gown she was naked, the outline of her ageing and undernourished frame showing through the thin material. As her caller left, she saw Calloway approach. She appeared to see nothing surprising in the hour of his arrival. She was a night bird and assumed he was too.

'You missed all the fun, Mr Calloway.' For a moment he wondered what fun she meant. 'Gun shots, a car crash, it was like the St Valentine's Day Massacre.'

'Did you see it?'

'No, luvvie. Didn't get to the window in time. I was a bit indisposed.'

He didn't doubt it. He played her along. 'The papers are right, Miss Logan. It's a crime wave. Too many guns brought back from the war. Too many folk knowing how to use them.'

She drew the robe closer together and made a half-hearted attempt to straighten her hair.

'We learned a lot of things in the war that we've brought with us into peacetime,' she sighed, before drifting back into the house and closing the door.

His basement room was a mess, his few possessions strewn across the floor. His collection of gramophone records had borne the worst of it. Shattered discs lay on the lino like haphazard tiles. He checked the gramophone, sliding his hand inside the cabinet and feeling for the envelope with Joe Smoke's photographs. They were still where he'd pinned them.

He stripped bare and scrubbed himself down in front of the stone sink. Then he lay on the bed still damp, letting the air cool him. He felt an overpowering tiredness. The fatigue of combat. He fell into a fitful sleep and dreamt.

It was 1945. There were three of them. McNally driving, Calloway riding up front, a Sten gun on his lap, and Cox the wireless operator in the back, his lanky six-foot frame twisted into the jeep's mean back seat. They drove at speed through a dense pine forest. Dangerous country for a lone, un-armoured vehicle. The three men sat upright and alert, their eyes scanning the forest walls and the road ahead. They had met no resistance since leaving their unit in Wesel. The enemy was in retreat and in poor shape. The remnants of the German 89th infantry division pulling back from the Rhine. Calloway had orders to investigate an enemy camp beyond the forest near Bergen. RAF reconnaissance photographs suggested there was a barracks. Calloway, McNally and Cox were to approach from the south west, assess its strength and report by wireless to 6th Airborne Division headquarters.

Two miles from the map reference they had been given, they

slowed the jeep, mounted the verge on the roadside and drove beyond the first few lines of trees. The three men shouldered their weapons and dismounted. McNally and Cox unrolled a camouflage net and dragged it over the vehicle. Calloway checked the map. It showed a network of forestry tracks they could navigate on foot, out of sight of the road. He marked a route in cinograph pencil on the transparent cover of the map case. The track was damp and rutted and made for slow going. It was still early, a grey mist hung above the track in the forest half-light. They trod silently and cautiously, stopping at intervals to check ahead for signs of the enemy. It took an hour to reach the clearing Calloway had marked as their observation point. As the cover of the forest gave way to open ground, they crouched low then lay on the damp ground. The barracks was six hundred yards in front of them.

It was the smell they noticed first. A smell of death so strong it burned their throats.

Through binoculars Calloway could see the perimeter fence, but the last of the morning mist hung low and prevented a proper view. Behind the fence, a grey mass masked the huts behind. It seemed to ripple gently in the breeze, a tarpaulin he thought at first, stretched between the concrete fenceposts. As the mist drifted from the dead ground in front of him, the mass took on its true form. There were people pressed against the wire, three or four deep. They wore simple oversized uniforms, some with caps, most had shaved heads. Their faces were gaunt and androgynous. All of them looked close to death.

Calloway swore under his breath.

'What is it, Sarge?'

McNally had known Calloway too long to call him sir after his promotion. He also knew him well enough to sense something was very wrong.

'I'm not entirely sure.'

All Calloway knew was that this wasn't war. It was something altogether more terrible.

SIXTEEN

It took a day for the first medical units to arrive. They were ill prepared to deal with what they found. Starvation and typhus on a mass scale. The medics were equipped for battlefield medicine, not this. A neutral zone around the camp was declared to stop the spread of disease. The Royal Engineers did their best to establish basic sanitation and the medical corps oversaw the building of temporary medical facilities.

Calloway and colleagues who had arrived from 316 Field Security Section processed the guards. The kommandant and his cohort of SS officers seemed resigned to the point of nonchalance. Most were drunk. They cooperated in line with the expectations of their rank. When questioned they exhibited a kind of defiance, the bravura of schoolboys about to be caned. The other ranks had mostly fled. Those that remained milled about without purpose until one of the medical corps officers set them to work piling the corpses.

Several days later 316 Section was recalled to division with orders to proceed as planned to the Baltic. Calloway suggested to his CO that he remain at the camp with a small intelligence detachment. There were offices here full of documents, filed with the meticulousness of Nazi bureaucracy. The kommandantur had made no effort to destroy them. Calloway wondered whether they were proud of their work. And the kommandant's staff had yet to be interrogated, save for questioning necessary to help with the handover to the British forces. The CO gave Calloway orders to remain.

The interrogations had proved fruitless, the SS officers' defiance turning to silence when questioning moved beyond routine subjects. Calloway handed them to the military police. With McNally, Cox and three others, he spent the days that followed working through the files. They held reports on the running of the camp. They were written with utter detachment, like the accounts of a well-run business. Between the carefully typed lines, the carbon copies and rubber stamps, the unwritten human cost of this terrible place became clearer to Calloway as he read. The intelligence was of no military use. This was not a military establishment in any conventional sense, yet it had very efficiently been producing a level of cold brutality rarely found in battle.

Calloway received instructions from the Army Legal Service to send the processed documents back up the line to divisional headquarters. They would be used as evidence for war crimes trials following the German surrender that now seemed inevitable.

Calloway and his men took turns helping the medics, under the direction of a medical corps major who was trying his best not to let the near futility of his efforts show. The spread of typhus could not be halted and feeding the starving was not simply a matter of giving them food. Their bodies couldn't handle normal nutrition. He heard talk that Bengal Famine Powder might help, if the supply lines could provide such a thing.

The mortality rate from starvation and disease was running at five hundred a day. Civilian doctors and nurses from neighbouring towns had been drafted in to assist the medical corps personnel. Some showed a genuine willingness to help, whether through compassion or guilt. Others looked like the whole affair was an inconvenience. There were also volunteers from among the inmates, mostly from the overflow camp nearby, where newer prisoners had been held. They were generally fitter, healthier and more able to assist. Calloway noticed one volunteer in particular. A woman of around twenty-eight, perhaps thirty. The overflow camp had not ravaged her looks, as the main camp would have done in time. She still had hair as dark and lustrous as her eyes. Though clearly undernourished, she had not succumbed to the emaciation that characterised the inmates of the main camp. She wore a simple dress from the bundles of confiscated clothing they had found piled high in one of huts. In spite of its gruesome provenance, she wore it well, with elegance and poise. When they worked together in the makeshift infirmary, Calloway couldn't help but watch her. In time she noticed and would return his look, but briefly and with no indication as to whether his attention was welcome. Their first interaction was unspoken. He had found her resting after a shift in the typhus ward. He offered her a cigarette, which she accepted without acknowledgement. They smoked together in silence, before she returned to her work on the ward. It became a routine, which continued for a while, with neither speaking. In these silences Calloway found himself hoping that she found them as comforting as he did. Small moments of purity amid the horrors.

One evening he was returning to the room in the hut he had made his billet and office, when he noticed her standing in his path, as if she had been waiting for him. She turned and walked towards the far perimeter of the camp. Though no words were spoken, he knew she intended for him to follow. It was an hour past dusk and the rows of huts were lit up against the dark and empty sky. He followed her past the special camp, the star camp, the camp for Hungarian Jews and the clothing store, until they reached a larger, more substantial building with a tall brick chimney. Calloway recognised it as the camp crematorium. He followed her inside. There was just enough light to see. She stood in the sickly yellow glow of the electric light, which shone through the high windows. Still she said nothing, but he knew she had brought him here for a reason. There was something she wanted him to see. He let his eyes adjust to the half-light and looked around him. It could have been any abandoned factory, a foundry perhaps. There were trolleys and tools, shovels and piles of coal for the furnaces and long-handled tongs with jaws wide enough to grip a man's head. The oven doors hung open, the furnaces piled high with ash. A deep layer of ash and cinders carpeted the floor below them.

It was then Calloway noticed a figure, shrouded in sacking, huddled against the brick half walls of an empty coal bay. He looked to the young woman for affirmation that this was the thing he was supposed to find. She stared back expressionless. Calloway reached forward and removed the sacking. Beneath it was a man, alive and trembling. He wore the striped uniform and yellow star of an inmate. He sat on the floor with his knees raised and his arms clasped around them. His head was low, his chin pressed deep into his chest so that Calloway could not see his face. Calloway spoke to him softly, but the man buried his head deeper. Gently, Calloway leaned forward and raised the man's head by the chin so that he could better see his face. The man's flesh felt warm and pudgy, his face full and rounded. It wasn't the face of an inmate. It was too healthy, too well fed. The eyes were keen and alert, lacking the despair he'd seen around him every day since arriving at the camp. Calloway then realised what he'd been shown. He grabbed the man by the collar and dragged him across the concrete floor into the light cast by the window. He pushed up the loose sleeve of the uniform. The man's wrist was blackened with coal dust. Calloway rubbed it away. There was the tattoo, but it was different to the tattoos that branded the camp inmates. This was an SS blood group tattoo. The man now knew he had been discovered and the mask of fear fell from his face. In its place the same school-bully defiance the other SS men had shown under interrogation. This was enough for Calloway. He fell on the man with his full weight. He knelt hard on his shoulders, pinning him to the ground. He started pounding with his fists. He split the man's nose and broke his teeth. With repeated blows he pulped his face until his lips split so many times they pared away from his jaw. He grabbed him by the hair and slammed his head onto the concrete floor, again and again. With each blow the impact become softer, as the skull smashed into a patchwork of bone fragments and hair. He continued his savage attack until he realised the body beneath him had become limp.

Calloway stood, panting like an animal. Only then he realised the woman was standing beside him. She was calm, almost impassive, despite his savagery. She looked down at the bloodied corpse and spoke.

'He ran the overflow camp. He hurt me. He hurt all the women.'

She reached down and tore a wide strip of fabric from the hem of her dress. Taking Calloway's big hands in hers, she used the soft material to wipe the blood and cinders from his fists.

Her name was Miriam, he later found out, and she was twenty-nine. She was from Breslau, where she had taught music in a school. She fled to France while travel for Jews was still possible, settling in Paris and earning a meagre living as a private tutor to the children of affluent French families. When the Germans invaded in 1940, she was taken in by one of her clients and lived as the family governess. Monsieur Berteaux, the head of the house, was a man of resource and influence, with friends in both the resistance and among the occupying army. He arranged false papers for Miriam. In return she became his mistress, a role she did not want but in time came to accept. Madame Berteaux came to accept it too, after very soon discovering her husband's infidelity with the young Jewess, as she took to calling her. These were not times to be leaving the security of a marriage, especially one to a man who enjoyed the privileges and relative security of having friends on both sides.

The arrangement lasted for almost four years, until Berteaux's duplicity became his undoing. He was arrested and sent to Natzweiler-Struthof, a labour camp in Alsace. With no more need to harbour her husband's mistress, Madame Bertaux turned Miriam in to the Paris Gestapo, claiming she had been duped by her husband into believing the girl's new identity was bona fide. The Gestapo believed her story and Miriam was transported east with other French Jews. She spent a month or more in transit before arriving at the overflow camp.

After the incident in the crematorium, Calloway and Miriam had started to talk, in snatched moments while helping in the infirmary. He had learned her story a little at a time as he grew to earn her trust. Neither mentioned the death of the relief camp kommandant.

One afternoon, as his work on the camp files neared completion, Calloway left McNally in charge and took a jeep into the nearby town. It had been a pleasant enough place in its day he imagined, but now looked drab and uncared for. But it had avoided any significant bomb damage and its town square retained that gemutlich charm that seemed obligatory in the provinces here. The townspeople in contrast were joyless. They eyed the jeep with suspicion, with looks that implied that their indifference to the horrors of the neighbouring camp was about to catch up with them.

As he left the main square, he noticed a villa at the top of the road ahead. Three storeys with a chalet roof and well-tended window boxes. The whitewashed walls were clean and bright, as if five years of war had never happened. It stood in stark contrast to its neighbours. He drove the jeep through the gates and parked on the drive. This too was well maintained and the adjacent lawn with its beds of brightly coloured flowers was edged with precision by a skilled gardener.

He dismounted the jeep and rang the doorbell. A woman answered. She was thirty-five perhaps, handsome and well dressed. She looked Calloway up and down with an air of superiority and an expression that suggested his stained battle dress and mud-caked boots offended her. Only now he realised how shabby he had become after his days at the camp, where the punctiliousness of military life had given way to humanitarian expediency. He pushed past her despite her protestations. The house was well furnished showing little sign of wartime hardship. There was heavy oak furniture and polished silverware and a baby grand by the window of the drawing room. He crossed the room leaving a trail of mud on the expensive Persian carpet and picked up a framed photograph that stood on the piano. The husband, he assumed, wearing the uniform of an SS Obergruppenfuhrer.

The woman continued with her protestations, with a righteous indignation she was too arrogant to accept was no longer deserved. Calloway tossed the photograph to the floor. The woman gasped as the glass broke in the frame. He noticed a full decanter of what looked like brandy. He poured a glass and swallowed it on one gulp. The warm liquor burned his throat. It emboldened him. He searched the house room by room before coming to the couple's bedroom. It was light and airy with a cool breeze from an open widow, rippling newly pressed curtains. He rifled through the drawers and wardrobes, deaf to the woman's objections. He picked out clothes, which were all laundered and pressed, and laid them on the bed.

'I'm requisitioning this property. You have twenty-four hours to leave. Take what you need but leave these.' He gestured to the clothes he had selected.

'But where will I go?'

It was a complaint more than a question.

'I don't care.'

He took Miriam to the villa whenever he could. It was their private sanctuary. They feasted on tinned food from larder and drank from what remained of the Obergruppenfuhrer's cellar. Miriam wore the dresses Calloway had chosen. They weren't entirely to her taste, but she forgave him. The luxury of water to bathe in and clean clothes to wear was the best gift he could have given. In return, she gave him music. She played piano and picked records to play on the gramophone. Like good Nazis the Obergruppenfuhrer and his wife eschewed the Jewish composers, although a Mahler symphony seemed to have survived the ideological purge. And Calloway learned to appreciate Beethoven, Schumann and Strauss.

When they first made love it had happened quite naturally. Neither had made overtures. Both felt it was right, savouring the passion and the tenderness that circumstance had denied them for years. Then to sleep in clean sheets just for a few hours, inured from the continuing misery of the liberated camp, brought them a comfort that was beyond value. Though he never said as much, in his head Calloway was imagining a life for them both, away from the camp and the war.

At first he didn't notice the pain she was in. She hid it well. But the more she relaxed in his presence, the more she let it show. And though they continued to enjoy those moments of tenderness in the sanctuary of the villa, Calloway knew this happiness wasn't lasting.

She died from an internal haemorrhage, the surgeon explained to Calloway. He was German and had been transferred from a civilian hospital in Duisburg. His English was poor and he struggled to find the words at first.

'A result of appalling violation,' he managed to say.

A week later Calloway rejoined 316 Section. He wished he had a photograph of Miriam. Instead he returned to the villa one last time and took gramophone records of the music she had taught him to love.

SEVENTEEN

Rough hands shook him awake.

'Christ Mr Calloway. What happened here? You have a party?'

Calloway's eyes adjusted to the light. It was Bert Webber. He stood amid the chaos of the turned-over room, shaking his head. Calloway sat up, feeling the dull ache of bruising from the fight.

'What the hell are you doing here, Bert?' he grunted.

'Pattie sent me. She was worried, with you not turning up for two days. Not like you, chief. Everything alright?'

Two lost days. He cursed himself inwardly. He thought he was over this. He had kept himself from going under for more than two years now. He had convinced himself he'd beaten it.

'Everything's fine. Flu, that's all,' he lied.

'Rough kind of flu. Did it break your door in and turn your place inside out?'

Calloway ignored him. He waved vaguely towards the gas ring. 'Coffee?'

'Coming up, chief. Looks like you need it.'

Webber looked uncertainly at the coffee pot on the shelf. 'How do you make coffee?'

'Tea then.'

Webber lit the gas and filled the old enamel kettle. He started to pick the records up from the floor.

'Leave them.'

'It's no bother. There's a few still alright.'

Calloway snapped. 'I said leave them.'

Webber shrugged. He turned his back and spooned tea into

the pot. Calloway crossed the room and splashed water on his face, drying himself on the tea towel. Webber passed him a cup of the treacle-brown brew. He noticed the scabbed-over cuts on Calloway's knuckles.

'Sorry, Bert. Out of sorts.'

Webber slurped his tea. 'Yeah. Alright. But you better get yourself down the stadium. Pat's doing her nut.'

'Pat can wait.'

He sent Webber away and did his best to clean up the room. He gathered up the shards of shellac from the floor. All but a few of the records were broken or scratched beyond being playable. He should have been angry. Instead he just felt numb. The anger would come later.

He called the stadium from the hallway phone. Les Birkett answered.

'Les, it's Calloway.'

'Yes, sir. Everything alright sir?'

Calloway ignored the question. 'Is Billy Riley at the track today?'

'I believe so sir.'

'Get him for me, will you. And when you've done that, find Pat Moxon and tell her I'll meet her tomorrow. Call me at home with the time and place.'

Birkett was not the type to question an instruction. 'Will do, sir. Now if you'll just hold on, I'll fetch Mr Riley.'

Calloway heard the clunk of the receiver on the desktop. In the distance he could hear the roaring engines of the riders practicing. He waited ten minutes before Riley came to the phone. He sounded wary.

'It's Calloway. We need to speak. Can you meet me tonight?'

'I've got nothing to say to you.'

'You've no need to worry, Billy. I just need to talk. It's important.'

'Why would I be worried?'

'I think you know why. I just need to talk. Sort a few things out between us. I don't want to have to take this to Pat.'

There was silence for a moment. 'Alright. I'll meet you at

nine, but not near here.' He suggested a meeting place. 'You know where that is?'

'I can find it.'

Calloway hung up. A woman's voice behind him said: 'You look very pale, luvvie. Another late night?'

It was Miss Logan. She was done up like a fashion plate. Only the fashion was two decades late. She examined him through kohl-rimmed eyes and frowned with her Cupid's bow lips.

'You need a holiday, darling,' she said, placing a gloved hand on his arm. 'Or a good woman.'

He allowed himself a laugh. Many a true word. She muttered something about having a lunch date and tap-tapped down the hallway and out of the front door.

Calloway went back to his basement. His half-drunk tea was lukewarm. He reached under the sink for the gin and poured the last of the bottle into the cup, then downed it in one. He let the alcohol work its way through his veins. He lay on the bed and made a mental report. Some facts connected, others didn't. The Fenton-Riley connection was clear now. The Fenton-Simpkins connection was obscure, save for a handful of wartime photos which had meant something to both of them, something that put Simpkins behind the theft of the notebook and a series of lies when questioned. The photos, or at least their subjects, were also important enough for Sammy Mackay and his birdwatchers to fire a warning shot across Calloway's bow. The intruder connected with the photographs too, although had failed to find them. He was professional. More henchman than thief. He carried a service revolver and a commando knife. Even in this so-called crime wave, those were not the tools of a work-a-day burglar. Who the henchman and his driver worked for was unclear. It could have been Simpkins or Mackay, Riley at a push. Now he was dead, floating down the Thames with a hole in his forehead that Calloway had put there. It was the big loose end that he couldn't leave untied.

He parked near the river in a street of bombed-out shells

awaiting demolition. The sun had long set and the sky loomed dull-grey over the estuary. The fumes of the approaching ferry hung heavy in the damp night air, mingling with the soot of the power station. Across the water, the masts of giant freighters in the Royal Docks cast a skeletal semaphore against the fading light. He crossed the street towards the blackened brick cupola that marked the entrance to the foot tunnel. The lift was stopped for the night. He stepped into the spiral of the descending stairs.

The tunnel was empty. The last of the dock workers had headed south for the night. The dim electric lighting buzzed and flickered. Midway through the tunnel he heard footsteps ahead. Heavy steps which echoed off the white ceramic walls. Then the steps seemed to double time. There were two men approaching, one ahead of him, another behind. Dockers or seamen he judged from their clothing. The man ahead stopped. He was a pug-faced bruiser, five foot ten and barrel-chested, with muscled arms and ham-hock fists. He was big enough to block the tunnel all by himself.

'Are you Calloway?'

His Liverpudlian accent was deep and phlegmy.

'Are you going to let me by?' Calloway replied.

'Answer the question, pal. Are you Reg Calloway?'

Calloway looked behind him. The other man was short and wiry, with dark leathery skin and swallow tattoos on his neck and hands. He would be the dangerous one. He'd compensate for his size by fighting dirty.

'If I'm Calloway, what then?'

'Then I've got a message for you.'

'So pass it on and get out of my way.'

'Steady, pal. I don't see reinforcements showing up any time soon.'

'Who says I need them?'

'Fighting talk, eh?'

The big man laughed to himself and spat between his feet. The small man behind said nothing. Calloway braced himself.

'Billy Riley's changed his mind. He doesn't want to see you.

And if you keep on at him the way you've been doing, well...'

He heard movement from behind and felt a sharp blow to the kidneys. He'd been expecting it and had tensed to deflect it. The pug face followed up with a punch to his jaw. It had weight behind it but no technique. His attackers paused, waiting for his reaction. The blows were warnings. If they intended a beating they would be all over him by now. Calloway put his full weight onto his right leg and stamped hard on the small man's shin. A cry of agony echoed down the tunnel. The pug face swung at him. Calloway sidestepped. Pug face lost his balance and stumbled forward. Calloway aimed a rabbit punch at his neck. The big man slumped. He crouched on all fours, gasping. From the corner of his eye Calloway caught the glint of a blade. The small man gripped a knife in his tattooed hand. He danced on light feet looking for an opening. He knew what he was doing. The small man lunged forward with the knife. Calloway stepped back but the blade connected. He the felt pain as blood seeped from a gash in his forearm. Behind him, the big man struggled to his feet. He grabbed Calloway's arms and used his weight to anchor him where he stood. The blade flashed beneath the electric light. Calloway tried to remember his training, but his head spun too much with adrenaline. He struggled in the grip of the pug face, his heel aiming for the big man's shin bone but stamping thin air instead. Calloway saw the sinews in the knife man's neck tighten as he prepared for the kill.

A voice hollered down the tunnel.

'Don't, Charlie! Put the fucking knife down.'

It was Riley.

The small man stood firm, his knife hand poised.

'Call off your dogs, Riley. I'm not here to make trouble for you,' Calloway shouted.

The two men looked to Riley for instruction.

'Charlie, Ron. It's alright. Let him go.'

Charlie slipped the knife into the pocket of his reefer jacket. Pug-faced Ron loosened his grip on Calloway's arms and shoved him in the direction of the tunnel's southern stairway.

The pub was a hole. It stood alone on the street corner, having defied the bombing of the docks that it served. The dim streetlight lit up a grim facade with peeling paintwork beneath a single, smog-black upper floor. Etched glass windows screened the interior from passing eyes. A babble of voices hit them as they walked through the doors. The place was full. It was a drab place, a comfortless dock pub. The clientele wore the same reefer jackets and wool caps as pug-faced Ron and his friend. They knew Riley. They acknowledged his arrival with turned heads and subtle nods. They eyed Calloway with curiosity and suspicion.

Ron turfed two drinkers off a table and gestured to Riley and Calloway to sit. The displaced drinkers raised little objection. The pug face and the knife man Charlie had a reputation here. A fat landlady with a music hall laugh poured them pints from the crowded bar. Charlie brought them over, laid them on the table, then left them to talk. They kept a watch on Calloway from the bar.

'An odd choice for a man of your means, Billy.'

'I prefer my own kind.'

'Been to sea often have you?'

On the surface it was a typical dock pub. Seamen and dockers, loud and drunk. But there were others here too. Better dressed men, out of place but clearly at home. And the talk was different. Part Silvertown, part Soho, ports of call with hints of polari. It was the looks Calloway noticed. An interrogator learns to read the small signs, the sideways glances and the eye contact. He'd seen the same looks on the faces of the men in Fenton's photographs. When patrons left, they left in pairs.

Riley downed half his pint and set the glass down.

'I suppose we had better talk.'

He looked down at the table like he was expecting the worst.

Calloway leaned forward and spoke, as quietly as the noise around them would allow. 'I know Fenton was blackmailing you. I've seen the photographs. Tell me what he wanted.'

Riley took another gulp of beer. 'He threatened to send

copies to Ken Kilminster.'

'Police?'

Riley shook his head. 'He writes for Speedway Gazette. He's always down the track. Sweaty bloke with a bald head. Smells of moth balls. Fenton used to go crawling round him. Glory hunting.'

Calloway recognised Kilminster from the description.

'Would Speedway Gazette run that kind of thing?'

'No, but Ken is a stringer for the Sunday Pictorial. They'd lap it up. Fenton wanted a third of my winnings for keeping quiet. He also told me I was never to win a race when I was paired with him.'

'What did you do?'

'I paid him, didn't I? And I pulled back on races. I was at the top of my game when he first got onto me. The next star rider. But it was him who shot up the tables. Left me as an also-ran.'

'And you never told anyone?'

'Are you having a laugh? Of course I fuckin' didn't. It would have been the end of my career, not to mention two years in jail with the nonces. Do you know what they do to people like me inside?'

His voice had risen to a shout. He looked around to see who might have heard him. He needn't have worried. The hubbub in the bar drowned out their conversation.

'I only told Charlie and Ron so they'd warn you off.'

Calloway glanced at the dried blood on his sleeve. 'They did a pretty good job.'

'Look, I never knew Ron would pull a knife on you. They were only supposed to rough you up a bit. It was a stupid idea.'

Riley gulped down the rest of his pint. He looked scared.

'Are you going to tell the police?'

Calloway shook his head. 'I've seen a lot of bad things in my time Billy. Those pictures aren't one of them.'

He pulled the prints and negatives from his pocket and slid them across the table. 'Take them and burn them.'

Riley looked doubtful, as if he didn't believe his boss's head of security. Calloway passed him a second bundle.

'There's a list of names on the back. Do you recognise any of them?'

Riley read through the list. He raised his eyebrows at a couple of the names. 'One or two.'

'Tell them you've burned the lot. I'm not interested in you or the others. I'm only interested in Ray Simpkins.'

Riley looked puzzled. 'Why Ray?'

'Fenton had something on him. He was taking money from him and getting him to pull races, same as you. Is Ray like the other men on that list?'

Riley laughed. 'You're joking aren't you? Ray Simpkins? He's a proper cunt chaser. Spends his winnings on whores. Real rough ones an' all, from what I've heard.'

'Rough enough to blackmail him over?'

'Nah. He boasts about it. He's a dirty bastard.'

'Then Fenton must have had some other kind of dirt on him. Simpkins's score card shows the same tail off in form as yours. All the signs point to him making regular payments to Fenton. The only way I can connect them is through the tramp that used to doss down under the stands. The tramp had photos from the war.'

'Photos of Simpkins?'

'No, Germans. SS soldiers.'

'Fuckin' hell.'

'Can you think of anything that might make sense of all that?'

Riley shrugged. 'Honestly, Mr Calloway, if I could I'd tell you.'

The young rider paused to take it all in. 'Why do you need to know, Mr Calloway? Fenton's dead isn't he?'

'Pat knows something was up. She thinks the accident was suspicious.'

Riley rolled his eyes. 'Seriously? Speedway's a dangerous game. We all know the risks. We don't get many deaths in the sport, but when they happen, it's not like anyone's surprised.'

'That's what I thought at first. But when I started asking around, well Billy, it felt like I'd kicked the hornets' nest. You ever see Fenton and Simpkins arguing? Or talking about the war?'

Billy thought about it. 'I didn't spend much time with them two, to be honest. Didn't like 'em. Even before, well you know. I like a drink with the fellas but it's usually with Bert and Six Gun, sometimes the skipper, if his missus will let him out.' He sniggered at this. 'They're good blokes. Bert's everyone's mate and O'Donnell, well he's a bit flash, but he's got your back, you know?'

Riley noticed Calloway's glass was empty. 'You want another? It's the least I can do.'

Calloway accepted. Riley signalled two more pints to Ron who was maintaining a keen watch from the bar. They sat in silence for a moment, then Calloway noticed Riley turning something over in his mind.

'There was this one time, thinking about it. Something a bit odd, if you know what I mean.'

'Tell me.'

'We were away to White City. The Rebels. A few of us were having a post-race drink-up. We'd lost as it happens, but they were being, you know, gracious about it. One of 'em knew Simpkins from before the war. Ray's not local, you see. He's west London, from Acton way. This Rebel rider, I forget his name, kept calling Simpkins blackshirt.'

'Blackshirt? Meaning fascist?'

'Yeah. Said he remembered him when he was following Mosely around. Simpkins denied it, but this Rebel rider kept on. Pulling his leg, but a bit serious about it too.'

'What happened?'

'Simpkins told him to fuck off and left.'

'Did anyone mention this again?

'Nah. By the end of the night we were all too pissed to remember. It's not like it was a big deal. There was enough of 'em around before the war.'

'Blackshirts?'

'Yeah. My old man knew a few round here.'

'Was he one?'

Riley choked. 'Christ, no. He was practically a communist.

Told me he fought the fascists in Cable Street.'

'A man of principle.'

'Yeah. He had a lot of principles. Not all of 'em worked in my favour.'

He looked reflective. 'He was shop steward for the union at Surrey Docks. That was until a bomb got him. Direct hit. He was helping unload aggregates for the Mulberry harbours. Mum never got over it. She died of lung cancer a year later. Me and my sister looked after each other after that. We were both underage, but my sister managed to convince the Peabody Mum was still alive. That way we got to stay in the flat.'

As they spoke, Charlie and pug face Ron walked up to their table.

'Everything alright Billy?' the pug face asked.

Riley slipped the photographs into the pocket of his blouson jacket. He smiled at Calloway.

'Yeah, everything's fine.'

EIGHTEEN

The hotel bar was a jazz-era throwback with a drinks list to match. Every cocktail told a story which came at a price. The decor was Tinseltown on the Strand. Chrome, walnut and zigzags. Calloway could hear his father's voice. A cocktail bar? Who d'you think you are lad, Franchot bloody Tone?

'We could have met in my office,' he said.

Pat was already seated with a drink in front of her. He guessed it wasn't her first. 'Or mine.'

She was reminding him she was still the client, even though he'd refused her money.

'Sorry for dragging you here but I had to meet with a couple of chaps from Ealing Studios.'

She enjoyed saying this, he could tell.

'They want to make a film.'

'Another newsreel?'

'No, a proper feature film. They've bought the rights to some book or other, about speedway riders. They want to film it at the stadium, use the Bullets for the race scenes.'

More bloody show business. Calloway heard his father's voice again. This time he agreed with him.

'Can I be in it?'

She laughed. 'A big brute like you?'

She sipped from her drink. It was pale pink and had a cherry in it. The cherry matched her lipstick.

'They're thinking of casting that young Dirk Bogarde.'

'Good is he?'

'Well he's a looker. No offence.'

A waiter came over. Calloway ordered the most expensive cocktail on the list.

'Not too ill to drink then.'

She put the cocktail stick to her lips and bit on the cherry. 'This film would be good for the club. Good publicity. But I don't want this Fenton business hanging over it.'

'No, you don't. It's dirty business.'

She seemed unsettled by the word.

'Dirty how?'

'Fenton was running a blackmail racket. I found a stash of photographs in his workshop, photographs of men importuning. Enough to put them in jail. One of them was Billy Riley.'

He waited for a reaction but she didn't seem surprised. She took it in and let him continue.

'Billy was paying him a third of his winnings and letting him win races. I've found evidence to suggest Ray Simpkins was doing the same, but for different reasons.'

'What reasons?'

'I don't know yet. But Fenton had something on Simpkins, something he'd learned from a dosser that used to sleep under the stands. I went looking for him. I found him dead. He'd drunk himself to death on meths down by the estuary. I found photographs on him from the war.'

'Photos of Simpkins?'

Calloway shook his head. 'Photographs of SS soldiers.'

It was the first thing he'd said that seemed to surprise her.

The waiter brought Calloway's drink and set it down on the table. He was worn and sallow-faced, his white steward's jacket too big for his skinny frame. Pat waved her empty glass at him. He acknowledged the order with a servile nod and withdrew to the bar.

'Simpkins has denied any knowledge, but he's lying. Somehow those photos connect him to something he'd sooner keep quiet about. Something serious. And he's not the only one who wants it kept quiet.'

'Meaning?'

'Someone broke into my flat. A professional. My guess is they were looking for the photographs. I caught them at it before they had a chance to find them.'

She looked shocked this time. 'What happened?'

'Best you don't know. But this is more than a spat between teammates.'

'And the accident?'

'Probably just that. An accident. Granted, one that was convenient for Simpkins. But even if Simpkins did intend to run Fenton off the track, it would be nigh on impossible to prove.'

'Even if Fenton was blackmailing him?'

Calloway nodded.

'So I just forget about it?'

'The accident? Yes. That's the answer you wanted, wasn't it?'

She looked annoyed. 'Yes, Reg, that was the answer I wanted.'

'Then I'm happy to oblige, at least on that front. It's the dirt Fenton had on Simpkins you need to worry about.'

But it was Calloway that needed to worry. The dead burglar could wash up at Deptford steps where all the bodies wash up, right on his doorstep, shot through the forehead at point-blank range. He may have been seen, he may have left fingerprints during the fight. It would be hard to argue self-defence if it came to it. More likely he'd be dealt with through less-formal means.

His mouth was dry. He drank the expensive drink. It was hard liquor with a drop of something to take the edge off it. He felt the alcohol course through his veins. It calmed him.

'So what do we do now?'

'You do nothing. I need to brace Simpkins. I also need to call a friend of mine. Someone else that's lying to me.'

She toyed with her drink, buying time. She had something to ask him, something he was expecting. 'The photographs you found in Des's workshop.'

'What about them?'

'Were they just of men? Blackmail photos of queers?'

'No. Fenton liked to photograph women too. Only much closer up.'

She lit a cigarette. 'What have you done with them?'

'They're safe.'

He felt a frost descend. She had dropped her cocktail bar act. 'I need those photos, Reg.'

'I'm keeping everything until I've sorted this business out.'

He didn't trust her. He didn't trust anyone right now. He was holding the cards and this wasn't the time to play them. Her face tensed. She lit a cigarette and drew on it hard.

'How much do you want?'

Calloway scoffed. 'Don't insult me.'

'If not money, then what else?'

'I want to deal with the Simpkins situation. Like you asked. I'll tie up the loose ends afterwards.'

Liz Francis lived with her mother and three younger siblings in a tenement flat on the Old Kent Road. Bert Webber had given Calloway the address. Like Billy Riley said, Bert was everyone's friend. The tenement was cramped. It smelled of a place where people slept and fried food in the same room. Washing hung from a line across the room. Children's vests and pants, grey and frayed, nylons and women's underwear, cheap and worn out.

Liz was embarrassed to see him. She had answered the door in a dressing gown. It was three in the afternoon and she had slept in her make-up. She kept him at the door, making excuses. He'd insisted they speak in private. She made him tea and they sat at a mean-sized table, penned in by two iron beds and an old stone sink. The sink was full of dishes. Calloway struggled to squeeze his big frame into the space. She put two cups without saucers on the table in front of them. There was a film of grease on the surface of the tea.

She pulled the dressing gown tight across her and made a half-hearted attempt to tidy her hair.

'Late night?' he said.

'Working. Didn't get home until five.'

'Night shift was it?'

'You could call it that. I'm a waitress at a club.'

'A gentleman's club?'

'Believe me, they're not gentleman.'

She held the tea with both hands. Her painted nails were chipped.

'So this is me.'

She waved a hand around the dismal room. 'Des said he'd take me away from all this.'

'Men say a lot of things.'

'Don't I know it.'

She lit a cigarette and tossed the match into a filthy ceramic ashtray. It was a present from Margate.

'He didn't seem in any hurry though.'

'You told me he was raising the money for a flat.'

'So he said. I'm beginning to wonder. Anyway, you can't miss what you've never had I suppose.'

'Did he tell you how he was raising the money?'

'Just said it was a sideline. Something different to the speedway.'

Calloway supped the tea reluctantly and looked around the room. He guessed Liz and her mother shared one bed and the children shared the other. Neither beds were made. There was an un-emptied pot beneath one.

'I need to tell you something Miss Francis. It might shock you.'

She raised a pencilled eyebrow. 'I'm not easily shocked, Mr Calloway.'

'Des Fenton was a blackmailer. Homosexuals mostly. Irene Fenton was in on it, but not all of it. Fenton kept one of his victims from her. His teammate, Ray Simpkins. He wasn't like the others. Fenton had another kind of dirt on him. Something going back to the war. My guess is he kept this from his wife so he could use the money he extorted from Simpkins to pay for the flat he promised you.'

He gave her time to take it in. She folded her arms and looked down at the grubby table. 'Des Fenton was a bastard.'

'But you were lovers.'

'The two aren't exclusive. Des was charming, generous when

he felt like it, exciting to be with. He took me to parties and restaurants and clubs. He showed me off, it was flattering. I 'spose I knew he would never leave Irene. She had her claws into him too deep. He didn't have the balls. But I kidded myself willingly, imagined a life, you know. A nice flat up West, glamorous friends, being photographed on his arm. The speedway star's beautiful wife.'

She corrected herself. 'Second wife.' She glanced around the cheerless room. 'I mean, look at the alternative.'

A baby screamed in the next door flat. It could have been in the room with them. Its mother screamed back. Then a man's voice shouted. A door slammed. The mother started sobbing.

'Did you know Fenton was a blackmailer?'

She shook her head. 'No, but it doesn't surprise me. He'd often let on that he knew people's secrets. It was bit of thing with him, you know? "See him over there", he'd say. "I could tell you a thing or two". He got a kick out of it. Probably said things about me too.'

Calloway didn't doubt it. He'd seen the photographs. Fenton seemed the type that might show them around.

'Did Des ever mention anything about Ray Simpkins to you?'

She shrugged. 'He didn't like Ray. Didn't have a good word for him. They were chalk and cheese.'

'And he never talked about the war? Never suggested he knew a thing or two about Ray?'

She shook her head. 'Sorry.'

The baby next door was wailing, competing with the clang and clatter of the trolley busses in the street below. Children's feet in heavy boots rumbled along the tenement balconies where two women argued. The smell of damp and bad cooking was all pervading. The place made the pit village back-to-backs of Calloway's childhood seem as genteel as the Fenton's suburban idyll.

'Fenton processed his blackmail photos in a darkroom at his workshop. I went there. I found these.'

Calloway took the photos of Liz from his raincoat pocket and laid them on the table. She snatched them up and rifled through them. Her hands trembled. She tossed the pictures back on the tabletop. They fanned out as they landed, the pin-ups on top, the explicit poses underneath, the worst of their depravity visible to them both.

'Alright, so you've seen them. I'm not proud of them. He said he'd take publicity shots, to help with my career. I was still at the Centurion school and couldn't afford to pay for a professional shoot. Des took a good photograph. Of course I accepted. He had borrowed a flat from a friend. A nice flat. We went there one evening. It was all set up. He kept telling me to have a drink. Said it would relax me. Bring out the best in the photos. After a while I said I'd drunk too much but he kept insisting. He started asking me to do things. Things I didn't want to do. As you can see, he got his way.'

She picked up one of the explicit shots and held it up so Calloway could see. 'That's not me, Mr Calloway. That's Des Fenton.'

She threw the photo down. 'He was a bastard.'

Anger gripped at her face through the smeared make-up. But if he was expecting tears, he was wrong. She was full of fight. Calloway gathered up the prints, pulled the negatives from his pocket and added them to the pile.

'Destroy them all. You're worth more than that and you know it. Fenton's gone. Forget him and move on.'

'Move on?' She laughed. 'Do you know how hard it is to get out of a place like this? Do you think I want to be here? The charm school was my big chance. I've got the looks, I've got the figure.'

He couldn't help but look her up and down.

She saw him. 'Yeah. In case you hadn't noticed.'

She shook her head and sighed. 'I thought I'd got the talent too. Who was I kidding? Like it or not, if a girl like me wants out, chances are she has to find a man. Des seemed like that man, at least at first.'

She stubbed the cigarette out hard. 'Boy, can I pick 'em.'

He had no advice to give. No suggestion of a way out, although God knows he wished he had one. He managed a sympathetic look, which made him seem weak.

'I'm sorry,' she said. 'You're not seeing me at my best.'

'I wouldn't say that. At least I'm seeing you. Not the charm school hopeful, or Fenton's mistress or the girl in those photos.'

He offered her another cigarette.

'I prefer this version.'

She looked down, embarrassed. 'Thanks. But I reckon you're the only one.'

He sipped his tea. He felt obliged to. It wasn't so bad.

'Where's the family?'

'Mum went up to the World Turned Upside Down. They'll have called time by now, so Christ knows where she's ended up.'

She rolled her eyes. 'Or who with. The boys will be out smashing up bomb sites and scrounging cigarettes.'

They sat in awkward silence until she spoke again, 'Des fucking Fenton.'

Calloway stood up to leave. She stopped him. 'Wait.'

She hesitated, then stepped over to the little mantlepiece above the cast-iron fireplace. There were papers in a plain wooden rack, the sort prisoners of war used to make. She rifled through them, coupons, leaflets, a letter or two.

'Des asked me to look after this. Said it was insurance.'

She passed Calloway a sealed envelope. 'He told me not to open it.'

'Do you know what it is?'

'I don't know and I don't want to know. You take it. Perhaps it will help with whatever it is you're trying to find out.'

He thanked her and slipped the envelope into the inside pocket of his suit jacket.

She turned to face him as she opened the door. 'Thanks for listening Mr Calloway. Not many do. Men don't want to hear that sort of thing.'

He thought about the times he had spent in the villa in the small German town.

'You're welcome,' he said. 'I liked having someone to listen to.'

The greasy tea had turned to acid in his stomach. He couldn't remember the last time he had eaten. He felt nauseous and light-headed. He took a trolley bus to Deptford and ate pie and mash at Manze's, soaked in thick green-white liquor.

He had settled himself in a booth at the rear of the shop with his back to the wall. He pulled the sealed envelope from the pocket of his jacket, wiped his knife clean on the edge of the plate and slid it under the flap. There were three photographs inside, the missing shots from the vagrant's album. He examined them under the harsh overhead lighting.

The same uniformed men, only three of them this time. The first photo was taken in a field hospital. One soldier lay on a cot, his face half covered with a dressing but managing to grin. His two comrades squatted either side him, giving the thumbs up to the camera. The injured soldier and the comrade to his right had featured in the all of the photographs Calloway had removed from the album. The face of the third soldier was overexposed and indistinct. The second photo was taken subsequently, the injured man recovered with his healed wound visible. The three were rounding up civilians at gunpoint. Again, the third face was obscured. The civilians held their hands in the air. Two old men, one too frail to walk unaided, being assisted by the other. Two women, alike enough to be mother and daughter. And a child of no more than ten, in shorts with loose socks bunched around the ankles of his stick-thin legs. In the final photo, the three SS men stood with their arms extended, aiming pistols at the heads of the two old men and the child, who kneeled in front of them on the mossy floor of a pine forest. A few feet beyond the kneeling men, three shovels stood in the ground next to the grave they had been used to dig. In the background, a group of Waffen SS soldiers looked on as spectators.

Calloway held this last photo up to the light and squinted to better see the detail. He saw that the three executioners were smiling as they squeezed the triggers. He could also see that one of them, holding his pistol to the frail old man's head, had a lightning-fork scar on his face. And this time he could clearly see the face of the soldier that held his gun to the head of the child. It was Ray Simpkins.

NINETEEN

He parked behind the Fenton's Alvis. Overnight rain had left a patina of soot-black circles on the polished maroon coachwork. He saw the front room curtains twitch. Irene Fenton opened the door moments later and crossed the paved driveway towards him. Her expression was lacking the suburban propriety of his previous visit.

'What do you want?'

No chance of tea in china cups this time. This was the un-gentrified Irene, the Kentish twang of her south east London accent cutting through the quiet of the morning like a rusty scythe.

'I need to talk to you again Mrs Fenton.'

She stood toe-to-toe with the big man, arms crossed, chin jutting forward like an unvoiced threat.

'I've told you all I know. Now please leave. You've no business here.'

'I wish for your sake I hadn't.'

'For my sake?'

'For your sake, Mrs Fenton. You see blackmail carries a sentence of up to fourteen years. I imagine Holloway prison would come as quite a shock after the leafy suburbs.' Although, judging by the look on her face right now, he suspected she might just get by inside. 'I'm sure your neighbours would agree.'

By now other curtains twitched in the street. Irene noticed them.

'Shall I carry on, Mrs Fenton?'

She dropped the fighting stance. They went inside, into the kitchen this time. It was pristine and looked like an advertisement. He settled himself on a chrome-legged chair.

‘Sit down, Mrs Fenton.’

‘I’d rather stand.’

‘As you wish. I won’t waste time. You ran a blackmail racket with your husband. Ran it, or at least were complicit in it. You blackmailed homosexuals with incriminating photographs. You said yourself, your late husband took a good photograph. Seems he put his talents to use.’

She rolled her eyes. ‘This is rubbish.’

‘Is it? Your husband had a darkroom at the back of his workshop. He kept the photographs and negatives there. I’ve seen them. In fact I have them.’

She frowned, disbelieving.

‘The workshop’s all locked up.’

‘I’m the resourceful type.’

‘I don’t know anything about this.’

‘Then you won’t mind if I go to the police. I have to, you see. It’s track business. I’d be negligent if I didn’t.’

‘I said I know nothing about this.’

‘You knew enough to squeeze Billy Riley for money in the Four Bells last Saturday.’

Her eyes flashed. The muscles in her jaw tensed. ‘You can’t prove that.’

‘Actually, Mrs Fenton, I can. Billy Riley made a statement for my report. He signed it.’

She shook her head. ‘He’d never do that. It would be the end of his career.’

‘Very possibly. But he’s prepared for the consequences. The lad’s had enough you see. He wants the whole thing to be over.’

She clenched her fists, digging her manicured nails into her palms. ‘He’ll deserve everything he gets. He’s a dirty little queer. They’re all dirty queers. Des hated them, hated their type. He hated Billy the most. He couldn’t stand having a dilly boy for a teammate.’

‘And rather than report him, he decided to blackmail him. Him and half a dozen others. That’s hardly the moral high ground.’

She spat her retort. ‘They deserved it. Hit them in the wallet where it really hurts, that's what my Des said. Prison's too good for their sort. A nancy boys' holiday camp, he called it.'

Calloway felt his anger rise. Veins pulsed in his head. He had seen homosexuals at the camp in Germany. The faded pink triangles sewn to their lousy prison jackets. The hollowed-out faces filled with desperation and confusion. He'd been ambivalent up to then. He'd used the words everyone used, sniggered when others sniggered, called them nancy boys along with the rest. He wasn't scared of them, but he'd no great concern for their lot in life. The camp changed that. He saw the humanity in all its victims. The Jews, the communists, the gypsies and the queers. It was the common denominator that trumped the prejudice.

'Spare me the moral crusade. Now sit down.'

She ignored him, out-staring him with hating eyes. He leapt to his feet and grabbed her by the arm, dragged her across the showroom-bright lino and pushed her down hard on the chair opposite his. She bared her teeth like a cornered animal.

'If you lay a hand on me again I swear I'll...'

'Shut up and listen. You're going to jail, Mrs Fenton. A cold filthy women's prison. I have evidence and a witness, enough to put you away for years. Long, cold, ugly years, far away from the niceties your filthy racket has been paying for. You have one chance to avoid that happening. One chance, if you do exactly what I ask.'

She threw her head back and laughed, play acting derision. 'If you think I'm going to sleep with you, you've got another think coming.'

'Don't drag me down to your level. Now listen. Do you have writing paper and an envelope?'

She nodded.

'Fetch them.'

When she returned from the living room he made her sit again and dictated a letter. She started to write then stopped. 'What's this about?'

'Just write.'

'What if I refuse?'

‘Then you’d better hope there’s a hard-as-nails brass inside Holloway that will be your friend. Of course she might want something in return.’

She hissed, ‘You’re a bastard.’

‘They say the same about your Des, as it happens. Now write.’

She did as she was told, gripping the fountain pen hard and scratching the letters into the velum paper as if to spite him.

‘Sign it.’

She looked up. Her eyes narrowed and her tensed lips showed white through her lipstick. ‘I’m not signing this. It makes no sense.’

He leaned back in the kitchen chair. He didn’t speak until he had her full attention. Then he spoke calmly and quietly, ‘There’s an ex-army sergeant-major on my staff, reliable sort he is. He’s at the stadium right now with my report in an envelope addressed to CID and ready to take to New Scotland Yard. He’s instructed to deliver the report at three o’clock sharp today.’

Calloway looked at his watch.

‘He’ll be preparing to leave now I reckon. I’ve got about five minutes to call him from the phone in your hall and stand him down. Sign that letter and I’ll make the call. Refuse and you take your chances in a court of law.’

He crossed his arms and waited. She picked up the pen and scrawled a signature.

‘I hope you burn in hell.’

He crossed the room to the hallway and closed the door behind him. He dialled the stadium number and asked to be put through to security. Les Birkett answered.

Calloway spoke quietly, ‘Les, go to the personnel files and find me an address.’

From the kitchen he heard crying. A deliberate, self-pitying wail for his benefit. Birkett retuned a few minutes later and Calloway memorised the address. Calloway didn’t mention the report to Birkett. There was no report. There was no signed statement from Billy Riley either. He returned to the kitchen.

He found her with her head in her hands, sobbing, but not so much that her make-up ran, not even so much as a smudge.

'You can stop that. I'm not interested.'

He grabbed her hand roughly and thrust the pen in it. 'Now write this address.' She complied. He sealed the letter, slipped it into his inside pocket and left her to her crying. On the drive back to the stadium he stopped a post office, bought a thrupenny stamp and posted the letter in the local mail slot. The next collection was four pm. With luck the letter would arrive tomorrow.

He drove to the stadium and parked in Canal Road. Les Birkett saluted as he passed through the main gates. Curiosity showed on the old NCO's face. Calloway blanked him. He was in no mood for conversation. As he approached his office, he saw movement behind the frosted glass panel of the door. Slowly and silently he tested the door. It was unlocked, when it shouldn't have been. He gave the door a shove and stepped inside.

Pat Moxon sat at his desk rifling through the drawers.

'Find anything?'

Her expression implied she had every right to search his office. 'Your filing's impeccable. A proper shiny arse.'

He shook his head. 'I did my reporting in the field. No desks to jockey there.'

'A man of action, clearly,' she leaned back in his chair, 'but very few words.'

'I speak when I'm spoken to, ma'am.'

'Don't start that again.'

He pulled a cigarette from his case and lit up. 'As you wish. Find what you were looking for?'

'You know I didn't.'

She was right. The last set of Fenton's photographs were in the safe along with the contents of Joe Smoke's album and the 'insurance' shots that Liz Francis had given him. Moxon would get them when he was ready. Right now there were still questions that needed answering about the whole affair. Until he had answers, he was trusting no one.

'Tried the bottom drawer yet?'

'I was rudely interrupted.'

'There's a bottle of Johnnie Walker in there and a couple of glasses. Pour us one each.'

'Is the sun over the yard arm?'

'It's over the west stand and I need a drink. I imagine you do too.'

She poured two glasses and waved one in front of him. 'Promise not to walk out on me this time? You still haven't redeemed yourself for leaving me at the party. Dennis drove me home four sheets to the wind. Nearly killed us both. Not the best end to an evening, what with that and his wandering hands.'

'I was following Riley and his man friend. It's how I tumbled the blackmail angle.'

'A proper Dick Barton.'

She passed him the glass. 'Chin-chin.'

The whiskey tingled through his veins. He relaxed into the chair. She dipped a finger into her glass and put it to her lips, holding his stare as she did so.

'So what's your story, Calloway? Was stadium security a lifelong ambition?'

'No, just the result of a lifelong need to eat. I was discharged in forty-eight. Honourably, in name if not in deed.'

'A bad boy were you, Reg?'

'I'll let the angels decide. My conscience is still unsure. Let's just say there was a war criminal who went to trail a little less hale and hearty than when I picked him up. I was escorting him to Nuremberg. On the way there he happened to say the wrong thing to the wrong man.'

Compared to the guard on the crematorium floor, the Nuremberg incident was nothing. The difference was Calloway let the man live and suffered the consequences.

'It seemed like a good time to leave the army. At least that's what my CO suggested, and in no uncertain terms. So I went home, if you can call it that. The army had been my home since grammar school. The war had been my life since thirty-nine. I had about as much in common with that tiny pit village than one of your Bullets has with a district nurse on a bicycle. I was offered a desk job by the coal board on account of my education and my short-lived commission.'

He shook his head dismissively. 'I packed a bag the next day and got as far away from that place as I could. I was down to the last few pounds of my demob money when I ran into an old pal from my unit. He was running security at a greyhound stadium on the south coast. He'd heard on the grapevine that Bermondsey was looking for the same. I knew nothing about the place and even less about speedway or dogs. But I knew how to keep people in line. The rest you know.'

He drank some more of the whiskey. It felt good. She poured him another glass. Sleep tugged at his consciousness. The fatigue of the past few days was taking its toll. He craved the onset of a gentle stupor. He wanted to relax, enjoy the company of a woman. But it didn't come naturally anymore. And he was still unclear how Pat Moxon fitted into the story. He scrunched up his eyes and blinked himself back to a safe state of alertness.

'So why no Mrs Calloway?'

It was a fair question, given his age, but one he was loathe to answer. He'd never spoken of Miriam and those precious weeks in the villa to anyone. It was a memory locked in the music he played to remember, the music that filled a very private place inside him. He'd allowed no one in, never wanted a shoulder to cry on nor a sympathetic ear. But as he sat in the gloomy office with the lady boss, a part of him that needed to pour it all out, lay the burden down if only for the duration of two cheap whiskies in glasses filched from the members bar.

'There was a future Mrs Calloway, once.'

'What happened?'

He stopped himself. The shell hardened around him once more. He felt safer inside it.

'A lot of things, not many of them good. What about you?'

'Me?' she huffed. 'Yet to meet a man good enough, Reg.'

He nodded in the direction of the circuit. 'You've got the

pick of the league.'

She knocked back the whiskey. 'Never love a speedway rider. I learned that lesson the hard way.'

'So why buy a whole team of them?'

She thought for a moment, then laughed. 'To prove a point.'

'To who?'

'Where shall I start? The ones that said girls don't ride. The ones that put me down when I did, the ones who denied me the credit and the ones that banned us from the sport.'

'That's quite a list.'

'That's only the half of it. Then there's the goosing, the groping, the promises in return for favours and the name calling when the favours are denied. Shall I go on?'

'I think you've made your point.'

'I've every right to, believe me.'

'Let's drink to that then.'

He pushed his glass across the desk towards hers and she refilled both. As she poured, he said: 'What made you suspect Fenton's accident might have been deliberate?'

He'd surprised her. She tried hard not to show it. 'There were rumours.'

'Word has it you started them.'

'Why would I do that?'

She was trying to sound casual but her tone was defensive. She looked away. She took a cigarette from her case and lit it with his desk lighter, inhaling deeply. When she turned to face him she was composed again. She pushed the glass towards him.

'I know them well enough, Reg. It's not what they were saying, it's what they were holding back. There was something wrong. You said yourself Des and Ray Simpkins were known to have fallen out.'

'It's a big jump from that to running a man off the track.'

'Des was a blackmailer. He had something on Ray. A convenient accident would be a good way out.'

'But you didn't know that when you asked me to look into this.'

'Then let's call it intuition.'

He left it there, but he wasn't buying it. She diverted the conversation, rummaging through the open drawers of his desk and pulling out a well-thumbed paperback.

'Zane Grey? Like a good western, Reggie?'

'Not especially. Bert Webber lent it to me. He's a big fan so he tells me. Read every one.'

'Bless him. He makes three thousand a year and still eats at the Civic Restaurant. Refuses to leave his prefab.'

She smiled with rare and genuine warmth. 'Fame hasn't changed that one.'

'I'd call that a virtue.'

His limbs felt heavy with the drink. He stood and stretched, walked to her side of the desk and took the book from her hand, dropping it back into the drawer and nudging it closed with his knee. She stood to face him, close enough for him to smell her scent and feel her warmth. He felt her breath on his face, the smell of the whiskey and cigarettes tingling his nerves. Her hand slid into his. She looked him in the eye and held his gaze, half tempting, half taunting.

'I need those photographs, Reggie. I beg you.'

Her closeness felt too good. He shook her hand free.

'You're not the begging kind.'

'I've tried money. What more can I offer you?'

'Nothing I'm prepared to take.'

She withdrew, poured the last of the whiskey into her glass and knocked it back.

'You'll get the photographs when I've dealt with Simpkins. I expect to see him tomorrow night. I'll sort things out, one way or another.'

'Then I guess I'm in your hands. But leave him in one piece, eh? I need him to race on Friday.'

He thought of the three photographs Liz Francis had given him.

'I can't promise that,' he said.

TWENTY

The heavy motorcycle rumbled over the cobbles down the dark mechanic's path. It was past midnight and deserted. The low throb of the engine bounced off the viaduct walls. The rider cut the engine, then it was quiet save for the distant screech of freight train wheels on metal rails further down the track.

Calloway heard the bike arrive. He had settled himself on a chair at the back of Fenton's workshop with a clear view of the big double doors in the railway arch. He sat in the darkness with a hip flask for company. He'd been there an hour, listening out and watching the chink of light between the doors for signs of movement. A man's shadow appeared in the chink. The figure hesitated, eased the door ajar and stepped inside.

Calloway had rigged an inspection lamp to face the doors. He flicked the wall switch. Ray Simpkins flinched and squinted through the glare. He could make out Calloway's shape but couldn't identify him.

'Where's Irene?'

'It's just me, Raymond.'

Simpkins recognised the voice. His eyes adjusted.

'Oh. You doing her dirty work, Calloway?'

'It's my dirty work, Ray.'

'Why'd she write to me then?'

'I wrote to you. She just held the pen. Sit down.'

Calloway gestured to a chair in front of him and tossed the hip flask at Simpkins. The rider caught it by reflex.

'Have a drink, Ray. We're going to have a chat you and I. See if we can't sort this little problem out.'

Simpkins squared up, stretching his jockey-like frame to full height. 'You know what your little problem is? You can fuck off, that's what.'

Calloway looked the lean rider up and down. 'Nine stone eight I reckon. Perhaps nine two without the motorcycle gear.'

Simpkins looked perplexed.

'They say Mr Pierrepoint can tell a man's weight just by looking at him. He needs to know the weight, you see, to know what length of rope to use, how long a drop from the trapdoor. He's very precise apparently. He's not vindictive. He likes a quick, clean, instant death. Painless they say, although they can't be sure, can they? He's busy mind. You might have to wait a while, in the condemned cell. A long wait, all by yourself, with a rope at the end of it.'

Calloway crossed the workshop and leaned forward. He spoke softly into the other man's ear. 'Very busy of late Mr Pierrepoint, what with this gun crime epidemic and the trips back and forth to Germany to hang the war criminals.'

Simpkins tensed. The sinews tautened in his neck.

Calloway continued. 'I met him once, at Hamelin prison in December 1945. I watched him execute eleven SS guards from a camp I had helped to liberate. I was no stranger to death, not after six years of war, but I'd never witnessed that many deaths in a single day. I suppose it would have been shocking had Mr Pierrepoint not been so professional. He hooded every one of them personally before pulling the lever. Most died instantly, but not all. The ones who took longer were harder to watch.'

Simpkins's bravura ebbed. He slouched into the chair and took a swig from the hip flask.

'Of course they wouldn't hang you in Germany. You're one of ours. Wandsworth, I imagine. Not too far from here, eh? I wonder if any Bullets fans would come to watch.'

The rider summoned some nerve. 'What the fuck are you on about?'

'Don't play the innocent, Simpkins. We're way past that stage. This is about you doing as I say and maybe, just maybe mind, saving your own wretched hide. I have the evidence see. The photographs. The ones your old mate Joe Smoke carried with him like some macabre trophy of your wartime adventures. There's one in particular, one of the three photographs Fenton kept for himself. The one he used to skim your winnings, the one that bought him points each time he finished ahead of his teammate Ray on the track.'

Simpkins tried to swallow but couldn't. He uncapped the flask and drained it. Calloway noticed his hands had started to tremble.

'What do you want?'

Calloway stood over him, hands in his pockets. 'Did you bring the money?'

'What makes you think I've got that kind of money?'

'What's this, Ray's a laugh? Spare me, son. I've never liked comedy. I know you're good for five hundred, even after Fenton skimmed his percentage.'

Simpkins coughed up a gobbet and spat at Calloway's feet. He managed a laugh. 'Christ, you're no better than him.'

'Perhaps not. But you're in no position to preach morals.'

Simpkins glared, defiant.

'Go whistle for your fuckin' money.'

The rider had not expected the blow. By the time he felt the smack of Calloway's fist he was already on the floor. When the big man's foot slammed into his guts, Simpkins's survival instinct took over. The rider gagged down the bile that rose in his throat. He summoned energy and scrambled to his feet. Calloway was ahead of him. He grabbed the rider in a neck lock and yanked him up, then pushed him face down on the workbench. He kept him there, twisting his arm to breaking point behind his back while he patted him down. He found the money zipped into a pocket of Simpkins's leathers. He kicked the rider's legs away and dragged his featherweight frame across the oil-soaked floor, dumping him back in the chair.

'Let's start again. Three men. One I don't recognise, one with a scar on his cheek and one that's quite clearly you, standing in a forest in Waffen SS uniforms executing geriatrics, cripples and children. I need this to make sense.'

Simpkins spluttered. The slam to the bench had split his lips and loosened his teeth. His nose leaked blood and mucus. He mumbled, but the words wouldn't form. Calloway barked.

'Speak up son! Let's hear it!'

The bust-up rider spat half-formed obscenities. Calloway's patience wore thin. There was a basin bolted to the workshop wall and in it a can catching drips from a leaking tap. Calloway picked up the can and doused Simpkins in the rusty water. The water shocked him into lucidity.

His screamed words echoed around the archway. 'They were rats. Fucking vermin!'

Something snapped inside Calloway. He bolted to the workbench, took up a wrench and swung it at the seated rider. A clanging blow caught the edge of the metal chair between Simpkins's legs. The rider snapped to attention. His face showed real fear this time.

'Tell me everything or I swear to God I'll kill you myself.'

Calloway tossed the wrench onto the concrete and grabbed Simpkins by the collar of his motorcycle jacket.

'You're a traitor and a war criminal with enough evidence to see you hang. Personally I'd like nothing better, believe me. I spent a lot of time putting scum like you on the end of a rope and you know what, Raymond? I enjoyed every minute of it.'

He loosened his grip on the stunned rider. 'Now the money keeps me from going to the police, but they're not the ones you need to worry about. There's others have an interest in you, son. And now they have an interest in me too. For both our sakes, I need to know why.'

He pulled his chair closer and sat, legs spread and hands on his knees. He leaned in and lowered his voice to a whisper. 'You tell me and I might just let you disappear. Lose yourself. You can clear your bank account and get the next steamer out of Tilbury. But I want answers, understand?'

Simpkins nodded keenly, his slitted eyes fixed on Calloway's.

'So tell me how a cabin boy from Acton ended up in a forest in Poland with a swastika on his cap and a Luger in his ratty little paws.'

TWENTY-ONE

They had drifted for three nights. Seven men with oil-blackened faces clinging to the Carley Float. The rest of the crew had gone down with the freighter. A U-Boat, loose from its pack and hunting alone, had snapped the five-thousand-ton vessel like a brittle twig, setting its cargo of munitions ablaze and lighting the clear night sky as if it were day. Men burned or drowned or choked on oil. Some swam for it but were dragged down by the vortex of the sinking vessel, the still-spinning screws dicing them to pieces.

For a day and a half the first mate, a solid Bristolian with a thick greying beard that aged him beyond his years, had kept his fellow survivors active physically and mentally with songs and filthy stories. But by midday on their second day adrift, even his reserves were all but used up. As he and the others drifted into a desperate half-sleep, Simpkins had watched the horizon, alert with fear, his young eyes sweeping back and forth for signs of funnel smoke.

It was near dusk when he spotted the fine wisp of black against the purple sky. A cruiser perhaps, or a frigate, too far away to tell if it were one of ours. He screamed and waved his numb, skinny arms, deluded by exhaustion into thinking he could be heard. He slapped and punched at the sailors who lay slumped over the float, urging them to join in. They rallied at the prospect of rescue, caring little about the allegiance of their rescuers. To the joy of his comrades the first mate produced a Very pistol from the pocket of his sodden bridge coat and with fumbling frozen fingers slid a distress flare into the chamber.

His crew as the bright crimson light streaked across the now dark sky. A lone firework, celebrating what remained of their hope. Then, following Simpkins's stare, they too looked to the horizon at the faint outline of the distant vessel.

They clung to the float in silence as they watched for a sign their flare had been seen. Some prayed, others muttered desperate encouragement as though the ship were a dog on which they'd bet their shirts.

Then one man cried out: 'He's changing course! Praise the lord if he ain't changing fuckin' course!'

A cheer went up. They flailed their arms in frantic semaphore. They whistled and hollered, their different dialects blending into a harmony of hope. It was true. The vessel had altered course, turning to port and heading towards them, waves breaking on its prow in the moonlight as it sliced through the black peaks of the sea. As its shadowy bulk loomed closer, an Aldiss lamp flashed a dit-dit-da message in morse. The first mate hushed his men so that he could better concentrate on the signaller's instruction.

A stoker broke the silence. 'For fuck's sake guv, what's he saying?'

The first mate's shoulders dropped.

'I don't know, stoker. He's saying it in German.'

A stab of reality intruded. Every man had heard the rumours. Machine gunning survivors, not picking them up. They knew the U-Boats did it. Why shouldn't the rest of the Kriegsmarine fleet? Their collective minds raced. Why change course just to shoot us up? We're going to die anyway, from cold or dehydration. Why not just steam ahead and leave us? They'll do the decent thing, surely. They've got to. It's the Geneva Convention isn't it? But whose gonna report 'em if they break it? They make their own rules out here.

Desperation won out. They continued to holler and wave their frozen arms.

'It's a cruiser. Leipzig Class by the look of it.'

'They're lowering the nets!'

They jabbered thorough trembling lips and chattering teeth.

'Thank fuckin' Christ.'

'If there's a cosy little bunk in a POW camp, I ain't complaining.'

'Get to it, lads. Paddle with your hands.'

The tiny Carley float bumped alongside midships, the bullying waves buffeting the little raft against the iron wall of the cruiser's hull. They had little enough strength to climb the nets. The German sailors hauled them up and over the rails, barking in guttural pidgin English. Six men fell limply onto the deck, their clothing sodden with sea water, oil and excrement. A seventh man floated on the waves below them, claimed by the cold minutes before rescue.

Simpkins lay flat, his arms spread like a crucifix, his narrow chest heaving as it sucked in the damp sea air. He stared at the stars thanking a god he barely believed in for this uncertain salvation. He felt a rough hand shake him. It yanked him upright and wrapped a blanket around his shoulders. Simpkins grabbed it with trembling hands and pulled it tight around his teenage frame. The same hand, gentler this time, held the back of his head and pushed a flask to his lips.

'Brandy,' the German sailor said in English. 'Drink it.'

The cruiser docked in Stavanger in Norway a day later. The British seamen had been held below deck and fed black bread and jam, which the Germans called marmalade, washed down with lukewarm ersatz coffee. From Stavanger boarded a troopship to Aarhus in Denmark. Simpkins blagged a pack of cards from a burly military policemen in Aarhus. Their Kriegsmarine guards called the MP kettenhund meaning chained dog, after the silly little breast plate that hung around the neck of his oversized wax greatcoat on a quarter-inch chain. On the train out of Aarhus they practiced their German, shouting kettenhund and barking like dogs. Their navy guards laughed and offered them cigarettes, while being graciously beaten at gin rummy for the next five hundred kilometres.

They were interned in Marlag X-B, a navy prison camp north east of Bremen, with other merchant marine captives. Dutch, Danes, Norwegians and Americans billeted in huts according to their nationality. They were treated in accordance with the Geneva Convention, fed and watered, worked but not abused and spent their free time playing football and keeping fit. They wrote letters home and enjoyed the Red Cross parcels when they arrived. No one thought of escape. Here they could sit out the war away from the U-Boats and the merciless ocean, while their pay accumulated back home.

The winter that followed was harsh. Temperatures dropped below freezing and the stoves in their flimsy barracks proved ineffective. The cold penetrated their clothing and the thin blankets on their bunks. It brought inertia and apathy towards the pursuits that had distracted them in the preceding season. Morale sunk and tensions rose. Simpkins's natural surliness and his growing irritability earned him a reputation as a troublemaker. Few allowances were made for the fact he was not yet nineteen. His mouth got him into fights and he fought back hard. A scrappy bantam weight who had few limits, he fought with feet and nails and teeth and could bring down the heftiest of sailors through sheer nastiness. His violence earned him nights in the cooler, his Kriegsmarine guards tiring of the disruption. They wanted a quiet war.

Camp conditions worsened. Germany was in retreat on the eastern front and resources were short. Too short to waste on foreign prisoners when supply lines were disrupted and troops at the front were the priority. Dissent spread among the prisoners, every man's emotions on a hair trigger which Simpkins knew how to squeeze. Whatever the dispute, be it over food or cigarettes or fuel, he would taunt fellow inmates with the old national rivalries. The Yanks came in late, the Danes gave up early, the Norwegians were quislings. He called them communists and Jews, revelling in his old blackshirt rhetoric, which since the outbreak of war he'd felt obliged to suppress. Before long he was isolated, his own crew members turning their backs on him. The stoker and a burly winchman once tried to knock sense into him, with a lengthy if restrained beating behind the latrines after curfew. It had little effect, silencing the lad for a week or so before his old ways came back with a vengeance. He took a razor to the stoker in the washhouse and might have cut his throat had not the guards heard the commotion and cornered him with fixed bayonets.

Simpkins sat his time out in the cooler muttering obscenities and harbouring grudges. It was a long sentence. Three weeks on half rations. No one had been banged up that long. Simpkins wore the fact as a badge of honour. His retribution would be harsh. He planned it each night on the hard floor of the dark and draughty cell.

He was released a week early and escorted to the guardhouse by the same two guards that had intervened in the fight. A lecture he imagined, from a pompous reservist officer who would read him the riot act. This didn't happen. Instead he was shown to a small and warm room with a roaring stove in the corner and a table and two chairs. The guards told him to sit, then one disappeared. The other held a big Mauser rifle at readiness and scowled. Simpkins scowled back. The second guard returned with a tray and set it on the table. Hot coffee, a sandwich and a pastry that could have been strudel had Simpkins known the name for it.

'Eat,' said the guard nodding at the tray, before the pair withdrew, locking the door behind them.

Simpkins ate like an animal. It was the best food he'd had for months. He pushed chunks of it into his mouth and slurped the coffee so fast it dripped down his face onto the table, leaving streaks in the dirt from a fortnight of not washing. When he'd finished he sucked his fingers one by one for every last sticky morsel. He belched loudly and deliberately, then dragged his chair over to the stove and warmed himself.

An hour passed and as Simpkins nodded into half sleep, the key turned in the door and a man entered. A smartly dressed civilian who spoke perfect English and introduced himself as Amersham. He was around thirty, foppish almost, with lustrous parted hair and a neat pencil moustache. He described himself as an Englishman and a friend. He had a battered leather briefcase bearing the initials JA from which he produced a hand bill.

'Can you read?' he asked.

Simpkins nodded. Amersham passed him the hand bill and said: 'Have a read of this.'

The young seaman was curious enough to comply. As he read, the man lit a cigarette from an expensive silver case. It was embossed with a swastika. He laid the case on the table so that Simpkins could clearly see the emblem.

'Well,' said Amersham, 'what do you make of that?'

Simpkins pushed the bill back across the table and helped himself to a cigarette from the case. Amersham lit it for him.

'I reckon there's truth in that.'

Amersham smiled. It was a long time since anyone had smiled at the young sailor, save for the forced pouts of the whores he spent his wages on.

'I reckon there is too,' he said.

Amersham leaned back, crossed his legs and draped an arm over the back of the chair. 'How would you like to get out of here, help me fight the real enemy? The Jew bankers and the Bolsheviks. The people who will bring our great nation to its knees.'

Simpkins looked confused. 'Which nation?'

Amersham grabbed his forearm and gave it a squeeze. 'England of course. The greatest nation. The nation that will become even greater when it joins the Thousand Year Reich. We need men like you, Simpkins. Strong patriotic men. Men that can lead the new order when the Germanic people unite to defeat those that would drag us down.'

Simpkins warmed to Amersham. He was a toff but he talked sense. He talked like Mr Mosely.

'There are plenty like us you know. In every POW camp. Men that can see the truth behind our so-called allies' lies. They've dragged us into an unnecessary war. Our comrades are dying because of a Jewboy communist lie. You know what I'm talking about, Raymond. We're the same, you and I. British to the core.'

The young seamen's eyes narrowed. He peered at the toff, cautious but curious.

'Was you a blackshirt?'

'A fascist, certainly. A proud one too. Fought alongside Franco in Spain in thirty-six.'

'I was a blackshirt. Youngest in the London area they reckoned. I lied about me age to get in. Done the same with the navy.'

Amersham nodded his approval.

'I knew you were a good 'un. That's why I'm here. Now listen.'

He learned forward and lowered his voice. He made Simpkins an offer. If he accepted, he would be released with immediate effect and would accompany Amersham to Berlin. There would be drinking and whoring, then he would be set to work. Honourable work, for which he would be rewarded and respected.

Amersham left the young seaman to think it over. He would be back in an hour for his answer. When he left the room Simpkins read the hand bill again.

As a result of repeated applications from British subjects from all parts of the world wishing to take part in the common European struggle against Bolshevism, authorisation has recently been given for the creation of a British volunteer unit.

The British Free Corps publishes herewith the following short statement on the aims and principles of the unit.

1. The British Free Corps is a thoroughly British volunteer unit conceived and created by British subjects from all parts of the empire who have taken up arms and pledged their lives in the common European struggle against Soviet Russia.

2. The British Free Corps condemns the war with Germany and the sacrifice of British blood in the interests of Jewry and international finance, and regards this conflict as a fundamental betrayal of the British people and British Imperial interests.

3. The British Free Corps desires the establishment of peace in Europe, the development of close friendly relations between England and Germany and the encouragement of mutual understanding and collaboration between the two great Germanic peoples.

4. The British Free Corps will neither make war against Britain or the British crown, nor support any action or policy detrimental to the interests of the British people.

Published by the British Free Corps

That evening Simpkins was on a train to Berlin.

TWENTY-TWO

Berlin was not the holiday Simpkins had been promised. Amersham had disappeared and his Waffen SS handler seemed disinterested in the young Englishman in his charge. He was issued with a uniform bearing the insignia of the British Free Corps, three heraldic lions on the collar tabs and a Union Jack shield on the forearm. It brought curious looks in bars and not a little hostility when he found himself in the air raid shelters alongside terrified Berliners, the RAF doing its worst in the sky above them.

He was left largely to his own devices during the first month, spending much of his time visiting the zoo and drinking in the Tiergarten, in the shadow of the enormous flak tower. He spoke enough German to order beer and food, learned in the navy from his visits to Hamburg before the war. His whorehouse German was passable too. He found a brothel off Potsdamer Strasse which satisfied his taste for big girls with few boundaries. He was paid the wage of a SS-Shutze and with little else to spend it on, became a regular visitor on speaking terms with all the girls and a few of their customers too.

He had no real desire for active service. It was enough for him to be out of the camp and enjoying freedom, with the benefit of a uniform which carried authority if not respect in all quarters.

Amersham returned to Berlin and Simpkins was summoned to a meeting in the Reich Main Security Office, a monstrous grey building on Prinz-Albrecht-Strasse. The young able seaman, whose experience of formality did not extend beyond refraining from spitting in the paymaster's office, was awed by the place. Sharp young men with earnest faces strode with purpose along polished corridors, darting in and out of endless rows of doors. There were women too, some of them lookers Simpkins thought, but a bit on the frumpy side in their serious grey uniforms.

He reported to room B16 and gave his name to a pimply clerk in an oversized Sharfuhrer's uniform, seated behind an Olympia typewriter the size of an armoured car. The clerk eyed the British shield on Simpkins's forearm suspiciously. He checked his day-book, running his finger down a row of names.

'Yes, you may enter,' he said.

Simpkins reached for the door handle. The clerk cleared his throat. 'Knock first.'

Simpkins sneered. He may have swapped sides in the fight against the reds and the Jews, but this little twerp was still a Jerry. He acknowledge the request by rolling his eyes, before knocking twice. A voice behind the door he recognised called 'Herein!'

The office was generous and well furnished. It smelled of sweet tobacco. A uniformed SS Obersturmbannfuhrer sat behind a mahogany desk, a small pipe dangling from the corner of his mouth. He was lean and fit, with well-cut hair and a tolerant smile. Behind him, a portrait of the Fuhrer stared down at Simpkins as if questioning his legitimacy. The newly inducted Shutze thought about giving the Nazi salute. He remembered Will Hay in that film The Goose Steps Out and decided against it.

'Raymond, old man!'

Amersham looked him up and down. 'My, my, look at you. A credit to the Reich.'

Amersham was draped over a chair in front of the Obersturmbannfuhrer. He held a cigarette high and away from his immaculate suit. He patted the seat of the adjacent chair.

'Sit yerself down then.'

The young Shutze looked apprehensive.

'Come on, we're all friends here.'

To Simpkins the toff looked liked a nancy, but he'd always

found it hard to read the posh ones. A Rottenfuhrer at the Lichterfelde barracks said Amersham was shacked up with a Berlin whore. A proper dirty bastard he was.

The SS officer pushed an ornate cigarette box towards Simpkins and gestured for him to smoke. Amersham produced the silver swastika lighter.

'This is Otto Bauer. He's the real boss. I'm just the tart who lures the boys in.'

Simpkins managed a deferential nod to the German behind the desk.

'Now Otto has a job for you. You see he's been running this holiday camp just outside the city for chaps like you.'

'Like me?'

'Chaps that recognise the Bolshevik threat and the influence of the Jewboys that pull the strings. At this camp they're well fed, they play sports, get a few trips into town to chat up the frauleins, that sort of thing. Otto's been showing these British POWs that their German foes are actually quite decent folk after all. Now the next stage is to persuade them to join the corps. That's where you come in. You will be our recruiting sergeant.'

'Sergeant?'

'Well, Sturmann at least.'

Amersham turned to Bauer. 'Comes with a pay rise I expect.'

The officer nodded.

'Do I have to live at this camp?' asked Simpkins. He had enjoyed his weeks at the barracks and not least its proximity to his adopted whorehouse. The camp sounded like a backwards step. Amersham shook his head.

'You'll be a regular visitor. You can boast about the freedoms you enjoy as a member of the corps. You'll also need to stir them up a bit. Appeal to their patriotism. Convince them that fighting the red is an Englishman's duty. You were a blackshirt, Raymond. This should be right up your street.'

This whole business was still strange to the former able seaman. But the role of recruiter sounded preferable to a posting to the eastern front.

'Alright,' he said, helping himself to another of the Obersturmbannfuhrer's cigarettes.

'Good man!'

Amersham clapped him on the back.

'Get yerself up to the camp at Genshagen as soon as you like. We'll find you some transport.'

He was issued with a brand new RT125 fresh from the Auto Union factory in Chemnitz. The peoples' motorcycle, the clerk at the SS motor transport depot had called it. Simpkins had never ridden a motorbike, but took immediately to the little two-stroke machine. A six-foot Teuton would have dwarfed it. Simkins's small jockey frame sat well in the saddle.

The recruiting drive did not go well. The POWs were content enough with their more comfortable conditions and suspicious of the Free Corps proposition. Even those who had been fascists before the war could not reconcile their patriotism with the prospect of a traitorous defection to the enemy. But Simpkins's efforts were not entirely without success. A young infantry private called Wood was a willing listener. A fellow Londoner, not much older than Simpkins, he too had followed Mosely and his blackshirts. His profound antisemitism led him quite effortlessly towards Nazi ideology. Before the outbreak of war he had more than once confessed to being pro-Hitler and only stopped his overt support for national socialism through fear of internment. Although a reluctant conscript into the British army, he had seen action in Italy and Sicily and had developed a taste for battle. In fact he enjoyed killing, not for the sensation of taking a life – he was not a psychopath – but for the feeling of power that his low status in both civilian and military life otherwise denied him. Simpkins recognised a kindred spirit and fixed on Wood as his best chance of success. He was coming under pressure from Bauer for results. The pair would go drinking and whoring in Berlin, Woods perched uncomfortably on the back rack of Simpkins's motorcycle, his legs trailing. While they drank together they fired each other's passion for the ideology of their adopted masters. They became committed Nazis and soon Wood was wearing the same uniform as Simpkins, with three lions on his collar and the union flag on his forearm. Together they continued their recruiting drive, but with little success. Acknowledging that the soft sell of the holiday camp was yielding few results, and under increasing pressure from the Fuhrer himself, Bauer resorted to other means – maltreatment and blackmail, the methods of the press-gang. These new techniques worked. Two dozen prisoners from Genshagen were conscripted into the Free Corps and transferred to its new headquarters in Hildesheim, under the command of Hauptsturmfuhrer Richter.

Frank Joseph Belper was a Waffen SS Hauptscharführer assigned to the Free Corps as an instructor. The son of Birmingham factory foreman, he had grown up in the industrial town of Smethwick, benefiting from a passable education and, in time, a good understanding of politics. A former blackshirt and fervent Nazi sympathiser, he had risen through the ranks of the British Union of Fascists to become one of Mosely's trusted men on the ground in the Midlands. At the outbreak of war, faced with the prospect of internment by the British, he fled to Europe and made his way to Germany, his goal being to enlist in the German armed forces and fight for the Reich. The Nazi authorities were suspicious of him at first, but through persistence he had convinced the Reich Main Office of his allegiance to the fatherland. He was accepted into the Totenkopf division of the SS in the spring of 1940 and posted to the Eastern Front.

Belper was unhinged. With his close-cropped hair and his manic stare, his face resembled a prison mugshot. His taste for violence and his unbridled hatred might under other circumstances have put him in a psychiatric institution. In the SS he found an organisation that could accommodate and indeed value the worst extremes of his behaviour. He proved a smart and determined Nazi, whose seething antisemitism was put to use at Sobibor concentration camp in Poland, where he served as a guard. He enjoyed his work, boasting to Wood and Simpkins later that he had personally killed twenty-seven Polish Jews. His extremism was unnerving, even to now-committed

Nazis like Wood and Simpkins. But they were drawn to Belper. He was a charismatic and they became willing followers. In time they became something akin to friends.

At Hildesheim, the Free Corps recruits settled into a routine of training and recreation. Belper drove them hard and could be brutal. But the evenings made up for the rigours of training, when the young Englishmen enjoyed the local hospitality and the attentions of curious local women. An English boyfriend soon became not just a novelty but a prize, a situation that the Free Corps members exploited.

Belper, Wood and Simpkins eschewed these outings, preferring to drink by themselves and use the local brothel. When they drank together, Belper would spew out beer hall rhetoric and as the evenings wore on he became darker, turning from politics to the mechanics of killing. These beer-fuelled talks became a regular fixture and in time Wood and Simpkins became desensitised to the near psychosis of Belper's keenness for destruction. They became converts to the collective madness of Nazism.

Amersham's grand plan to recruit a legion of Englishmen could not be fulfilled. His early attempts to drum up support from disillusioned POWs saw him driven from their camps by an angry rabble. When Free Corps recruitment was passed to the Waffen SS, they too failed to rouse a following. Even with their more coercive tactics, the Free Corps numbers never reached more than fifty. It was decided they should be absorbed into regular fighting units and posted east. The Hildesheim contingent were told they would be sent to the pioneer school in Dresden for training as assault engineers, then integrated into Division Nordland, the Scandinavian volunteer unit of the Waffen SS. Belper was reluctant to waste his talents on regular soldiering, even if this was under the auspices of the Waffen SS. He had a different plan for himself and his two English friends. He had become quite well connected with personnel in SS Obergruppenfuhrer Ernst Kaltenbrunner's office. He was able to persuade them to post the three of them to one of the remaining Einsatzgruppen, an

SS death squad charged with the mass killing of Jews, gypsies, partisans and intellectuals.

By the time of the German surrender in May 1945, Ray Simpkins had personally executed one hundred twenty-seven men, women and children.

TWENTY-THREE

Simpkins was alert now. He sat on the edge of the chair in the spotlight of the inspection lamp, telling his story with rising enthusiasm. At first he had seemed reluctant to shed the burden of the past half-decade of secrecy. Now he was revelling in it, the hero of his own story. Calloway had seen this before. There comes a point in any interrogation where the subject feels an uncontrollable need to confess. Not through duress, but to release themselves from the strictures of their own deceit. Calloway let him talk.

'We fell in with the Einsazgruppe in Lodz. We took part in the actions, rounding up Jews from the ghetto and packing them off to the camps. Some we had to deal with there and then, if there wasn't any transport.'

He made it sound like any regular job. He could have been a postal worker or a railway porter or a haulage clerk from the matter-of-factness of his tone.

'Then we moved further east. By the time the Russians were close to overrunning us we were at the camp at Chelmno, supervising the Sonderkommando. They were the prisoners we'd got exhuming the bodies from the mass graves and cremating the remains so the Russians wouldn't discover them. We had to deal with the Sonderkommando once they were done. Frank was given that job to supervise, on account of his experience at Sobibor. After that we dispersed.'

'Dispersed?'

'You know, every man for himself. Get the fuck away and cover our tracks. We ditched the SS uniforms for regular army ones. There were enough German dead around to take 'em off of. We were lucky. The Free Corps didn't have blood group tattoos like the other SS. The only thing we had to worry about was the language, but by then me and Wood had picked up enough German to get by and anyway the eastern front was full of foreigners, volunteers like. Danes, Norwegians, Hungarians, even Russians. We stuck together, me, Belper and Wood. Frank spoke German like a native and he was a canny bugger too. He got us back as far as the Elbe, which the British had reached. We could see the 11th Armoured Division from the other side of the river. We nicked some old civvies and wandered towards the British lines. Told 'em we were POWs who'd been banged up in a Stalag. Me and Woody anyway.'

'What about the third man, Belper?'

'He took off by himself. He wanted to avoid the allies. He was regular SS and had the tattoo. He said he'd burn it off with a hot iron then pull the same POW stunt as us.'

'Did you ever see him again?'

'Belper? Nah. Don't think I'd want to, to be honest. He was alright, after a fashion, but he was a nutter.'

'Shame that didn't occur to you before he persuaded you to join a death squad.'

Simpkins shot Calloway a look of defiance. 'I don't regret it. I'd do it again. I might have to. You read the papers lately? There's reds in the government and blackies coming over by the boat load. Then there's the Jews. Killing our troops in Palestine while over here they're buying up all the houses. The fight ain't over, Calloway. There's gonna be blood. Mark my words.'

Calloway felt his anger rise. The veins drummed on either side of his head.

He took a long deep breath. 'When did come you back to England?'

'Late forty-five. Me and Woody got back to London but he was right twitchy. He wanted to drop out of sight.'

'But you came back as British POWs. You'd got away scot-free.'

Simpkins shook his head. 'The trouble was this. When we was in the Free Corps they told us to change our names. I was Ron Samson, Woody was Pat Ladbroke.'

Sampson, Ladbroke and Belper. The three names on the notebook hidden in Fenton's toolbox. Names Fenton had been given by the tramp, Wood.

'It was a precaution, so we could come back to England after the allied surrender and not get flak for joining the other side. I could go back to me own name because no one knew I'd joined the corps. When Amersham took me out of the Marlag the other prisoners were told I'd been taken to a bad boys camp 'cause I attacked that stoker. It was different for Woody and the Genshagen lot. Their old mates knew they'd gone to the holiday camp. Wouldn't have been long before the military police clocked that.'

'And Belper didn't take an alias.'

'That's right.'

Simpkins seemed curious how Calloway knew this.

'He was regular Waffen SS. Half German too. He joined up under his own name and kept it. That's another reason he scarpered.'

'So where did you and Wood lay low?'

'We fell in with some deserters. They were in the same boat as us, but for different reasons. I tagged along for a while. We camped out mostly. I couldn't hack it for long. I like me home comforts, you know. Cash in me pocket, beer in me hand and a bit of female company. I went back to London and worked up the docks for a bit.'

'Then Pat Moxon gave you a try out.'

He nodded. 'I knew me way around bikes by that stage. I hung onto that little RT as long as I could. I got a real taste for riding. I traded up bikes and acted as despatch rider for the Einsatzgruppe.'

The word sounded odd from the mouth of the little London bike jockey.

'They gave me a big bastard Zundapp. I could barely get me leg over it at first. What I'd give for one of them now, eh? But there's no way you could ride a Kraut bike here. Not since the war.'

He sniggered. 'No one would talk to me.'

Calloway reckoned Simpkins had worse reasons not to be talked to.

'Then me and Wood got our hands on a BMW sidecar combination. It had an MG42 mounted up front. That's a very efficient weapon, I can tell you.'

He sneered at Calloway, taunting him. 'Saved the squad a lot of time and effort, that MG42 did.'

Calloway snapped. He made to grab the rider by the collar, raising his fist as he did so. A noise in the alley stopped him. Heavy footsteps approaching the workshop. Then the rattling of the lock. Calloway lowered his hand and gestured to Simpkins to keep quiet. Half comprehending, the small rider compiled. The workshop door opened a chink and a uniformed figure leaned in. Calloway swore. That bloody policeman again, 453, the young constable who had disturbed him when he was searching the place last time. Doing his rounds, trying doors and finding this one open. Simpkins turned. He saw the police uniform. He spat at Calloway.

'You dirty fucker. You set me up.'

His small frame sprung from the chair and leapt towards the door. Calloway tried to grab him but couldn't get a grip on the tough leather of his jacket. The rider threw himself at the copper, wrenching off his helmet and landing a head butt on him. The crunch of bone echoed around the railway arch and the young policeman rolled back like a kellyman, clutching his face. Blood from his nose seeped through his fingers. Calloway tipped the lamp over with force so the bulb smashed on the concrete floor. Hidden by the darkness he made for the door, leapt over the now-prostrate constable and followed the sound of Simpkins's boots down the cobbled path. Ahead of him a pale moon glowed behind fast moving clouds. In the moonlight the faint outline of the baroque church mocked its humble surroundings, the railway arches and the half-bombed streets with the all-pervading buddleja tearing their brickwork. Moments later he heard a police whistle behind him. He banked on 453 being too unsteady from the blow to keep pace. He prayed the young copper didn't have the wherewithal to jump on the big Matchless Silver Hawk Simpkins had left behind. Ahead he could just make out the silhouette of the rider turning into Church Street. Simpkins ran with the familiar monkey gait of the speedway rider, hobbled by the stiff racing leathers and rigid-soled boots. It allowed Calloway to gain ground. The pair crossed Church Street towards the creek, only a few yards between them now.

The streets narrowed. They were dark and featureless, a hotchpotch of cottages, small warehouses and jerry-built lean-tos blending into the gloom. Calloway drew deep breaths of the damp creekside air. It smelled of soot and decay. He was out of shape and his chest heaved painfully. Simpkins disappeared down a snicket between two low brick buildings. It was just wide enough to take the rider's monkey-boy frame. Calloway squeezed himself into the gap and did his best to run. The walls seemed to narrow as he neared the chink of grey light at the end of the passage. He stumbled over the discarded flotsam underfoot and snagged his clothes on the coarse brickwork. Reaching the banks of the creek, he drew breath and scanned the narrow creekside path in both directions. To the north, only the lone chimney of the power station. Simpkins was heading south towards the mill. Calloway summoned the reserves of his strength and gave chase. The path had petered out and the two men slid along the damp grass border of the open riverbank. He heard Simpkins curse at the tangle of barbed wire and planks that blocked the path ahead. Calloway was within feet of him when the monkey-boy leaped feet first onto the riverbank and started to wade through the sucking mud.

In the distance the roar of an engine and the shrill ting-a-ling of a police car's bell. Young 453 had summoned help. Too far away to worry about. Calloway jumped into the creek and followed Simpkins, heaving himself out of the mud with each step and plunging back in again. The young rider was lighter and leaner and had gained ground. Calloway's big frame seemed to sink deeper into the mud with each step. His chest hurt deeply, phlegm rose in his gullet and his windpipe constricted. His leg muscles cramped, pinning him upright in the mud like a scarecrow swaying in the wind. Inside his head a white light was threatening to engulf him. He fought against it and lost. When he came to, minutes later face down in the mud, Simpkins was gone.

TWENTY-FOUR

Two young boys pissed against the corrugated-iron fence. Calloway cuffed their heads midstream.

'Do that again and you're banned.'

The boys skulked off, zipping up their shorts with piss-wet fingers.

Bouncer and babysitter, that's all he was. Pattie Moxon's strong-arm boy and wet nurse to her paying punters. His cigarette hissed as he flicked it into the pool of urine. He'd not slept and his nerves were ragged. The thought of Simpkins evading justice had torn at him through the night. As he lay restless on the old iron cot, he saw the little rat rider's defiant face smirking at him.

'The fight's not over, mark my words.'

As he teetered on the edges of sleep that never came, the rat face merged into the mess of the SS guard he'd beaten on the crematorium floor, his pulped lips grinning through the gore.

'They were rats. Fucking vermin!'

He'd been called to the stadium that morning. The police had found Simpkins's Silver Hawk and were asking questions. Calloway denied knowledge.

'You'll probably find him drunk in a whorehouse,' he had offered as an explanation. The police didn't buy it. They were CID, a cut above the laughing policeman and his sidekick who had visited after the burglary. The detectives knew what they were doing. And 453 had identified Simpkins from his publicity photos as the man in the race leathers who had head butted him at the workshop. The detectives quizzed Calloway on who the second man might have been, the one who followed Simpkins into the night. Calloway was confident he'd not been recognised by the dazed constable. It was unlikely he'd been seen behind the harsh beam of the inspection lamp and when the lamp smashed, the darkness had hidden him as he bolted.

Part of him wanted to hand the whole thing over to the two detectives. The photographs, the notebook, the five hundred pounds and an account of Simpkins's confession, however much coercion was employed in its extraction. But as Basil Rathbone might say in one of those ridiculous mysteries, there was the difficult matter of the body in the Thames with a .445 calibre hole in its forehead. As loose ends go, that was a pretty big one still to be tied off. He had no plan other than to lay low, get on with his day job and wait for the fish in the Thames to do the rest. It wasn't a comforting plan.

He walked past the already-crowded stands towards the turnstiles. The fans were doubly eager tonight, shoving forward to buy their tickets.

'Full house tonight, sir. Bursting at the seams we'll be.'

Les Birkett stood sentinel at the turnpikes, his chest puffed out more than usual.

'Special night, Les. We've got royalty in.'

Birkett allowed himself a chuckle.

'Hardly royalty, sir. But he is very comical.'

The big ex-RSM was uncharacteristically chipper. He was even humming to himself. The Chinese Laundry Blues.

Calloway's fixed smile was hurting his face. The night was a big one for Pat Moxon and her twenty-five thousand paying punters, but on top of the Simpkins business, he could have done without it. He maintained only the facade of enthusiasm the job demanded. Inside, anxiety was eating at his stoicism. He wanted the whole affair brought to a conclusion. With Simpkins gone this looked unlikely. He cursed Pat Moxon under his breath for bringing him into the whole sordid business.

There was a different kind of excitement inside the stadium. The presence of a screen star at the track heightened the euphoria, the crowd desperate for a glimpse of the unlikely matinee idol with the jug ears and the horse teeth.

Calloway took his position in the commentary box. The commentator wore a dinner suit and had an extra layer of oil on his thinning hair. His cologne smelled like chemicals. He moistened his lips and held the big microphone close to his face.

'It's a big night tonight folks! The highlight of the season. Our VIP guest will be arriving soon and I want you to give him a rousing Bullets welcome.'

A cheer went up automatically, as if someone just pulled a lever.

'But first, time to introduce the real stars of the show...'

The commentator's sidekick, a pimply lad with bottle-end spectacles placed the gramophone needle into the groove of a worn shellac disc. Marching Along Together echoed around the stands.

The crowd roared like a reflex, conditioned by the ritual of countless Wednesday night fixtures. There was comfort in the certainty of it all. Calloway didn't begrudge them. The poor sods had survived six years of war and emerged into a world of shortage and dereliction. But they left it all behind at the turnstiles. He envied them. He craned his neck and eased his aching shoulders.

The spotlight followed the riders across the centre green. Billy Riley led them out with renewed swagger, waving to the crowd and enjoying it. Female fans blew kisses. He spotted Calloway in the commentary box and gave him a knowing nod. The Bullets lined up along the home straight, their opponents joining them to polite applause. Bert Webber was missing from the line-up. The announcer switched to amateur dramatics.

'Oh no folks. One of the riders seems to be missing. Where can he be?' he asked the crowd, sounding as convincing as a children's radio presenter who had failed the audition. 'Perhaps his motorcycle has broken down.'

The announcer passed the mic to the pimply boy and dashed for the door.

The spotlight swept over the green towards the pits. Bert Webber sat astride his motorcycle, behind him a squat figure in an astrakhan coat and mirror bright shoes pushed the bike onto the cinder track, helped by two of the pit crew. He mugged effort, tipping up his homburg and wiping his brow. His grinning horse teeth shone in the spotlight's beam. The crowd were hysterical. Driven by the collective consciousness of the sports crowd, they broke into song as one.

'If there's one thing that I like, it's riding around on a motor-bike.'

The man in the astrakhan coat let go the bike and waved with both hands, acknowledging his song.

'I once won first prize two and six, I know all the dirt track dirty tricks.'

Calloway snorted. The song was imbecilic.

The announcer was on the podium now, at the edge of the centre green. He looked out of breath. Smoothing down his oily hair with one hand, he raised another microphone to introduce the VIP.

'Ladies and gentlemen, boys and girls, give a rousing Bullets welcome to the boy from Wigan, Mr George Formby!'

Formby took the mic, a cigarette dangling from the side of his mouth. He threw them a catchphrase.

'Turned out nice again!'

Euphoria filled the stadium. The experience was religious. A picture-house deity with a hymn book of innuendo, right there in the flesh. He received the adulation with a bow as the supporters sang.

'In a fifty mile race I am the best, I ride five miles and skid the rest.'

Pat Moxon led the star down the line of riders like the bride's mother at a wedding. Calloway wondered whether her fixed smile hurt as much as his did. Formby glad-handed the Bullets, cracking jokes and pulling faces. Calloway had seen enough. He left the commentary box and crossed to the lighting gantry. It was the best vantage point for surveilling the crowd. From here he could spot trouble, not that there was much at a typical fixture. But tonight wasn't typical. The crowd were excitable and there was a VIP on the bill. Formby's wife and manager, Beryl, had reviewed security arrangements with Calloway personally. He like her. She was professional and not what he'd imagined from a show business type.

He kept a pair of old infantry binoculars in an oilcloth bag which hung from the gantry's tubular steel railing. Slinging the webbing strap around his neck, he scanned along the rows of spectators looking for the usual signs. Excitable kids, angry drunks or a knot of youths in the latest garb. Or the cosh boys from last Wednesday spoiling for a rematch. He saw nothing untoward. He looked up towards the members bar with its elongated window overlooking the track, like an aquarium for un-exotic specimens. Three men caught his attention. They weren't the usual types who sipped their pale ale and marked their race cards with pencil stubs. Two wore belted trench coats and sat facing the window. They were big and stony-faced with inexpressive eyes. Planted firmly in their seats, they sat straight-backed not touching their drinks. He recognised the type. Not police. More like former NCOs doing strong-arm work. It spelled bad news. A third man had his back to the window. He was smaller in build and wearing a dark suit too good for his surroundings. Though his face was not visible there was something about his build and his movements that was familiar to Calloway.

The first heat got underway. The four riders hit the dirt track, pushed off by their pit crews and accelerated into their warm-up laps. The smell of methanol filled the stadium. Calloway leant over the rail of the lighting gantry straining to get a better view of the members bar through the binoculars. Framed by his field of view the three men rose from their seats and wove their way through the regular punters towards the exit. It was then he caught a glimpse of the third man's face. A few pounds heavier with less hair and a neat new moustache, but still recognisable. It was Sammy Mackay.

Calloway descended from the gantry and headed towards the members bar exit. What the hell was Mackay doing here? If he wanted to pick up Simpkins he would send the police. The rat rider's wartime treason carried a death sentence but was a criminal matter, not something for Mackay and his security service goons. And there was nothing to suggest Mackay could make a connection between the name Ron Sampson that Calloway had mentioned when they spoke and the Bullets rider Simpkins. Odds on Mackay was looking for Calloway himself, and an explanation for the missing house breaker. It wasn't something Calloway looked forward to explaining, even to Sammy.

The three men were weaving through the crowd towards the rear of the west stand. Calloway picked up their trail, hanging back so he was obscured by the throng. He pushed past the tightly packed punters mumbling apologies. They were oblivious. The next heat was underway and all eyes were on the track. Behind him the announcer's voice raised an octave, broadcasting excitement to the crowd. Riley first off the tape and holding his lead. Webber close behind and gaining ground on the visiting riders. Five points for the taking. Mackay and the two NCO types ducked under the stand. They were heading for Calloway's office. He followed them, keeping two or three spectators between himself and the three men. But the crowd thinned out the closer they got to the office, depriving him of cover. He needed a vantage point from which to observe them unseen. He slipped between the supporters club and the workshop, into a small passage littered with cigarette butts and hotdog wrappers. From here he could climb the gantry that held up the north stand. The steel lattice work of the upright supports served as a ladder. He'd had to coax kids down from it in the past with the threat of a clipped ear.

Twenty feet up he hooked an elbow around one of the uprights and wedged his brogues into the angles of the cross bracing. It gave him a clear view of the door to his office, above the heads of Mackay and his strong-arm boys. One of the boys tried the door, which Calloway kept locked. He withdrew a small canvas tool roll from the pocket of his trench coat and selected a pair of wood-handled lock picks. He worked the lock as the other two men shielded him from the eyes of any passing spectators. It popped open with an audible click. Mackay and the second goon ducked inside while the third man kept watch. He lit a cigarette and tried to look like he should be there.

There would be nothing for them to find in Calloway's desk, unless they were fans of Zane Grey or in need of a drink so much they would drain the peg of whiskey he and Pat Moxon had left in the bottle two nights ago. And unless they'd brought explosives, which he doubted, SS Shutze Wood's sick photo collection were secure inside the heavy Banhams safe.

A collective gasp went up from the crowd, muffled by the underside of the stand above him. The announcer adopted his well-practiced shocked tone. Riley had over-banked and hit the cinders and Webber had lost his lead to the visiting rider. The marshal was allowing the race, four-two to the away club.

Mackay and the second NCO type emerged from the office as casually as they could manage. Their faces said they'd found nothing. The three headed back towards the track. They would be looking for Calloway now. A part of him wanted to stay where he was, hidden in the dark underside of the north stand. But he was already aching from the strain of clinging to the upright steel. He couldn't maintain that for the remaining ninety minutes of the fixture. He had to keep moving, away from Mackay and his friends. It should be easy enough to disappear with twenty-five thousand in tonight. At least he hoped.

When the three men were beyond his line of sight, he eased himself back down the lattice work of steel, shaking his numbing arm back into life. From the track, he heard the relieved tone of the announcer.

'It's alright folks. Billy Riley is on his feet. He's on his feet and walking back to the pits. Give us a wave Billy!'

Riley must have obliged. The crowd cheered in return. The rider would be heading for the surgery with Doc McArdle, the club medic. It seemed as good a place as any for Calloway to make for. He would be out of sight behind closed doors for a while.

The lights were on behind the frosted glass pane of the

surgery door. He tried the handle, which was locked. He pulled the pass key from the leather loop on his belt, unlocked the door and entered.

Pat Moxon sat on a bench in a corner of the empty surgery, her skirt hitched up and the soft white flesh of her thigh exposed above the dark silk of her stocking top. She was guiding the needle of a syringe into a green-blue vein. She looked up as Calloway entered the room.

'Don't look so judgemental, Reg. It's just a little pick-me-up.'

'From your gentleman caller in the tweed suit?'

'He's a Harley Street doctor.'

'I'm sure he is.'

He watched her as she eased the plunger of the syringe into the barrel. The needle left a tiny red puncture wound on her pale skin as she withdrew it. She placed the empty syringe into a small velvet-lined case and slid it into her handbag. Then she stood up and eased the tight-fitting skirt back down over her thighs, straightening out the creases with a wiggle of her hips.

'Get a good eyeful, did you Reg?'

'Something for your nerves, ma'am?'

'If you want to call it that. Put it this way, it's the George Formby Cup, it's ours for the winning but I'm fielding three novices, Clanger's laid up with his broken wrist, Fenton's riding with the angels and now Simpkins has gone AWOL. What the hell have you done with him? I told you not to hurt him.'

'And I didn't. Well not as much as I'd like to have done. He's a very bad lot that boy. Worse than you could imagine.'

'I can imagine quite a lot.'

'Not like this.'

She flicked her cigarette butt onto the concrete and stubbed it out with her toes. 'Fenton?'

Calloway shook his head. 'An accident. Plain and simple.'

'Then what else?'

Les Birkett appeared in the doorway, his white-topped commissionaire's cap touching the doorframe.

'They're doing photographs, Miss Moxon. You're needed on the track.'

'Christ, I have to go.'

She pulled a compact mirror from her bag and checked her lipstick. Then she took out a small half-moon-shaped perfume bottle and dabbed a drop behind each ear with her forefinger.

'Les, tell them I'm coming! And you,' she dropped the perfume bottle into the bag and turned to Calloway, 'You'll have to save your Bulldog Drummond stories for later. My office, once the stadium's clear.'

She pushed past him leaving a trail of Shalimar on the stale surgery air. She bumped past Riley at the door without apology and sashayed off.

'She means well,' said Calloway.

'Sometimes I wonder,' Riley replied.

'Not just me then.'

The young rider limped to the examination table and peeled off his race leathers, wincing. Calloway fetched him a beaker of water from the tap in the corner. Riley necked it down, the cold water running down the sides of his jaw leaving trails of clean flesh in the cinder smut. McArdle, a stocky balding man of fifty with horn-rimmed glasses and a shiny black, slug-like moustache, patted the bench. Riley lay back in his underwear while the medic worked him over with his big muscular hands. When he'd finished the examination, he stepped back satisfied.

'Someone up there likes you, Billy. Another lucky escape,' the medic said.

Riley looked up at him, expectantly. 'Fit to ride, Doc?'

The medic nodded. He took some powders from the cabinet and mixed a preparation of aspirin and caffeine in a glass of water. He passed it to Riley.

'Drink up, then chase it with this.' He poured a slug of cheap medicinal brandy from a bottle in the cream enamel cabinet. Riley drank the two liquids in succession.

'Now get your leathers back on, son. You're back in the race.'

Riley struggled into the stiff leather clothing and pulled on the red race jacket with its black flying bullet emblem. He saluted the doc as he left, easing himself stiff-legged through the surgery door, swinging his lead soles by their straps. Before the door could swing shut, O'Donnell appeared. He stood framed in the doorway, a giant among the Bullets with his rangy five-foot-eleven frame.

The medic rolled his eyes. 'Gawd, not another one. What happened to you?'

'Nothing Doc, go take a walk. I need to talk to Calloway here.'

'Haven't you got a heat to win?'

'I'm done for the night. Straight deuces all. Not a single race win. I'm gonna sit here with Calloway and bask in my own mediocrity.'

The Doc rolled his eyes again, took a nip of the medicinal brandy and left as he was asked. When they were alone O'Donnell said: 'I've got a message from Birkett. He says some old friends are looking for you only he didn't think they looked the kind of friends you'd want to meet anytime soon.'

'An officer type and two goons?'

'I'd say that's a fair description. Limey officer, mind. Stupid little moustache.'

'My old CO. The fact he brought two goons means he's not here to reminisce.'

'Birkett thought as much. Told me to tell you on the QT while he kept them busy.'

'A good man, that Les.'

'He's certainly got a nose for trouble. What's the deal, Calloway? Something to do with Simpkins blowing town?'

He needed an ally. He couldn't hide from Mackay and his friends all night. They were too good. They'd catch up with him sooner or later. His best chance was to meet them, bluff his innocence and buy time. If they caught him running there would be no telling where he'd end up. Some basement under an abandoned country house with very thick walls and two ex-Guardsmen to bounce you off them. If he could buy time he could slip away, but he would need help. O'Donnell seems like a good sort. He'd just have to trust the lanky American.

Calloway told O'Donnell the Simpkins story, minus the Riley

angle, the photographs Pat Moxon was desperate to get her hands on and the fact he'd put a bullet through the head of one of Sammy's black bag men. When he'd finished all O'Donnell could say was: 'Dirty limey motherfucker.'

Calloway nodded. 'Yep, that about covers it.'

'So who are the goons, police?'

Calloway shook his head. 'Sammy's military intelligence. The other two will be army muscle. There's something behind Simpkins's story that runs deeper than aiding the enemy.'

'That's deep enough.'

'Yes but it's history. If Sammy Mackay's involved, there's another angle I haven't worked out. Something still current. What I do know is I can't avoid him all night.'

O'Donnell clapped a hand on Calloway's shoulder.

'Listen man, if there's anything I can do, then name it.'

He made it sound like a drunk doing the old pals act, but Calloway knew he meant it. There was a half-baked plan in his head. He poured them both a slug of brandy from the medicinal supply in the doc's cabinet and let the plan bake a while longer.

'Who are the most popular Riders with the fans?'

'Since Fenton died? Well Riley's got the looks and I got the animal magnetism, baby.'

'I can work with those qualities. Now listen. First you've got to take a message to Les Birkett. Then you get hold of Riley and the pair of you do exactly what I'm about to tell you.'

When he finished he poured them both another shot for luck. 'You reckon you're up to that?'

O'Donnell gave the high sign and chinked his glass against Calloway's.

'As we say in the 82nd, All the way!'

TWENTY-FIVE

'Evening, Sammy. Getting a taste for the dirt track?'

Mackay and his two goons were back at their table by the big window of the members bar. The goons' expressions hadn't changed.

'You know I think I might be. Once you get the hang of it, well, it's really quite thrilling. Although the chaps do spend a lot of time sliding along on their arses. Strange little men. I do hope they don't get too badly hurt.'

'And your friends seem to be enjoying themselves.' He nodded to the two stone-faced goons. 'Do they speak?'

'They're more the physical type.'

'Unlike you, Sammy. Never liked to get your hands dirty.'

'No, that was always your job, Cab. You liked it rather a lot, I seem to recall.'

'That was then. Times were different.'

But it wasn't just then. He was still quick to violence. Too quick for civilian life. Like the Burma railway victim he'd watched beat the dog, there was a rage inside him that would fester until it burst. It was best not to be around him when it did.

Sammy was the only one touching his drink. The other two each sat with a full glass of Britvic on the Formica table in front of them, next to a copy of the night's race card. Through the big window behind them, George Formby was presenting the cup. Moxon was watching with forced grace as the Lancashire comedian handed the trophy to the visiting club. Calloway hoped her pick-me-up was easing the pain.

'So I'm glad we've caught up, Cab. You've been treading on my turf rather.'

‘I doubt that. There’s nothing I do here that would interest your department. Unless the Russians are recruiting greyhounds now.’

‘I wouldn’t put it past them. No, it’s people I’m interested in. Three in particular. Sampson, Ladbroke and Belper. The names you mentioned when we spoke. How does a washed up ex-sergeant running a dog track come by those names, Cab?’

‘Novice riders, doing tryouts. I check their bona fides for the club boss. We get some chancers through here. The boss likes to know what she’s buying.’

‘And the places, Genshagen, Hildesheim?’

‘We get services types trying out. Dispatch riders who rate themselves. I ask where they served. Check they’re not spinning a yarn.’

‘That’s very diligent.’

‘I was taught by the best, Sammy.’

Mackay took the compliment with mock grace. ‘And these novices, Sampson, Ladbroke and Belper.’ He waved the red-and-black race card. ‘Not on the team?’

‘Didn’t make the grade. The boss is very strict.’

‘Ah, yes.’ He peered at the cover of the race card. ‘Miss Patricia Moxon, Managing Director of South London Speed Stars.’ He tossed the card onto the table. ‘Never saw you working for a lady boss, Cab. What on earth is that like?’

Calloway shrugged. ‘Like working for a male boss but in higher heels.’

Mackay laughed and shook his head in disbelief. ‘What’s the world coming to? I need to watch my back, clearly. Some popsie from the WRACs might be after my job.’

‘And might do it better.’

‘Well, I suppose anything goes, like the song says.’

Mackay leant over the table and spoke into Calloway’s ear. He dropped the supercilious tone. ‘I need some fucking answers, Cab. If you don’t give me them, then we’ll have to dig them out of you.’ He gestured to the two goons, who were staring blank-faced at Calloway. ‘Like I said, they’re more the physical type. You should get on well.’

There was a commotion at the doorway to the bar. Right on cue, God bless them. O'Donnell and Riley pursued by fifty excitable supporters, young girls mostly, holding out race cards for autographs. Another twenty from the bar ran over to join them, arms outstretched. Their young voices rose to fever pitch. O'Donnell made a play of fending them off, but his face was egging them on. He spotted Calloway and led the crowd towards the table where the four men sat. Irritation showed on Sammy's neat little face. From behind, Les Birkett laid a hand on Calloway's shoulder, true to the plan.

'Apologies gentlemen, but Mr Calloway is wanted down at the track. A security matter. Urgent, I'm afraid.'

Calloway rose from his seat. One of the goons grabbed his forearm and tried to pull him back down. O'Donnell stumbled into the goon and a swarm of supporters with red-and-black scarves engulfed them like bees round the hive. Calloway pushed through the swarm towards the exit. Mackay and the goons were pinned to their seats by the screaming fans. Calloway looked back as he left the bar. O'Donnell winked. He raised a hand showing five fingers and mouthed 'five minutes'.

Calloway's heavy shoes clattered down the iron stairs. He snaked his way through the crowd who were by now heading to the exit gates. He had to barge through, drawing looks of consternation and shrill protests in soft south east London accents. He was heading for the workshop. O'Donnell had left a set of race leathers and a helmet inside, the biggest he could find. Calloway hoped the riders' garb would conceal him for long enough to meet O'Donnell at the rear gates. Here he would be waiting with his road bike, a big Vincent Black Shadow, its near-thousand cc engine running. If they could make it out of the stadium before Sammy and his men, they would be clean away.

The workshop was unlit. Calloway entered into the darkness, with just enough glow from the high windows for him to make out the helmet and leathers draped over the bench. As he crossed the room, he saw movement in his peripheral vision. A darkened figure moving quickly towards him, something glinting in its hand. Then an artillery shell burst inside his head. And then another. He saw white light and heard a noise so loud he buckled at the knees and fell hard onto the oily concrete, clutching his skull for fear it would explode into a thousand fragments. More blows came, from boots this time, to his guts and to his face. Pain dragged at his consciousness with barbed claws. His senses were failing. He heard a voice singing an imbecilic song. He recognised it as Ray Simpkins's.

'I once won first prize two and six, I know all the dirt track dirty tricks.'

The ground was slick. An upturned can of Castrol oozed rank-smelling fuel to engulf him. It soaked into the fabric of his suit, seeped into his hair and clung to the exposed flesh of his hands and face. His legs jerked in spasms as his heels slid around on the workshop floor. His fingers clawed at the legs of the workbench, desperately seeking a grip but failing.

He sensed he was alone now. The smell of burning fuel filled the room. He felt heat, intense burning heat. Acrid smoke crawled its way into his lungs as he gasped through searing chest pain. Then there was another voice. A familiar voice. An American. He felt strong hands dragging his ankles, his inert frame gliding slowly through an oily sea. More voices, angry this time. Shouts and scuffling. Then a heavy body falling onto his, sending his pain right off the dial. He gasped more of the acrid fumes into his lungs. Then a calm, quiet blackness pulled him down through the hard concrete, bone fragment by bone fragment, and into the netherworld below.

TWENTY-SIX

He came to on the hard metal floor of some kind of truck. Beside him another body, a dead weight that buffeted against him as the vehicle took corners. He was hooded and his hands were tied. He couldn't find a piece of him that didn't hurt when he moved. He sensed a presence over him, perhaps two people, the sound of breathing and the smell of cigarette smoke cutting through faint diesel fumes.

They drove for another hour at least, Calloway drifting in and out of consciousness, an overwhelming fatigue dragging him into bouts of fitful sleep. At first, in his waking moments, he heard other vehicles passing them at regular intervals. Now they seemed alone on quiet roads.

The truck stopped. He heard the driver exchange words with another voice outside, as you would with a sentry. The vehicle drove on, slower this time, before pulling up. He heard the rasp of the handbrake being applied and the metallic clink of small chains being released as the tailgate was dropped. The body next to him was dragged out first. Out cold or dead, it made no sound. There were heavy footsteps and the sound of a door opening, then swinging shut. Minutes later, the footsteps returned. Arms grabbed him roughly and dragged him over the tailgate. By reflex his legs felt for the ground. He attempted to stand but his legs gave way. Two heavy-footed men frogmarched him in the direction of the door he had just heard slam. They yanked his outstretched arms over their shoulders to keep him upright as his feet dragged along the hard concrete beneath them.

Inside the building the air was stale and damp. He could smell the fug of abandonment, even through the dusty canvas of the hood. It was cold too, the kind of cold you only get in places that haven't been heated for months. Ahead of him keys clanked in a lock and a heavy door screeched on his hinges as it was opened. Beyond the door the smell was worse.

They dumped him on what felt like a wooden bunk. The pain he felt all over suddenly grew more intense, as his injured body connected with the hard surface under it. He sensed another presence in the room. He felt practiced hands probe him, like the doc had done to Reilly on the examination bench. Then a rough hand yanked off the hood. The room was dark, except for the beam of a pen-torch in the hand of the man examining him. He raised each eyelid in turn with a calloused thumb and shone the torch into Calloway's eyes. The two other men stripped off his jacket, causing a shaft of pain to spread down his arms and across his ribs. Calloway yelped like an animal. He felt the pressure of a cuff over his bicep and heard the puff of a blood pressure gauge being pumped then released. He felt a hand on his wrist and the light touch of fingers taking his pulse to the faint ticking of a wristwatch.

His examiner then fumbled in a case and tinkered with an instrument Calloway could not make out in the darkness. A sound like a small bottle top being unscrewed, a short pause and the tap-tapping of a fingernail against something small and glass. Hands fumbled with his limp forearm. The needle of a syringe bee-stung through the fabric of his bloodied shirt. A thousand tiny ants scurried through his arteries. He felt becalmed. Then the eddying wooden surface under him seemed to swallow him whole.

He woke. A barbed wire skullcap was clawing its way into his brain. Pressure and pain. His limb joints constricted like rusting monkey wrenches in the hands of an angry mechanic. Simpkins at the workbench tossing tools around. There was light in the cell now, a big floodlight illuminating the Bullets as they saluted the crowd. He heard Marching Along Together inside his head. He scrunched up his eyes against the glare. His eyeballs felt pumped to bursting. He tried to summon proper consciousnesses but just kept drifting. He felt his bicep. It felt bee-sting sharp, like the puncture wound in Pattie Moxon's soft white thighs. Pat was there, standing over him, her skirt hitched up. She spoke with the voice of Liz Francis. 'Des Fenton was a bastard.'

Hours passed. Perhaps days. A window in his consciousness opened, but whatever was outside was fog bound. He shifted where he lay and tried to audit the damage. The hurt had shifted. The truck he'd arrived in had parked on his chest and dumped a ton of cinders into a chute in his forehead. A light blinded him. A golden, heavenly light rising up from the maggot-ridden body of the tramp Wood, permeating the concrete roof of the pillbox and spouting skywards to the stars. He tried to raise an arm to shield his eyes but it wouldn't budge. He was filled with concrete, the more he tried to move the more it solidified. He lay still and breathed hard. The air was damp and dusty. Floodlit dust specs floated around him. He scrunched his eyes to shut out the light. They felt over-ripe and mushy. It made him nauseous. The dust cloud smothered him. It suffocated his consciousness. He faded out again.

Giant hands shook him awake. He complied. He struggled to his feet like a rusted-up automaton. The body was working half capacity. The brain was still dormant save for enough nerve endings to instruct his limbs. They shuffle-marched him along a corridor. He heard himself singing Marching Along Together. His joints ground metal, his blood supply had hit the reserve tank. He felt his head bobbing like a kellyman. His bare, aching feet scraped on the gritted floor. His toes tingled with a million tiny agonies.

Then came a moment of clarity, as if a gallon of new blood had flooded his brain. He was alert, but he knew it would not be for long. He felt the urge to act, almost by reflex. He lashed out. A red haze frenzy took over. He struggled free and swung at the biggest of the two men holding him. It was a mistake. They pushed his face into the painted brick wall. His lips splayed and he tasted damp dust. The man he'd struck made a swift retort. Calloway's kidneys took a well-practiced jab. His nerve endings crescendoed pain. He kicked back, aiming for a shin. A bone snap would have given him an opening. But he donkey-kicked thin air with bare feet. A second kidney blow made his legs buckle. His body slimed down the wall in an ooze of hurt.

They scooped him up and dragged him through an open door into an interrogation cell. Two metal chairs flanked a tarnished metal table. They dumped him on one of the chairs. He fell like a half-full sack. The big hands grabbed his wrists and snapped on cuffs. There was enough light for him to recognise the two men. Mackay's stooges. They muttered too indistinctly for Calloway to make out. The words meant nothing but the tone was menacing, a prelude to something worse to come. It came. An elbow jack-hammered into his jaw. The crack echoed around his skull. He tasted his own blood. Then the door slammed. He was alone in the room, save for the spectre of his own private terror.

He must have slept as he sat. When he awoke Sammy Mackay was seated in the chair opposite, rocking back on its legs while he puffed on a pipe. There was a heap of pipe ash in an ashtray on the table in front of him. There was also an unopened packet Players Navy Cut, Calloway noticed.

'About time,' said Mackay. 'You certainly were out for the count.'

'I generally am when I've been beaten by professionals and pumped full of junk.'

Mackay raised an eyebrow. 'Happened to you before?'

'Fuck off, Sammy. Give me a cigarette.'

Mackay tossed the unopened packet at him.

'And take off the manacles. I'm not going anywhere.'

Mackay waved his head from side to side as if deciding whether this was a good idea. He dug in his pocket and fished out a key. He gestured to Calloway to hold out his hands, then unlocked the cuffs. Calloway rubbed some life back into his wrists and lit himself a cigarette. The hot tar burned his lungs but it felt good. His head swam with the right kind of giddiness this time. Mackay spoke without his characteristic superciliousness, the way he used to speak in the field.

'I had hoped that we could have avoided this. But you left me no choice, Cab.'

'I'm difficult like that.'

'I don't know who you're trying to protect.'

'Would it shock you if I said the reputation of the club?'

'Those motorbike jockeys? Are you kidding?'

Mackay laughed. 'Or is it your boss, the lady Patricia?'

He quoted from the race card.

'Managing Director of South London Speed Stars. I suppose she's not in bad shape for an old boiler, but really, Cab, are you that shallow?'

Calloway felt the urge to defend her but he bit his tongue. It wouldn't make any difference, not with Mackay.

'What do you want?'

Mackay leant over the table and looked him in the face. Calloway knew the look. This would be the crux of it.

'I want to know what names Ron Sampson and Pat Ladbroke go by these days.'

'Why?'

'A matter of national security.'

'You'll have to do better than that.'

Mackay thought about this. He sighed. 'I suppose I could have asked my boys to beat it out of you, but you always were a stubborn old shit. And strong as an ox.'

'Intelligence from torture isn't reliable Sammy. I reckon your lot should have realised that by now.'

'It never stopped you trying.'

Calloway shrugged. It made his shoulders hurt. 'Perhaps I enjoyed it, like you said.'

Mackay sighed again more deeply this time. He sat back in the chair and sucked on the pipe.

'You're still covered by the Act, Cab. If what I'm about to tell you goes beyond this room, I'll make sure you swing for it.'

Calloway shifted his weight in the chair. He recalled the kidney punches. Two swollen kidneys made sure he was reminded.

'I may be a fool, but I'm not a traitor, Sammy. Your official secrets are safe with me. Say what you've got to say.'

Mackay clasped his hands together on the desk and leaned forward. He looked liked the headmaster at a second-rate private school about to share the benefit of his wisdom with a disinterested pupil.

'You called me with three names. Sampson, Ladbroke and Belper. Three men who went by these aliases were members of the British Free Corps. Nazi volunteers. You had the names of Free Corps barracks and a description of their insignia, which I'm guessing came from the photographs we found in your safe.'

'Go on.'

'We've been trying to find Sampson and Ladbroke, but we've never known their true identities.'

'Why go to the trouble? For a charge of assisting the enemy? Even if you found them they'd be out of jail within five years.'

'We're not interested in their Free Corps membership. As you say, they would barely get more than a slap on the wrist if they had good lawyer. There's more to it.'

'Like membership of an Einsatzgruppe?'

Mackay waved a hand dismissively. 'Oh we know about that too. Nasty business, but hardly in the interest of national security. That's all in the past.'

'Unless you're a Jew, or a gypsy, or a homosexual, or a communist. I imagine that sort of nasty business is still very much part of their present.'

Mackay gave a condescending nod. 'Of course, Cab, you probably feel that more than most of us, what with that poor little Jewess you fell for. What a sentimental brute you are. But really, the war crimes trials are done and dusted. Waste of time digging around in that old nonsense again.'

Calloway had never felt more like punching someone.

'We found Frank Thomas Belper in Berlin. He was passing himself off as a German under the name Franz Baumann, working in the Russian sector. He'd burned off his blood group tattoo but we identified him from the records that survived from Prince-Albrecht-Strasse. The Nazis were so wonderfully bureaucratic. Unlike the other two, Belper was regular SS. He transferred to the Free Corps later. He was also a very bad boy indeed. We had enough evidence to get him an appointment with Mr Pierrepoint. It seems when faced with the end of a rope his willingness to die for the fatherland dissipated somewhat. We saw in him the makings of an asset. We tossed him back and made sure he found gainful employment within the state apparatus. He's been supplying us with intelligence ever since. Not chicken feed. Good quality gen. He's one of our best sources in the Soviet sector.'

'And to protect his cover, you want his two old Free Corps pals out of the way.'

Mackay nodded. 'Something like that.'

'Is that really necessary? What are the chances of them identifying him? He's behind the Iron Curtain. It's not as though their paths are going to cross.'

'That all depends what they're up to. But of course you'd know that, wouldn't you Cab? That's why we brought you here. You and that bloody American.'

The second body on the truck floor, out cold.

'O'Donnell's here?'

He realised it was O'Donnell who had dragged him from the workshop when Simpkins had left him to burn. Mackay's men must have snatched him too.

'Is that his name? I was trying to work it out from that little pamphlet I picked up at your stadium. Yes, he's here and bloody awkward it is too. If the cousins find out we're holding one of theirs there will be an almighty stink.'

'So let him go. He stumbled into this. It's not his lookout.'

'Actually you got him into this. That's your lookout. He'll get the same deal I'm about to offer you.'

'Go to hell.'

Mackay stood up and stretched. He checked his watch. 'Tiresome, Cab. Very, very tiresome. I'm half inclined to ask my men to beat some sense into you after all.'

'Be my guest.'

Calloway couldn't hurt more than he did.

Mackay leaned against the painted brick wall, sunk his hands into his pockets and stared at the filthy floor.

'The East Germans are forming a new ministry for state security. Franz Baumann is tipped for a top job in one of its departments, something called the Administration for Struggle Against Suspicious Persons. I do love these ideological names. It seems Herr Baumann's peculiar talents have been recognised. Essentially, he'll be spying on westerners, some of whom of course will be working for us. Well, you can see what a useful sort he's going to be.'

Now it made sense. Sammy had recruited a butcher as his favourite errand boy. The psychopath Belper would be deep within East Germany's intelligence apparatus with a direct line on which foreign agents were under suspicion. Even Calloway could see the value of protecting such a source.

'Find Sampson and Ladbroke. I don't care how you do it. Then we'll do our best to leave you and the American alone.'

'And if I refuse?'

Sammy let out one of his theatrical sighs. 'Then there's something else I should mention. I sent a black bag team to your flat to see what they could find. Two men. Only one came back. He described a man your height and build pursuing him and his colleague down the street. Four days later the river police fished the other man out of the Thames at Rotherhithe. He'd been shot at point-blank range with his own revolver.'

Calloway shrugged. 'There's a gun crime epidemic. Haven't you heard?'

'Your neighbourhood is a godforsaken place but I'm assuming executions aren't a daily occurrence. And don't even think of crying self-defence. Point blank, Calloway, dead centre, through the forehead, close enough for powder burns even that toxic river water couldn't wash away.'

Mackay pocketed his pipe, picked up the Navy Cut and lit one, tossing the pack back across the table. Calloway took another and shared the light. Mackay pulled on the cigarette and exhaled hard.

'I miss these. I took up the pipe because they're better for your health. Not the same though.'

He savoured the rough tobacco for a moment before continuing.

'We look after our own kind, Calloway. We don't need a court of law to do it. We're a long way from anywhere and no one knows you're here. Don't make me spell it out.'

They took Calloway back to his cell. It was light and he could see through the windows of the abandoned building. Outside was the vehicle he'd arrived in, a rugged light truck with a tilt cover and big suspension. Beyond it, a runway overgrown with weeds, next to that the familiar shape of Quonset huts, paint peeling on their curved corrugated tin roofs. In the distance a control tower, its windows broken and its distinctive Mickey Mouse camouflage fading. The runway was long, stretching as far as he could see. An old bomber station he presumed. He was most likely in the guardhouse.

One of Mackay's heavies shoved him into the cell and slammed the heavy door shut. He heard the key turn in the lock.

He lay on the hard bench. Above him the faint crying of crows cut through a howling wind. An east wind, he surmised. He would be in one of those featureless flatlands in Lincolnshire, Cambridgeshire or Norfolk. There would be nothing as far as the eye could see except black earth and intermittent rows of poplar trees, an ineffective windbreak against a biting wind blowing straight off the Ural Mountains two thousand miles to the east.

In the gloomy half-light of the cell he read the graffiti on the grey painted brickwork. Obscene sketches and Hitler caricatures. He dozed a little and dreamed half dreams. Shutze Wood's photographs flashed behind his closed eyes like a depraved magic lantern show. He heard Simpkins's voice carried on the wind outside.

'They were rats. Fucking vermin!'

He jumped up and banged on the cell door.

'Mackay, you bastard! Come here Mackay!'

Heavy footsteps echoed down the corridor and the key

turned in the lock. The two heavies entered with Mackay behind them.

'What's all this, Cab? Had a bad dream?'

'Pat Ladbroke's real name is Wood. He was an infantry private with the British Expeditionary Force. He lived as a tramp and drank himself to death on meths. I saw his corpse. Ron Sampson's name is Ray Simpkins. He's a speedway rider. He rides for the Bullets, or at least did. I braced him and he confessed to his wartime exploits. Then he did a runner.'

'So he's at large?'

Calloway nodded. 'I can find him. Release me and O'Donnell and we'll bring him in.'

Sammy shook his head and laughed.

'Bring him in? I don't want him, Cab. I want him out of the picture altogether. Make that happen and you might just get to go back to your dog track with your big American friend. Are you up to it?'

'You said yourself I was always quite good at that sort of thing.'

'Is Simpkins dangerous? It's not that I care for your safety or anything. I just need to know you can do the job without fucking up.'

It was Calloway's turn to laugh, but it hurt him to do so. 'You mean more dangerous than beating a man my size half to death and setting fire to the stadium? Yes, I'd say so, wouldn't you?'

'Is he armed?'

'Considering half of all demobbed servicemen came home with a Luger as a souvenir, I'd say there's a fair chance. And he'd probably have more emotional attachment to a German weapon than most of them. He seemed to have enjoyed using one.'

'I can get you firearms. Do you know men who can use them?'

'Men? What am I doing, raising a posse? Do you like the novels of Zane Grey, Sammy?'

'If you go this alone, you'll fail. A manhunt is a team play.'

Calloway nodded. 'I've got some friends.'

'Good. You'll be strictly freelance on this. You realise if you're caught we'll disown you?'

'I had assumed as much.'

'But better that than the alternative, eh?'

'Fuck off, Sammy. I'll need a vehicle too. Like the one I arrived here in.'

Mackay recoiled at this. 'You're not having my Land Rover.'

'Land what?'

'Rover's new overland vehicle. Like a jeep, only it doesn't roll over at the sight of a bend. I've been waiting two years for one.'

'I want it.'

Quite suddenly Calloway found himself desperately in need to ask Mackay a question. 'How is the stadium?'

His old commanding officer looked incredulous. 'Well I'm no expert but I reckon you'll need a new workshop. Everything else is still standing.'

'And the spectators?'

'Your boys got them out, so I'm told.'

He felt a pang of relief he hadn't expected. But in this whole disgusting business, the stadium had become some kind of constant he could cling to. When he'd first arrived in post he had arranged a fire drill with the stadium staff and fire brigade crews from the divisional headquarters at New Cross. He'd timed the fire crews at nine minutes from station to stadium gates. The drill had paid off. He felt a warmth inside that overcame the hurt from the beatings. For the first time since leaving the army, he felt like he belonged.

TWENTY-SEVEN

There were four of them in the Land Rover. Calloway, O'Donnell, Webber and Birkett. Webber drove. It was more than they could do to stop him. He gave a running commentary as they rumbled down the Kentish lanes. How the vehicle handled, its responsiveness, the suspension. He was in his element behind the wheel of the newly designed marque.

O'Donnell had raised the posse, like the sheriff in one of Webber's westerns. He picked military men. He played on their sense of outrage at the London boy turned Nazi. All three volunteers thought they would be handing Simpkins over to the authorities. Only Calloway knew of the deal he'd made with Mackay. He would honour that alone. The other three need never know.

Calloway was playing a hunch, but an informed one. This wasn't the first time Simpkins had gone to ground. He'd lost himself in the marshes once before, with Wood and the deserters. Calloway wagered he'd do it again.

As the road petered out he recognised the gate where he'd parked previously.

'We're out of road, Bert. Pull her up just ahead.'

Webber drew close to the gate and applied the handbrake. He killed the engine and doused the headlights.

'Sweet as a nut,' he said, patting the dashboard with his four remaining fingers.

The four men disembarked. Calloway dropped the tailgate and hauled a long canvass bag from the deck. He unbuckled the webbing straps. There were two Webley service revolvers, a Browning HP and a MkIII Lee Enfield.

O'Donnell whistled. 'Planning to start a war Calloway?'

'Let's hope we don't have to.'

He had worried O'Donnell would blame him for ending up in a cell at the bomber station. Sammy was right. Calloway had got the innocent American into this. But O'Donnell's grudge was with Simpkins. He saw the whole affair as a betrayal by a teammate and it hurt.

Calloway handed a Webley to Bert Webber and tucked the second one in his own waistband. O'Donnell grabbed the Browning automatic.

Webber smirked. 'Wouldn't you prefer a six shooter?'

'What, to thirteen rounds in the clip? Are you kidding?'

'Who's starting a war now?' said Birkett dourly, sliding the bolt back on the Lee Enfield and putting a round in the chamber.

Calloway was firm. 'No war. No cowboy antics. Use the weapons as a deterrent or in self-defence at the absolute worst. No one's leaving this place with hole in them that God didn't put there.'

Webber sniggered.

Calloway took Birkett to one side. 'You don't have to do this, Les. You've earned your stripes and then some. You've nothing to prove.'

The old RSM bristled. 'With respect, Mr Calloway, I've spent the last four years watching those punters file through the turnstiles with no more action to be had than bollocking them for dropping litter. This feels like the life I remember and if you think I'm too old for it, just try fucking stopping me.'

Calloway clapped him on the back. 'Then keep watch here, Les. Secure the exit route. If Simpkins bolts for the road, your job's to stop him.'

'You're Johnny on the spot, Birkett,' said O'Donnell. 'Make it count.'

Calloway beckoned the three men to him. 'So Birkett's holding the rear. The remaining three will fan out, one man on the path, such as it is, and two either side at fifty-yard intervals. If you see something, holler. The rest of us will close in. Don't go taking on Simpkins alone. He's unpredictable and fights dirty.'

'You think the 82nd fights clean?'

'Stow the bravura. There's to be no unnecessary risks.'

Webber raised his hand. He gestured towards the estuary. 'The light's fading and that looks like a pea-souper blowing in. The biggest risk is that we end up clobbering one of our own.'

'We'll use a sign and countersign. If you see another man, give the sign. If he gives the wrong response, you'll know he's not one of us. That doesn't mean it's Simpkins. I've been here. There's a colony of vagrants. Don't get the wrong man.'

'So what's the sign?' asked Webber.

O'Donnell offered one. 'The call is, "How d'ya like your eggs?", the response is, "On the Jersey side". That's one for Cab.'

'That'll have to do,' said Calloway.

Webber was right. A thick mist was blowing in from the river. The light had all but gone and above them a full moon glowed through the cloud cover.

'Time to move. Best of luck, gentlemen.'

O'Donnell stopped them. He put a hand to his lips for quiet. All four strained to hear above the rising wind. In the distance they heard the faint rumble of a motorcycle engine. As the engine noise grew louder, Calloway made out a single headlamp weaving its way through the lanes towards them. He instructed the men to scatter, each finding cover and readying their weapons. As the motorcycle approached, its headlamp picked up the reflectors of the Land Rover casting a faint red glow over the mist. It was a heavy bike which crunched over the gravel of the path as it pulled to a halt. The rider killed the engine and dismounted, crossing to the Land Rover and peering through the side windows. Then the figure stepped back and removed its helmet. Recognising the rider the four men broke cover. A female voice broke the silence.

'Jesus. What do you think you look like? A bunch of bloody Boy Scouts.'

Calloway ran forward, anger rising in his veins. 'What the hell are you doing here Pat?'

'What am I doing here? I could ask the same of you. Have you seen yourselves? Like Karno's bloody army.'

'You need to leave.'

'Oh, I'm going nowhere mate. Not till I've yanked that Simpkins by the ear back to my stadium. No rider goes AWOL on me, not on the night of the George Formby Cup.'

Calloway let out a frustrated growl. 'How the hell did you know about this?'

Moxon looked at Webber. Even in the darkness the small rider looked sheepish.

'You don't want to tell him your secrets, believe me.'

She shook her hair loose and pulled down the zip on her leathers. She turned to Calloway.

'So do you have a plan or are you going to run around all night like a big girl's blouse?'

There would be no arguing with her, Calloway knew that much. He ran through the plan. Moxon seemed to approve.

'Right. So I'll take the left flank and that way we can cover an extra fifty yards between us.'

Webber raised his hand. Moxon sighed. 'Yes, Bert?'

The small man stuttered. 'If you see someone, you say "How d'ya like your eggs?". That way we'll know it's you.'

'Oh behave yourself, Bert Webber. I'll do no such thing.'

Undeterred, Webber raised his hand again, this time looking at Calloway. It was Calloway's turn to sigh.

'We haven't got a gun for Pat, Mr Calloway.'

Moxon let out an incredulous squeal. 'Who do you lot think you are, the Texas bloody Rangers. If someone comes near me I'll knock his teeth out. It wouldn't be the first time. Guns my Aunt Fanny!'

Birkett signalled the end of the conversation, laying his rifle on the bonnet of the Land Rover and lighting a cheroot. 'You lot better get going then. You've lost the light. Best just get on with it.'

Calloway led them forward, then as agreed they spread out at intervals. From the estuary the sound of a steam whistle carried on the wind.

It was boggy underfoot, more so than last time. There had been rain. The four picked their way through the long grass, eyes sweeping from side to side and peering through the mist which surrounded them now on all sides. Overhead, gulls cried. Then Calloway heard a voice singing a bawdy shanty. He looked down. A blackened face peered up from a bivouac and cackled, 'Fuck me, it's a will-o'-the-wisp.'

Calloway pressed on. He'd lost sight of the path and was using the moon to navigate as best he could. It lit up the fog through breaks in the fast-moving cloud, like a lighthouse beam rotating. To his left he heard muffled profanities. Webber finding a ditch the hard way, he imagined. His own boots were sodden now too and a fine film of moisture clung to his jacket. The mist was turning to mizzle. He felt it trickling down his neck and into his shirt collar. Through the occasional break in the mist he made out the pin-prick of a torch beam from one of the other hunters. They should have left the torches behind. They were no use in these conditions. All they would do was advertise their presence to Simpkins and risk giving him a head start.

Through the gloom he made out the outline of a low structure. As he drew closer he recognised it as the shelter of the man he'd given cigarettes to. It was securely fastened and as Calloway drew nearer, he heard the snoring and muttering of a fitful sleep from inside. As he passed, as light footed as he could, he saw the last embers of the sleeping man's fading campfire glowing through the ash.

The shelter gave him a bearing. A quarter mile ahead was the tramp Wood's pillbox. He played a hunch and headed for it, keeping the moon in a constant position above him to stay on course. Conditions underfoot deteriorated. It was slow going now and took him a quarter hour to cover the distance. Clouds covered the moon fully, ahead only a grey-black darkness. He trod deliberately and carefully, then paused. Two eyes glared thorough the mist, as if from the face of an invisible demon. The rifle loops in the pillbox, lit from inside. Joe Smoke's castle had a new king.

Calloway advanced at a crouch, steadying himself with this fists on the sodden ground that rose in clumps the nearer he drew to the tiny blockhouse. He pulled the Webley from his waistband and slid off the safety catch that nestled discreetly above the trigger on the weapon's cold metal body. He hugged the damp walls of the building listening for movement inside. The rising wind bounced off the bricks and drummed against his ears making it hard to hear. He scrambled around to the front. A crack of light shone down the side of the hessian sack that served as the pillbox door. Still no sound from inside that Calloway could hear above the wind. He rose to his feet and steadied himself. Adrenaline coursed through his veins and his heart pounded in his still-aching chest. In a snap, he ripped down the sack and lunged through the blockhouse door, pistol arm extended. No one inside. Joe Smoke's corpse was gone and the fug of death had dissipated. The place had been cleaned out and was arranged in a soldierly fashion, with a Primus stove, water canteen and a bedroll stowed along the far wall. A tilly lamp hung from a rusting hook on the underside of the roof. In its glow Calloway noticed a kitbag, stuffed to capacity, leaning against the sidewall to his left. The new king of the castle was going somewhere and soon.

He ripped the kitbag open and tugged out its contents. Spare clothing in small sizes, wash kit and a small tool roll of motorcycle tools. Buried at the bottom an envelope of cash, plenty of it, in sterling and French francs. Against the same wall, a jacket hung from a nail in the brickwork. He recognised it as Simpkins's. He rifled the pockets. Loose cash, a switchblade and a dozen 9mm cartridges. Also a folded slip of paper. He unfolded it and held it up to the light of the quietly roaring lamp. A line scrawled in pencil read The Channel Queen, Ramsgate, midnight, followed by today's date. He pocketed the note.

He crawled out of the pillbox and stretched his aching body to full height. Gripping the revolver in readiness he swept three hundred sixty degrees, using his peripheral vision to more clearly see through the darkness. Simpkins was out there, perhaps observing him right now.

The wind had dropped leaving an eerie silence. He edged back to the walls of the pillbox and dropped to a crouch. He heard the sound of sodden ground being trodden underfoot and strained to hear from which direction it was coming. The blackness was disorientating. Before he could get a fix on the nearing footsteps, the hard butt of a pistol stuck him from behind. There was a flash inside his head and he buckled. A figure pushed past him and ducked into the blockhouse. He heard scuffling as the figure hastily gathered up the strewn kit. Calloway thought he heard the chink of the dozen brass cartridge cases being pocketed. Then, like a will-o'-the-wisp, the small figure fled from its cave in the direction of the road a half mile behind them.

Calloway struggled to his feet, a searing pain from ear to ear and a ringing inside his skull. He levelled the Webley to his eye line and aimed at the faint outline of the running man illuminated against the moonlit mist. He fired two rounds which cracked like thunder through the silence. The will-o'-the-wisp ran onwards. Calloway aimed again and fired two more rounds. The wisp-like shadow stopped, turned and spat fire of its own. The first round ricocheted off the pillbox wall before Calloway had seen the muzzle flash. The second round caught his left shoulder and slammed him back against the hard brick wall. As he slumped he saw the wisp turn, then disappear into the darkness. He slid his hand under his shirt and checked the wound. It was light, just nicked flesh, arteries intact. Behind him he heard shouting – O'Donnell voice, then Webber's.

Calloway drew breath and hollered, 'Fall back to the truck, he's heading for the road!'

He stuffed his handkerchief under his shirt as a makeshift swab and followed O'Donnell and Webber's voices back towards the gate where they'd left Birkett. Birkett would have heard the shot and would be covering the marshes with the big .303. Calloway hoped the old soldier's eyesight was up to it. In these conditions it would be just as easy to fire on one of his own.

The three men met at the path and ran together towards the road. There was no sign of Pat Moxon. By now Calloway had figured she could take care of herself. He pictured Simpkins being dragged along by the ear, his two front teeth missing. Then another image of Moxon flashed through his mind, water-stained and faded like one of the sick photos from the tramp Wood's album. She lay in a ditch half naked with a bullet through her head, a trickle of blood running down her dead face and seeping into the silk of her torn slip. Amid the pain of exertion he found the strength to run faster.

As the three men neared the road the outline of the Land Rover loomed into view. But between them and the gate a fourth figure crouched in the reeds.

O'Donnell gave the sign to halt. Webber whispered, 'Is it Pattie?'

'I can't tell. Too far ahead and too dark.'

O'Donnell drew back the slide and put a round in the Browning's chamber. Ahead of them a shot rang out and the muzzle flash lit up the crouching figure of Simpkins. He bolted for the gate and fired twice more. Someone flicked a switch and the Land Rover's big headlamps lit up the marshes like a stage set. Calloway scrunched up his eyes to peer through the glare, looking for Birkett. There was no sign of the old RSM, nor any sound from the .303.

In silhouette against the beam of the lights, Simpkins raised the pistol again, this time in his direction. Two more shots rang out. Under this covering fire the small rider scrambled over to the reeds and tossed clumps of foliage aside. Beneath the camouflage was a motorcycle. Simpkins kicked it into life.

O'Donnell spat: 'That's my fucking Vincent.'

They heard the deep clunk of the gears engaging before the powerful bike crashed through the rotting gate, passed the Land Rover and headed for the road.

Birkett lay propped against the nearside wheel of the small truck. Moxon crouched over him, using her scarf as a compress to stem the flow of blood. Birkett looked up at Calloway.

'Bastard fucking winged me before I could loose off a round.'

Moxon shouted at Webber, 'Bert, hold this, press as hard as you can.'

She passed the compress to Webber and crossed over to Calloway and O'Donnell. 'He'll live, if we get him to a doctor right now. You know where Doc McArdle lives?'

O'Donnell nodded.

'Then you and Bert take the Land Rover and get him over there pronto. You drive, Bert needs to hold that compress tight.'

Webber called across to them, 'It's a fucking bullet wound, Pat. What if Doc calls the police?'

'Tell the old soak if he wants to keep his job, he'll keep this to himself.'

'Will he do that?' Calloway asked.

'He will if he wants me to keep quiet about the backstreet abortion clinic he runs on the side.'

She grabbed Calloway by the arm. 'Now you, come with me.' She nodded towards her motorbike. 'If were going to catch the little bastard up, we've got to get going. Any idea where he's heading?'

'Ramsgate, for midnight.'

She looked at her watch. 'Come on then, get on the back.'

Calloway stopped. Only then did it occur to him he'd be riding pillion. He sensed the other men were watching him.

Pat cocked her head and raised an eyebrow. 'Unless you can ride a motorcycle, Reg.'

She knew he couldn't. They both knew she was the professional rider. He fought with his pride and won by a slim margin. He climbed onto the rear seat of the motorcycle.

'Hold me tight, Reg,' she shouted above the noise of the gunning engine. 'I won't break.'

TWENTY-EIGHT

They picked up Simpkins's tail-light a mile ahead. He was throwing himself into the bends and Moxon did the same, in spite of the additional weight on the mean passenger seat of her Series C Rapide.

'Lean in, Reg, you're like a sack of coal back there.'

He pressed himself closer to her and gripped her waist, pushing his chin into the crook of her neck below the line of the tightly buckled helmet. For a second he felt her nuzzle closer. The rain was heavier now and the visibility worsened. She tugged the flyers' googles down off the helmet and onto the bridge of her nose.

She turned her head and shouted above the roar of the slipstream, 'Is he meeting a boat?'

They were touching eighty miles an hour and the oncoming rush of air sucked the words from his chest.

Calloway shouted back, 'Crossing the Channel on a contraband run I reckon. One of those fast-motor vessels. A ration-buster fetching brandy and God knows what back from France. Simpkins will try and lose himself in Europe, maybe even head to Germany. He speaks the language.'

The small red tail-light faded in and out of the mizzling rain. Moxon dropped a gear and squeezed more power from the throttle. She clamped her legs around the tank and merged with the machine.

The cry of the wind had risen to a scream. She could no longer hear him. The two motorcycles cut through darkened towns and villages, their whirring wheels spraying rainwater over the slick bitumen of the empty streets. Rochester, Chatham, Rainham, places Calloway knew from maps but had never been.

They left the streetlights behind. Their eyes adjusted to the darkness, but at best visibility was down to the two dozen yards of their headlamp's beam. The full moon was lost behind thick cloud now. The distant red dot of the tail lamp disappeared.

Calloway shouted above the scream of the engine, 'Have we lost him?'

Moxon responded with a clunk from the gearbox and a shriek of acceleration. They powered through the darkness for another half mile. Then something glinted in the headlamp a hundred yards ahead. Moxon cried out.

'Jesus Christ, hold on.'

Simpkins had stopped dead, broadsiding the Black Shadow to block the single-track road. He sat astride the motorcycle gripping his pistol with both hands. Two shots flashed from the barrel. The first went wide, whistling past Calloway's head. The second clipped Moxon's helmet sending a spark off the metal cowl into the darkness. There was no room to brake. She accelerated and lugged the heavy bike up and onto the verge to the side of them. Their back wheel struggled to grip the grass and the soft earth beneath. Moxon decelerated, then revved once more, manoeuvring the bike back onto the road and gliding to a halt. Simpkins was back on the Vincent. He accelerated past them and disappeared into black night ahead.

Moxon gunned the engine aggressively, let the clutch out and gripped the bike hard as it lunged forward in pursuit of the Black Shadow. Calloway's head snapped back with the inertia.

'Lean in for Christ's sake Reg! You'll have us off.'

He complied, clasping her around the waist and pushing his head into the crook of her neck. The rain eased as they passed through Faversham. They were able to keep the tail-light in sight for another half hour. Calloway's damaged frame ached in new places but he held tight to Moxon, their bodies and the motorcycle moving as one.

They entered Ramsgate from the west, both motorcycles cutting a swathe through the red neon haze cast by the sign of the grand Odeon cinema. The posters advertised Adam's Rib.

Calloway managed a laugh. Ahead of them the harbour lights glistened. Moxon dropped a gear and squeezed more life from the Rapide's hot engine. Their rear wheel skidded on the slick wet cobbles as they descended through the deserted coastal town. They were close enough to Simpkins now to see the beam of his headlamp lighting the wet road that led to the western arm of the harbour. As they approached the Royal Parade and dropped down towards the harbour wall, Calloway loosened his grip on Moxon and peered at his watch under the streetlight. Five minutes to midnight. Sensing the urgency, Pat dropped another cog and gave the throttle every last drop.

They were closing on Simpkins. The two motorcycles shot along the long curving arm of the West Pier towards the lighthouse, its constant red light soaking the two machines in a wash of blood red.

The bike ahead was yards from the end of the harbour wall and showing no signs of stopping. Simpkins gripped the throttle with his right hand and swivelled his body back towards them, his left arm outstretched. He let fly the last rounds in the pistol's clip. Calloway saw sparks glance off the harbour wall to their right. Simpkins's motorcycle wavered, his body snapped back attempting to wrest control of the big Vincent and failing. The bike glanced off the lighthouse, flinging Simpkins's bare head into the curved brickwork. They saw a red spay of blood against the harbour lights before the Black Shadow dragged its unconscious rider over the end of the jetty and down into the black water below.

Moxon pulled up just ahead of the jetty's end and both she and Calloway dismounted, running to the water's edge and peering down into the spume that crashed against the stone harbour wall. Bike and rider were gone, swallowed by the Channel that was to have been the young traitor's escape.

Moxon took Calloway's hand and led him back to the motorcycle.

'We need to leave here, find somewhere for the night.'

Calloway continued staring at the water. Ray Simpkins' angry little saga had reached its end. It gave Calloway no satisfaction, just a cold sense of relief that the job had been done.

They rode to the top of the town and found a guest house with its lights still on. Pat fed the elderly landlady a line about a motorcycle holiday and a blown gasket. It seemed to work, even if the last guest remaining awake in the lounge raised an eyebrow at their lack of luggage.

She led him to the room and locked the door behind them. He walked to the window and stared down towards the harbour. Behind him he was aware she was undressing. He heard the unzipping of race leathers and smelled the sweet scent of Shalimar cutting through the musk of the rough black hide.

She crossed the room to the window and eased off his jacket and waistcoat, now sodden with rain. Then she circled him with her bare arms and unbuttoned his shirt, slipping it down over his shoulders and onto the floor. His handkerchief, caked in congealed blood, fell onto the worn rug. He heard her wince in sympathy. She pressed herself against his bare back and clasped her arms around him tightly. She was warm. She traced a line down his chest and over his clenched stomach with her fingernail.

'What are you doing?' he asked.

'Helping you make up for lost time,' she whispered.

He turned to face her. She was naked save for an oil-stained slip and stockings snagged by the zip of the leathers. Her hair was mussed, her lipstick smudged. The small puncture mark left by the syringe had faded.

He cupped her chin in his mud-streaked hand and pulled her lips onto his. From the harbour he heard the bells of a police car, its flashing light casting a blue neon glow onto the damp-stained ceiling of the cheap guest house room.

TWENTY-NINE

He woke to the sound of gulls crying in the sky above. The sun was rising, flooding cool white light through the open-curtained windows. Pat's head lay on his chest. Her arm rested on his stomach, her nails tracing shapes down his side.

'Are you awake?' she asked.

'Yes.'

A thought was tugging at him. He voiced it. 'There never were any rumours about Simpkins running Fenton off the track.'

She stopped stroking him. 'I needed those photos. When Fenton died it was my last chance to get them. I reckoned someone like you would find them, given the opportunity. The circumstances of Des's death created the opportunity I needed.'

'So you were prepared to accuse an innocent man of murder?'

She scoffed. 'Ray Simpkins was hardly innocent.'

'But you didn't know that when you dragged me into this business.'

She rolled off him, reached for her cigarettes on the bedside table and lit two of them. She put one between his lips and drew hard on the other.

'No harm would have come to him. It was an accident, plain and simple. You said so yourself. There was no evidence. Nothing that would stand up. The police weren't going to take a few rumours seriously.'

She laid her head back onto his chest. 'I knew he was a nasty piece of work long before Bert told me about this Free Corps business. I had no great qualms about spreading some gossip.'

Calloway pushed her head away. 'Ray Simpkins tried to kill

me. He tried to burn down your stadium. Do you have qualms about that?'

She sat up and laid the ashtray on her lap. 'I didn't think things would get out of hand like that. Christ, I know they all think I'm a hard-nosed bitch, but I'm not that hard.'

He should have been angry. God knows he had reason. He'd been beaten to a pulp, threatened with death and shot at. Even by his standards that was beyond the call.

'Tell me about the photographs,' he said.

She turned to face him. 'Have you seen them?'

He nodded. She laughed. 'And you're still here.'

'Did Fenton take them?'

She let out a deep sigh.

'It was a long time ago. The early thirties. I was a show rider down at Catford. Des was the star of the home team there. We became lovers.'

She tutted at herself. 'I liked them flash in those days. I was young. Too young to know better. And they were mad times, Calloway. Des and his gang were hell raisers. Parties, drinking, snow. A blizzard of snow. I didn't need any encouragement. I was wild. When you risk your neck on a motorbike, recklessness becomes a way of life. I didn't care.'

She climbed out of bed and walked naked to the window.

'I love the sunrise. I like to think it wipes the slate clean from the previous day.'

The previous day's slate was quite a full one, Calloway thought.

'Des bought a camera. A good one and all the darkroom kit. He said he'd take publicity photos for the club.'

She laughed to herself. 'Publicity photos my arse. He was peddling smut. He had expensive habits and his speedway winnings didn't cover them. That workshop he's got down in Deptford? That was decked out like a boudoir back then. All plush and gold paint. He'd pick up girls, young ones mostly. Brasses some of them, but not always. Sometimes just girls. Wide-eyed and susceptible. He'd get them high as a kite and photograph all manner of depravity.'

'And you were one of them?'

She shook her head slowly. 'I wasn't like the others. I was Des's girl. He persuaded me to do a private session, just for him. I was high as a kite myself most of the time, what with the snow and the booze. I didn't need a lot of persuading. I suppose I kidded myself that sort of thing was normal. I'd be lying if I said I hadn't developed a taste for decadence. My judgement was a little off, you might say. I did two or three shoots in the end. Des would be flying too and we'd be getting up to all sorts, once he'd put the camera down'

'So what happened?'

'Des and I didn't last. I knew I had to calm down. My health was starting to suffer and my riding was turning to rat shit. I quit the snow and the booze for a while and got my life back together. Des didn't seem so great when I was sober. He found someone else and I wasn't too cut up about it. Then one day down at the stadium I caught some of the young riders sniggering. I asked them to share the joke and they fumbled around trying hide something from me. Des had been selling my pictures. Pretty Pattie Moxon, Queen of the dirt track, dirtier than you've ever seen her. That night I went looking for him. I searched all his old haunts and found him pawing a couple of young tarts in a club up west. I threatened to kill him. He just laughed. He said if I didn't want those photos all over the speedway scene I'd better play nice. That's when the penny dropped. With those pictures he would always have a hold over me. It's no coincidence Des had a glowing career, Reg. Sure he was a good rider, one of the best, but he always enjoyed a big helping hand from yours truly whenever he needed it.'

She turned away from the window to face him. 'He betrayed me Reg. He betrayed my trust. And I've been paying for it ever since.' She threw back her head and laughed. 'I suppose I was the start of his career as a blackmailer.'

Calloway crossed to the window and wrapped his arms around her. She tensed and bit hard on her lip. Then she spat, 'He may have owned my reputation, but I owned his fucking neck.'

‘That’s all in the past,’ he said. ‘For good. The photographs and the negatives are safe. You’ll have them by the end of today. Then you can get on with your life.’

He kissed her neck. ‘You deserve better Pat.’

They both looked down towards the harbour. It was low tide. The police were dragging the seabed. Behind them, the jagged outline of the Vincent Black Shadow poked through the shallow waves, skeletal and macabre. There would be some explaining to do. Calloway would think of something. He had good reason now.

THIRTY

They took some convincing, but in the end the police bought Calloway's story. Fenton's death had sent Simkins off the rails. He blamed himself for the accident. His behaviour became erratic, he had taken to drink and in a fit of melancholia had set fire to the stadium, before stealing a teammate's motorcycle and attempting to flee to France. The club's owner, Patricia Moxon, had signed a statement corroborating these facts, so too had McArdle, the team medic, and the rider, O'Donnell.

It was Wednesday and Pat was at the stadium coaching Riley before the evening's fixture. She had a new star rider and intended to keep him at his peak. Calloway watched from the stands. He was growing to understand the sport.

When Riley took a break, Calloway called him over. He handed him an envelope. Inside was the five hundred pounds he had taken from Simpkins at Fenton's workshop.

'That should go some way to replacing your lost winnings.'

Riley counted the money. He looked quizzically at Calloway and opened his mouth to speak but the track security boss cut him short.

'Don't ask questions. Your slate is clean, Billy. There's nothing holding you back now.'

He turned his back on the young rider and walked towards the turnstiles. Birkett was there, his arm in a sling. He clicked his heels in lieu of a salute.

'As you were, Les,' said Calloway as he passed.

He took a trolley bus along the Old Kent Road and jumped off at the Bricklayers Arms. Liz Francis walked towards him as he approached the soot-black tenement buildings, returning from her shift at the nightclub. She looked tired and drawn.

'I'm glad I caught you. I won't keep you long.'

She looked apprehensive. 'I suppose I've got five minutes. Can we talk here though? I don't want you coming up when Mum's in the flat.' She looked coy for a moment. 'Embarrassed I s'pose.'

'You've no need to be.'

She snorted. 'So you say, but I'd sooner be far away from this place, believe me.'

He smiled with genuine warmth and she noticed. 'Open your bag a moment.'

'Are you being funny?'

'Don't make a fuss, Liz, just do as I ask.'

She did, in spite of the obvious suspicion that was showing on her face. He palmed an envelope into the bag discreetly, and she snapped the bag closed.

'That's rightfully yours,' he said. 'The money Fenton had been putting aside for the flat. You can get as far from this place as you like now.'

He had Sammy Mackay to thank for the fact the money was still in his safe. All Sammy's goons had taken when they arrived with a warrant were Wood's SS photographs. They had left the cash.

'But how?' she's asked.

'Let's call it balancing the books.'

She looked blankly for a moment then small tears welled in her eyes. They were beautiful eyes, he thought. She leant forward, placed a hand on his shoulder and kissed him lightly on the cheek. Then she turned, looked up and down the busy road and flagged an oncoming taxi. The cabbie pulled up, set the meter running and said, 'Where to miss?'

'Up West,' she said.

Calloway returned to the stadium on foot. He enjoyed the walk. Pat was still coaching Riley, using his motorcycle to demonstrate cornering. Calloway caught the familiar smell of Castrol R as he ducked under the shower of cinders. Pat completed the lap and let the bike slow up alongside him. She pulled off her helmet and untied her hair. It shone in the light of the late morning sun, which had broken out from behind the cloud.

She shouted over to Calloway, 'Turned out nice again!'

He smiled, surprised that for once the catchphrase didn't irritate him. He gave her a wave as he crossed the track, then strode over the centre green. There was a lightness in his step that was pleasantly unfamiliar to him. But beneath the pleasure of the moment was fear. A terrible nagging fear. Reg Calloway was a violent man. A violent and unpredictable man. And one day that violence would erupt again. When it did, he wanted to be as far away as possible from anyone he cared about.

He climbed the steps to his office and closed the door behind him. He lugged the big Remington typewriter from the top of the filing cabinet beneath the frosted glass window and set it down on his desk. He wound a sheet of paper onto the roller and typed the address of his basement room in the top right-hand corner. He typed the date beneath it. Then he wrote:

Dear Miss Moxon,

I hereby tender my resignation as Track Security Officer for Bermondsey Stadium...

He withdrew the letter from the roller and signed it R Calloway. Taking an envelope from the drawer, he sealed the letter inside. Webber's western novel lay at the bottom of the drawer. Calloway picked it up and slid it into his jacket pocket. Then he left the office, locked the door behind him and placed the envelope and key on Pat Moxon's desk.

He walked to the turnstiles and saluted Birkett as he passed. It was the last time he would see the stadium.

THE END

About the author

DDC Morgan lives in South East London. He has written professionally as a journalist and consultant for more than thirty years. Crime writing fills the rock'n'roll-shaped hole in his life left by no longer playing in bands.

You can follow him on Twitter @DDCMorgan

More great books from Fahrenheit Press…

Pills & Soap by DDC Morgan

Six months after his adventure in *Blood & Cinders*, Reg Calloway finds himself working as head of security for a London film studio turning out low-budget Brit flicks.

When the studio boss's car is blown up, Special Branch suspects Irish terrorists are responsible but Calloway doesn't buy it. He saw a woman fleeing the scene. Finding the woman and uncovering her connection to the case becomes his obsession.

Calloway's under pressure from all sides - Special Branch and his studio bosses are convinced that the IRA are behind the bomb but when the terrorists give Calloway an ultimatum to find the real bomber or else, he knows for sure that the mysterious woman who fled the scene is the real key to everything.

His investigation takes him into the dark side of the London film business - its exploitation of starlets, its underworld connections and its Faustian star makers who trade young souls for broken dreams.

As Calloway delves into some of the seediest recesses of 1950s London he risks everything in an attempt to find the truth and see that justice, in some form, is served.

Abide With Me by Ian Ayris

Abide with me is the story of two boys forced to walk blind into the darkness of their shattered lives and their struggle to emerge as men. It's also a story of loyalty, of community, and of powerful friendships shaped by adversity and celebrated on the football terraces of England.

With power, sensitivity and wit, Ian Ayris has crafted one of the most authentic snapshots of working class life you will ever read.

Black Moss by David Nolan

In April 1990, as rioters took over Strangeways prison in Manchester, someone killed a little boy at Black Moss.

And no one cared.

No one except Danny Johnston, an inexperienced radio reporter trying to make a name for himself.

More than a quarter of a century later, Danny returns to his home city to revisit the murder that's always haunted him.

If Danny can find out what really happened to the boy, maybe he can cure the emptiness he's felt inside since he too was a child.

But finding out the truth might just be the worst idea Danny Johnston has ever had.

Find more amazing books

www.Fahrenheit-Press.com

www.ingramcontent.com/pod-product-compliance
Lightning Source LLC
Chambersburg PA
CBHW020334310726
48979CB00015B/2362/J
* 9 7 8 1 9 1 4 4 7 5 5 6 6 *